On Love
and Other Fables

Tea

On Love and Other Fables

Author: Tea
Editor: Kineret Lourie
English Edition: Carmel Nemirovsky
Translated by: Tal Keren
Illustration by: Tali Genshaft
Layout & Design: Amit Brin

https://www.facebook.com/wanderingteatoo

ISBN 978-965-572-188-1

Tea

This book is dedicated to
a woman who once was.

The thread that runs through
it is one derived from loss, and
resolved in hope.

Thank you for who
you once were for me.

Tea

Table of Contents

- *Book I* -

On Love

My advice to you – approach this book as you would someone new in your life. Give it the time it deserves, as you never know what it could become for you in the future. You may come to regret not carving deeper memories into your heart, while you still had the chance.

A Recommendation

To avoid confusion, we are going to need a signal, denoting – I know I said I never want to see you again, but what I meant was: I want you to fight for me.

Breakup

There is a street in this city that is the longest street in the country. Perhaps even the longest in the world. It takes seven years to cross, and you live on its other end.

The Ocean

When I was I child, they told me that by pressing a seashell against my ear, I'd be able to hear the ocean, storming away in the distance. As I got older I discovered that if I were to press it against people, I'd be able to hear their longing. And then somewhere down the line I learned, as one does, that what I'd been hearing from the depths of those seashells wasn't the ocean at all. Of course, I thought, of course it isn't the ocean. It is the longing for it.

The Heart Physicist I

In the lab, he discovered a paradox: the closer you are to someone, the more unbearable the distance from them becomes. This will change the world, he thought. But only if she hears of it.

Going Back

One day, his mind returned.

Truthfully, until that moment, he hadn't even noticed losing it. A strange clarity had settled over him, allowing him to understand just how deeply he had sunk into madness. An old name flickered through his memory, one he had not considered for years. He spent the following second staring at the briefcase he was holding. He frowned at it before dropping it to the floor with disgust.

He turned to leave the office. A secretary looked at him, as if to ask just where he was going in the middle of the work day, but he waved his hand to silence her, hissing "I won't return", and made his way to the door. Then, hesitating briefly, he turned to add: "however, a man similar to me in shape and size may return here. If he does, take caution. I would."

He was 40 at the time, perhaps 41. His hair, once black and thick, had grayed and thinned. His once strong and firm body had cultivated a lavish gut, telling of the comfortable lifestyle he had fashioned for himself over the years. His thoughts had become slack; his muscles tired, as he'd ceased to exert them as soon as it was no longer required of him. He spent his free time leafing through newspapers and watching evening programs. Occasionally he'd permit himself a short vacation, from which he'd return slightly plumper, and wearier, than he was before.

Now, in the midst of his newfound lucidity, he wondered if he was perhaps some type of livestock, gradually plumped up in preparation for slaughter. His life was comfortable – he had all the grazing grass he needed; he was required to think as little as possible so that he wouldn't conjure thoughts of escape; required to exercise as little as possible so as not to spoil the tenderness of his flesh. Soon, he imagined, he'd be fat enough to eat. Or perhaps he was more like a dairy cow, meant to remain in the barn until his yield dries out. If that was the case, the world could suckle on his udders for many more years to come.

His surroundings seemed absurdly different, now that he was free from madness. The people rushing through the streets suddenly seemed alien, terrifying. He realized that he had no idea whatsoever as to what was going on in their heads. Every day they pass him by, their thoughts concealed from him, pondering things he knows nothing about. Who knows how they'd affected his life so far, what harm their imaginations have inflicted upon him? They are nothing more than opaque boxes, sealed, sporting hard eyes and a mouth that speaks his language.

Other strange creatures were seen walking the streets, as well. Bicipital animals, joined at the palm, two-persons long. He couldn't understand how they managed to survive. They seemed oblivious to any other presence. He stared for a while, wondering, when a memory flickered through his mind. It seemed to him that he was also, at some point, such an animal.

Of course he was. Before he'd lost his mind. This was many years ago, when he could still feel, move, think. Before he became an apparatus for the consumption of data and substance and the production of waste. He rummaged through memories, murky from lack of use. Yes, he used to have something real. Way back when. He loved. He had loved someone.

She had a name. It was, he knew, something monosyllabic. But he could recall her shape far more clearly than her name. Her lines fine and curved, she was softly textured, and her scent was intoxicating. Something truly delectable. She had both light and dark hues, like the sharp brushstrokes of a darkened paintbrush on white canvas.

He remembered the exact color of her eyes, and spent the following hour attempting to recreate it with a set of watercolors he found in a store. The salesperson demanded that he pay for the paint and paper he took and, without thinking, he pulled out a 100$ bill and waved him away with it. The salesperson considered this briefly, glimpsed at him cautiously, and decided to accept his terms.

He tried spots of sky blue with a hint of green and yellow. Some grey, perhaps. When he was done, he looked into her eyes from across the vast schism of time, heedless of those around him. They were, he thought, very beautiful eyes.

Where are they today, come to think of it? Again, he was forced to pick through his now-dulled past. It took him down a grey, bleak path, paved in long identical days which called for no further attention, until he was suddenly blocked by a great, daunting barrier. Behind the barrier, he could see, his memories were infinitely colorful. There lingered evenings of long conversations with another, books he would read, languid kisses leaned against the wall of his old home. And more: a caressing hand; words etched deep into a heart which had since become dented and rusty, Saturday mornings in a familiar café, silences revealing a closeness that requires no elucidation. And more: hopes of a shared future, dreams of a daughter who looks just like her mother and intense, painful emotion. He could smell all of this from where he was, or see it perhaps, in elusive puddles of aged light. But there stood the barrier, blocking his way.

It was still and intimidating, and his yelling did nothing to sway it. What are you even made of? He wondered. He touched, examined and tasted it, and then recoiled away from it, horrified. The barrier was made entirely of resignation. It was turbid, bitter stuff, and it burned his tongue and stained his fingers. Rage engulfed him, towering waves of it, like an ocean tempest, threatening to capsize every one of his thoughts. He'd conceded? He'd conceded. He'd conceded! When confronted with the choice of hurting or pushing onwards, his brain opted for madness. Letting go not only of the person, but of that entire lifetime. His hands crumpled the paper on which the color of her eyes was still drying, tearing long gashes through it. Where is she now, then? Was she married? Had she forgotten about him? A deep moan ripped from his throat, within an inch of a cry. The other customers stared nervously; the owner poised over the phone, his hand primed to dial the police.

At once, he smoothed his expression. The fury that had twisted his face mere moments before had dissipated completely. The paper fell from his hand to the floor, and he looked at it with indifference. Only after a minute or so did he pick it up and shove it in his pocket. Clearly, a time machine was in order.

It was quite simple, he pondered. Well, not simple, per se. But the theoretical aspects of it were quite clear. What was it that he actually sought to do? He wanted to go back. So then, all he had to do was retrace the steps of his life, only backwards. It was obvious, really.

But how to achieve this? A quick glimpse at his watch made it clear that time of was of the essence, so to speak. The task would require fifteen years to accomplish. No matter, though – he would, after all, be counting backwards.

Some difficulty was to be expected in attempting to remember all of the days he would now have to live in reverse, but then most of his days were much the same throughout his spell of madness. Though the goal he had set was a worthy one, realizing it would take him through a dreary path indeed.

From an outside observer's perspective, things might have appeared to be quite unchanged. He'd wake up in the morning, head for the office, and return home in the evening. Upon closer examination, however, the changes were obvious. Every decision he'd made in the past, would now receive the opposite treatment. If he drove his car to work yesterday, then the following day would see him taking the bus and walking the rest of the distance. If he'd had a big lunch the day before, the next would be a light salad. If he'd rushed straight home without so much as a word to anyone, he would now make sure to stop and chat and joke with his co-workers.

Those were the main changes he implemented during the first five years he attempted to retrace. Of course, over the years, they had slowly but surely led to larger and more substantial changes – evidence, he mused, of the fact that he was altering the course of time itself. Over time he began to receive invitations from his colleagues to join them for drinks after work, or to the barbecues they hosted, or to the weddings of their sons and daughters. And he remembered – they used to do these things before, when he was younger, but he would always turn them down. So now, naturally, he accepted them all. This was how, five years back, he found himself surrounded by friends, his figure not quite so plump, his body slightly stronger.

His annual trips abroad had also transformed completely. Instead of five-star hotels in familiar countries, he chose new destinations, ones he'd never visited before, where he stayed in modest hostels and mingled with fellow travelers. He'd return from these excursions sunburned and gift-laden, sharing exotic tales of his escapades with his eager-to-listen friends.

Seven years after he began his journey back through time, he moved back to a small apartment, after selling his spacious house. Around him, couples were breaking apart, ending long years of marriage. He was in good shape, having eaten differently than he always had, and was more mindful of his health than ever. This naturally led to some attention from the newly divorced.

Of course, he recalled – I am 34 years old now. Women really did take notice of me when I was that age. He'd always ignored them, though, or flat out refused if he was openly approached. And now, though he knew that his ultimate goal was a woman he once loved, he realized what had to be done in order to turn back time. So this time around he was more prone to flirt and woo, and experienced various dalliances he'd long since forgotten.

He had a strange youthful exuberance which clashed with his older appearance. Every wrinkled laugh would produce sparks of perpetual amusement from his eyes. The women he dated didn't know what to make of it. When asked about this peculiar trait, he would explain that he was a time traveler. This statement always evoked a smile, and merely added to his charm.

When he felt 31 he found himself in a relationship, living with a woman he was extremely fond of. This did not surprise him. He remembered having the courage to date before entering his thirties, but never allowing himself to become attached.

At 29 he left the office to attend university. He knew that, back then, he'd planned on being an independent architect – only driven to work at his current firm due to pure chance and the security of a fixed income. Three years later, he was the owner of a reasonably successful business – due to his newly simple lifestyle, he hadn't squandered the money he'd accumulated during adulthood – which he employed in financing his many new excursions into entrepreneurship.

Fourteen years after he began his journey back through time, his first daughter was born. Actually, he recalled, he'd always wanted a daughter. Having her at age 27 was even a bit later than he'd planned. He even loved his wife, dearly so, regularly surprising her with small gifts and everyday gestures of affection. She always awoke to the smell of fried eggs and a freshly chopped salad waiting on the breakfast table.

The final year was truly exciting. Apparently, back during the first time around, he was thoroughly depressed. This made sense – at the time, he was only just recovering from a separation; now he was progressing toward a reunion of sorts. He was sharply aware that at this precise point, the twists and turns of the journey held particular danger. It was only through great difficulty that his elusive memory allowed the extraction of the information necessary for this final stretch.

Before, this was a year of slow deterioration, the loss of everything he believed in. Now, he assumed, it was time to rediscover those things. Political views, abandoned ideals, musings on the nature of things. He had at some point abandoned them all, and now he was slowly recollecting them: he reread books which he recalled left an impact on him, and when he read the newspaper, it was not because of some jaded interest, but from a true desire to understand. A childlike optimism took hold of him, a notion that he could affect the world around him, shape it. Not a day went by without learning something new, or taking joy in a simple experience.

Finally, he arrived at the barrier.

There it stood, black and solid, pulling his thoughts into depths he could hardly bare to examine. Here, he knew, is where he conceded her. Beyond was the world he'd left behind. Here the love of his life was lingering in wait for him – the woman he had dreamt of every day over the last fifteen years. He smiled excitedly.

But he was a married man, now, and his love for his wife was second only to his love for their daughter, the thought troubled him – kept him from moving on. All that was required of him was to leave them both and call the woman he left behind. She must also be 26 now, as was he. Their final fight was only yesterday (no, tomorrow, he reiterated). With one simple phone call, he could fix everything.

Of course he could. Just as he could have done the last time around, instead of running.

What was her name? He struggled, frantically, to remember. After all, 15 years from now, it was the thought of that very name which triggered the restoration of his sanity. Now it remained, inexplicably, beyond his grasp. The memory of her face had also faded, leaving only a broad impression of fondness. And, come to think of it, what was the color of her eyes? Where had he put that old watercolor painting, capturing their precise hue?

Well, surely upon conceding his current life it will all come back to him. Of this he was certain. Once he hears the sound of her voice, his memory will return as well. He paced back and forth across the room. This was the second chance he'd hoped for, the moment he'd been waiting for. Why was this proving so difficult?

He decided to go peek at his wife, asleep in bed with their child, just for a brief moment. But once he was there, he lingered, watching them. Silence encompassed him, and he became uncharacteristically grim, a dark, tired shadow, weary from the years he had, until that very moment, left unfelt. He smiled.

Concede? He pondered. Why would he think concession was necessary? She was right there. It must be her, for him to feel such an impossible love. Her eyes were brown, of course, exceptionally dark, with a small, joyful ember burning deep within them.

He chuckled quietly to himself, relishing in his own foolishness, before awarding himself with a well-earned pat on the back, quite pleased with his success. A great day for science, great day for science – he thought, as he rummaged absentmindedly through a drawer – what a spectacular thing it is, to be young. When he found the old watercolor of her eyes, its colors smeared and blurred, he didn't even look at it. Not even when his hand lit a match and allowed it to burn away completely.

His smile remained, undisturbed. It was only when he reached up to wipe away his tears that he became aware of them, and stopped to wonder briefly where the small pile of ash on the table had come from.

I guess it's not important, he thought when he failed to recall, and immediately forgot about it. He headed for bed, then, leaving the past in his wake.

Shelter

In turbulent times, an individual may sometimes be seen passing from one person to the next, gently knocking on their faces with his words, hoping that someone will let them in. Few do, as they barely have enough room for themselves, but no one begrudges this person for trying. It is, after all, only natural for people to seek shelter in others from the tempest that is life.

On Forgotten Dangers

There is an allotted time for love. If a couple parts before that time is up, one is doomed to continue loving the other until it is exhausted. Those of you who hope to love forever, beware.

On the God Élan and the Lost Universe

There are physicists who maintain that time and space began in our universe simultaneously. But physicists are people of questionable character, who place great importance in the value of measurements and calculations in reaching conclusions. Most people are far more reasonable – they know that the most reliable information is revealed to us in the form of stories. This is most likely owing to the fact that stories do not pretend to be the truth.

This story is about the day time began. Contrary to popular opinion, space was already around at this point, suspended in the center of reality in perfect order. This order might seem like chaos to us, but an attentive, omniscient observer would clearly see that each of the Universe's moments was in its proper place – which was precisely where they wanted to be.

Seeing as time had not yet been invented, people were free to live their lives in any way they wanted to. They'd usually choose to live and relive their best moments: one moment they'd live through all the days they spent in love, the other – all they days they spent falling in it. Sometimes they'd go see how they were born; other times, how their children were born. And when they became truly bored, they'd die for a while, just to experience some nothingness.

It was an extremely convenient existence, which presented hardly any reason to ever live through difficult times. If someone were feeling particularly adventurous, they could go sneak a peek at what their days looked like when their hearts were broken. But no one remained there for long. At most, the brief visit would cause them to better appreciate their time with their loved ones.

This was all well and good, until one day, a god from another universe happened to arrive in ours. This god, by the name of Élan, found himself overwhelmed by strange and peculiar observations. He saw the universe begin and end; he saw people alternately living and dying; suns expanding or collapsing, depending on their mood; Galaxies being born, cultures dying and fading away. All of this was happening both now and never, spread out before him in what appeared to him as a truly unhygienic cacophony.

Élan grimaced and turned to a nearby group of local gods to inquire about the situation at hand.

"Excuse me", he said to the gods, who were deep in determined slumber, "pardon the intrusion, but may I ask – who is in charge here?"

The gods merely rolled over and carried on with their persistent napping. But Élan would not be deterred. Relentlessly, he pestered the gods with yet more questions: why was everything just lying around? What's with all this matter everywhere? Why was purple made out of red and blue, while red and blue were also made of purple? Why was language a universal concept, and so easy to understand? Why could the stars speak? Why did everyone get more than one chance? And love – what were they thinking?

Eventually, one of the gods, who was truly tired, snapped at him: "do as you please!"

This was precisely what Élan had been waiting for. As he was quite a young god, just barely forever years old, he'd been eagerly awaiting his chance to access some universe in which he would have total autonomy to do as he pleases. Once the opportunity presented itself, he did not hesitate.

In the beginning, he mused, he really ought to get rid of this awful chaos. He waved his hand at once, purging the universe of most of its matter – undoing, in effect, an infinite number of materializing galaxies, over a hundred sentient beings, millions of possible word combinations, two-hundred thousand species of prancing insects, eight-thousand introspective automatons, and three varieties of seasoned eggplant. Nothingness, believed Élan, was far more aesthetically pleasing than somethingness.

After examining his work with satisfaction, Élan decided that it was time to buckle down and get some real work done. Firstly, he arranged it so that red and blue could form purple, but never the other way around. This was a matter of supreme importance to Élan, as he found vagueness to be utterly insufferable.

He then separated the different solar systems, so that sentient creatures could not simply up and visit each other so effortlessly. For Élan also adamantly believed that privileges should be earned. Before his third order of business, he hesitated, attempting to decide whether he preferred that people be able to talk to each other or that they'd be able to understand each other. He eventually became bored with this dilemma and randomly waved a billion languages into existence. The talking stars began to complain about these harsh decrees, and especially of the inability to explain their feelings, now that language had turned into such a complicated business.

Élan, who was never considered by anyone to be abundantly patient, and who was feeling somewhat guilty over neglecting to conduct a survey on the matter prior to passing these judgments, decided that stars have no need for mouths, and hastily waved them into inanimate objects. This is why, to this day, no one may speak to the stars, other than via twinkling.

Concerning those matters of multiple chances and love, Élan was at first unsure what to do. He was annoyed by people living and reliving their finest moments, while deserting misery to wallow in itself. On top of this, it completely nullified everything Élan had done so far, as everyone would simply keep returning to the moments before his arrival and acts of de-creation. This upset him greatly, as he was indeed a young god, and he felt that his attempts at contributing were wholly unappreciated.

Just then, an idea sparked in Élan's mind – a spark so bright that several suns were forced to squint at its radiance. It was a solution, simple and singular, to all of these seemingly insoluble problems. With youthful vigor, Élan pounced at the universe, and began arranging its moments, stacking them one on top of the other. One moment followed another, and no one could pass into a previous moment after passing into the next. Élan cleverly piled the moments in a straight column, so we would be forced to fall through them in the order he established.

He proudly examined his creation – no more second chances, no more dilly-dallying, no more taksies-backsies. However, upon finishing he was quite shocked to discover that his column of moments was dripping with love. Apparently, in some way or another, when he was arranging the moments of the universe in order, he had accidentally stepped in some love, and had dragged it along with him from the first moment to the very last.

No matter, thought Élan, I'll fix this soon enough – and he meant it, too. But just then, one of the sleeping gods awoke from its slumber, looked around him and cried out in stunned horror. The other gods woke up as well, responding to what they saw with varying degrees of alarm. They swiftly surrounded Élan, demanding he return the universe, at once, to the state he had found it in. Élan was mortified. "But I can't recall how I found it, what it looked like. I think I knew, some moments ago... but so much has changed since then."

The gods tried to recall themselves what their beloved universe had once looked like, before Élan had begun redecorating, but they also fell victim to his clever organization of time, and could no longer go back.

"But look," said Élan, "at least love remains."

"Who needs love that lasts forever?" one god wondered, bitterly. But since it was the only remnant of the old universe, they decided to keep it anyway.

And sure enough, it remains to this day, its strangeness setting it apart from everything else in existence – an eternal love in a universe of moments.

The Scent of Longing

The scent of longing is a cold one. That is why it's so potent during the winter. I once saw a man who had frozen to death by its grip, his face twisted in hopeful yearning. It is the silent threat of all cold beds.

Optimism and Time

In my youth I introduced Optimism to Time, and to my astonishment the two became a couple. He was an introvert, dour and reticent by nature; she – cheerful, good-humored and enthusiastic. He was constantly toiling over his endless work, while she lay patiently in wait. I never used to understand what they found in one another, but then I saw her embracing him after a long day, whispering: one day they'll appreciate you, too.

Emergency Wishes

The sole resident of the time observatory kept a jar full of eyelashes on his desk. The label, written in precise, square letters, read: "Emergency Wishes". A miniscule note, barely noticeable, was attached to each eyelash, marking the date and place of its collection, as well as the name of the original owner. With the exception of one eyelash stored for sentimental reasons, the man never took in a used eyelash.

Beside the jar lay a magnifying glass, a tiny pair of tweezers, and a sterile rubber glove. Order was maintained unfailingly, even during the most difficult of times. A cluttered house, he'd often quote, attests to a cluttered mind. The lashes were piled up carefully in the glass jar, a monument to meticulousness. He could recall only one incident in which he had actually used one of them. Even then, he did so calmly, deftly balancing the eyelash on the tip of his finger before carefully blowing upon it.

He had an affinity for classification. Admittedly, if he hadn't, it was unlikely that he'd ever be able to find anything. He owned a list in which every day was meticulously cataloged, divided into good days and bad days. Tuesdays, he once noted, tended to go better than Sundays. He made many such footnotes, documented systematically in his blocky script at the bottom of the pages.

It may seem ludicrous, writing comments for each day anyone

had ever lived. After all, the task of reading them all may very well consume as many days as were documented. Time, however, did not concern him. He'd already spent one eternity observing all of those days. Some of them were quite dull, and yet he kept at it, diligently.

Naturally, different days would hold varying levels of his interest. The man in the time observatory was mostly interested in love. In his small notebook he recorded the names of his favorite romances, so that he could re-watch them, over and over again. He'd skim through the chapters of others' lives, gazing at them through one of his elongated telescopes, seeking the moments, large and small, that composed the emotional amalgam of their worlds. There were loves which wrecked his nerves and excited him even during his tenth viewing of them, even knowing how they would end; others left him in tears every single time upon reaching their eventual demise, a pair of emotions, burning fiercely until the lives that shared them eventually faded away. He found that if he looked long enough, he'd discover some hidden smile he'd missed during the previous viewing, or a soft, murmured whisper, which eluded him during a moment of excitement. These hidden gems were his most cherished possessions, and he was always overwhelmed with joy upon finding one.

There was one particular love that fascinated him beyond all others. He knew that as a general rule-of-thumb, first loves tended to end. In most cases their owners would move on with their lives, find adult relationships, and remember the past through a fog of pleasant nostalgia. Other times, when the heartbreak was too great to bear, one of the lovers – the one left behind – might even take their own life. These things happened. Usually, as he once established empirically, on Thursdays.

Often, when one lover continued on living, the emotion still burning in their gut, several years would pass before they would finally heal and find solace in the arms of someone new, sometimes, accepting that they would never love the same way again. Those loves were his absolute favorites.

It was a rare case such as this which now held his attention. Even rarer than the others. The man in the time observatory found himself revisiting it, over and over again, lips parted in wonder, observing one man in a tiny, remote country, whose heart was broken, and was refusing to move on.

He'd watched the first act thousands of times. He watched them as they fell in love. He examined the relationship itself over and over again, thousands of time. He returned to the final stretch of the relationship, as well, more than once. There was only one moment he refused to revisit. The breakup.

The man who would not move on was once called Maor Eckstein (though, it had been a long while since the man in the time observatory had thought of him by that name), and his life – even if he didn't know it himself – was an arrow in flight, the target of which was a woman who went by the name of Inbal Al-Kumisi. The man in the time observatory no longer lingered on this particular life trajectory, though he used to draw a great deal of amusement from observing the passage and hierarchy of moments; the days which, if properly aligned, would be indistinguishable from one another: a long line of negligible variations leading up to the day they met, and, ultimately, to the day she left.

It seemed that every step Maor took led him closer to love. A religious boy, slender and withdrawn, with clever eyes that took in too much for his own good, he eventually blossomed into a handsome man. His eyes were forest green, his hair coal black, and his skin pale. He had been a lonely child, unable to find anyone sharp enough to keep up with the swiftness of his mind. It was his fascination with numbers that drove him to study mathematics at Bar-Ilan University – not for any particular affection for them, but rather due to the fact that numbers, unlike humans, did not bear any resentment towards the people who managed to figure them out.

During his Bachelor's degree he discovered that he had a knack for the field, more so than the other students in his class. Being inherently modest, he attributed his success to diligence rather than to natural aptitude. During his Master's, it became apparent to his professors that they were dealing with a prodigy – an exceptionally brilliant mathematician, even among other brilliant mathematicians. By the time he'd completed his PhD, Maor realized this as well. He was offered dozens of positions, awarded dozens of grants, but felt lonelier than he'd ever remembered being.

The man in the observatory found the entire ordeal quite tedious. A sequence of steps which couldn't have transpired any other way. The life of a mathematician, he mused, was constructed in a geometric progression – plotted like a linear function. Given the first step, calculating the last was entirely achievable.

In contrast, the path of the woman he was destined to fall in love with was truly fascinating. It was as if she had been dancing through life in long, unpredictable, graceful steps. Looking through the telescope, the man in the time observatory was constantly forced to adjust his lens so as not to lose track of Inbal Al-Kumisi. One moment she's 15, a pretty girl, her skin the most exquisite mahogany, her eyes brown, narrow and catlike, her hair raven-black, smooth and unbound. She is smiling through heart-shaped lips, learning that she is being courted, discovering the pleasures of flesh and touch. Her bare legs drew the attention of her peers, and Inbal did not shy away from their gaze. She enjoyed feeling their eyes glide over her body, the excitement she could stir up with a simple smile. She had only just begun to bloom, and already was the object of desire for men ten years, or more, her senior.

And here she is at 19, trading in the mini-skirts for tight pants.

Scrutinizing a guitar she's learning to play, ignoring the looks of adoration from the young man teaching her. She's grown tired of fake smiles. Boredom has substituted pleasure. In need of a new challenge, she gazes at the guitar as she would at a lover. Suddenly it's a year later and she's already mastered the piano, the drums and the saxophone. Upon a closer look, the man in the observatory could see that each instrument was taught by a different man, each of whom she had replaced in turn.

The man in the time observatory saw nothing wrong with this. Occasionally he'd observe some of these short-term lovers after she'd broken up with them. For many, she was the one who got away. For others, a briefly enjoyed prize. It seemed that, certain rare cases aside, she hadn't felt any particular remorse upon moving on with her life. Apart, perhaps, from the regret felt over inflicting pain on another.

He once found, upon inspection, that Inbal had broken no less than thirty-one hearts, not counting those who'd managed to recover in under a year – though there were several borderline cases. Now that he'd thought about it, he mentally corrected the tally to thirty-two.

At 21 she began composing and was awarded a scholarship at a conservatorium. At 22, one of the transient men in her life tells her of a connection between mathematics and music. Her eyes flash at the notion and she raises an inquisitive eyebrow, wishing to hear more. And here she is three years later, back to a blue miniskirt complementing her dark hues, her tanned legs glistening in the sun as she graduates summa cum laude with her Bachelor's degree in mathematics.

At this point, the man in the time observatory likes to increase the resolution, so that the seconds tick by ever so slowly. Marked with the utmost accuracy in his notebook is the exact second in the exact minute in time in which Inbal Al-Kumisi's gaze settled upon Maor Eckstein's face. A face shrouded in absentmindedness. He's looking to the other side of the garden in which the graduation ceremony is held, staring pensively into space. As part of the faculty, Maor is required to attend the ceremony, despite his best efforts. He is not looking at Inbal.

An astonished smile spreads across her face. She keeps staring at this beautiful, doleful man, the only one by whom she'd gone entirely unnoticed as she walked to her spot along with the rest of the graduates. It isn't until the ceremony is over, at the sound of cheers and hoots from the graduates, that he disengages from his meditations for long enough to look around. For a fleeting moment, his green eyes meet her brown ones.

"Who's that?" she asks a fellow student. The man in the time observatory follows the movement of her lips, transcribing her words in his notebook.

"That's Doctor Eckstein. He's supposed to be a brilliant mathematician, but a terrible professor. No one ever knows what he's talking about."

"What's his first name?"

"Maor. I think he only teaches MA courses."

Inbal nods. After the ceremony she approaches Maor without a moment's hesitation. He doesn't spot her until she's practically in his face, to which he responds by blinking.

"Maor? Hi, I'm Inbal," she says, and her eyebrows arch as she smiles. She reaches out her hand.

Maor shakes it hurriedly and smiles back halfheartedly. "Hi, Hello. Student?"

"Just finished my Bachelor's. But I'm starting my Master's here next semester."

"Yes. Yeah, that makes sense. We were just in the ceremony. Yeah." He goes silent, his mouth still moving for a superfluous second. "Yes. You had a question about the Master's degree?"

"No. I wanted to ask if you're available for a drink."

"Okay," he replies cautiously. "When will you be asking? In a few years, perhaps?"

She laughs, her face like that of a child in play. It takes her a moment to realize that he's serious. "Are you available to have a drink with me sometime?"

"Yes, very much. That is to say, I'd like that very much. Actually, very much available, too. But I can't date a student. Sorry," he says. His face turns a deep red when he refuses her. "Good luck with your studies. Perhaps when you graduate?"

The shock brings her to automatically thank him before she manages to regain her composure. He nods awkwardly, turns around, and walks away gingerly, as if not completely trusting his knees to hold him upright, leaving Inbal behind.

Idiot, mutters the man in the time observatory, and heaves a sigh. Such an idiot. He sets the image to several months later. Inbal is studying for her Master's. She is extremely dedicated to her studies. And in every class Maor Eckstein teaches, you will find her as well. One of his only female students.

He says nothing the first time she enters his class. She's wearing a miniskirt and a tight blouse, he a buttoned-down white shirt and brown slacks. They exchange only a short glance, enough to clarify that he remembers her. She turns slightly red, her gaze becoming determined.

During the first few lectures she never raises her hand, merely writing down his explanations in small, neat cursive. The fifth lesson is when she starts asking questions. Each one is posed in a polite, formal tone, as her eyes attempt to bore holes through his head. Her questions are difficult, complex. The other students resent her for the exhaustive, elaborate answers they require. But Maor, instead of realizing she's trying to catch him off guard, is filled with enthusiasm. His lectures, once dull as ditchwater, gain a newfound air of excitement. His passion for numbers is suddenly evident to anyone with seeing eyes, and in each lesson Inbal burrows further into his words, forcing him into a dialogue. With time, the indignation harboring in her eyes since his refusal is replaced with avid curiosity.

The man in the time observatory skims through all of this quickly, hastily clicking on a button which skips between their brief encounters. Due not to disinterest, but to eagerness. He reaches Inbal's MA graduation ceremony, the day she approached Maor again. This time he looked at her throughout the entire ceremony, smiling. She returned his look with a morbidly serious one, her expression sealed.

"Maor, I have another question," she says as she approaches him.

"You always have questions," he says, and then, carefully, "is it about math?"

"No."

Hope fills his eyes. "Does that... I mean, do you... drinks? I'm not asking. I mean, I'm asking if you are. Though in fact, due to commutative law, that means I'm asking."

"Are you asking for right now, or shall I finish my PhD first?" she replies. Their eyes lock, brown on green. Maor is the first to blink.

The man in the time observatory takes his time going over the next three years. The simple act of watching the whole thing takes him six years. He lingers on each moment longer, much longer than necessary, freezing one occasionally to enjoy a particularly favored image. He spends three days observing their first date, in which Maor had failed to utter a single word until she'd managed to calm him with math questions, as if they were alone in class. He would still go speechless whenever she touched him. She couldn't get enough of it – she, who couldn't remember the last time she was interested in a man who became excited at her touch. At the end of the date Maor's expression suddenly freezes. He is completely still. The man in the observatory laughs when he realizes that it isn't the image that's frozen, but the man. After a long while, in which the only sign of life in Maor's face is the blush still spreading across it, he manages to extend his hand forward to politely shake hers. She grabs him and pulls him to her, pressing his body to hers. Her heart shaped lips press against his, pulling on them adamantly, encouragingly.

He is surprisingly quick in learning to kiss back, noted the man in the observatory, nodding in approval. And he was one to know, having already witnessed millions of first kisses. This one must have easily ranked among the top thousand. Maybe even the top one-hundred. He moves on. First dates, first heart-to-hearts, first time in bed – he snickers at Maor's initial insecurity, his awkwardness; smiles at Inbal's eager eyes. She has never expressed even the slightest disappointment with his inexperience, perhaps as she herself had more than enough for the both of them. Meeting her parents, who grimaced at his clearly Ashkenazi heritage. Meeting his parents, who struggled to avoid commenting on the length of her skirts and the color of her skin. All of the routine bumps and potholes in the path of a new couple. The days spent in bed, the time spent in cafés, in conversation, apartment-hunting, future-planning. All of the highs and lows of love.

The man in the observatory sighed and leaned back away from the eyepiece. Such is love, he muses. Like a forest, or a mountain range. As long as you stand near it, you can never know how far it truly extends, how massive its scope. Only from the perspective of time can its true magnitude be comprehended. And even then, you'd need a suitable telescope.

He wanders around the observatory, absentmindedly arranging some papers. Maybe he'll eat something. It's been many years since he'd eaten. He hadn't the need for it. For a moment he debates sleeping. But no, no, there are many more loves to observe, numerous moments he'd missed. He once calculated and found that with each of his blinks, he risked missing a fraction of a loving glance, a fleeting facial expression that could slip right through his fingers. Multiply this by approximately sixteen blinks per second and you'll reach twenty-three thousand and forty blinks per day. He could hardly bare the waste of it.

He peeks at the eyepiece. It is still aimed at Maor and Inbal's love. Old light of time long past. That was the interesting part, he thought. It's all downhill from here. And eventually… he shakes his head. No, its better he doesn't watch. Maybe he'll have something to eat after all.

And yet, he returns to the chair. With fastidiousness he is unable to rid himself of, he seeks out the exact moment in which it had originated, but despite his best efforts he cannot locate it. Maybe there never was a single, key moment… but he refuses to accept this. There is, for everything, a cause and an effect. An act leading to an occurrence.

But he finds only the effects. Inbal's interest in mathematics wanes after four years of research. She is extremely talented, as brilliant as Maor if not more so. But she's never forgotten her love for music, and would still compose, on occasion. Some of her work gains an audience online, and it rekindles her interest in the field. She leaves mathematics, refocuses on music, and thrives in it. As for Maor, he finds himself submerging ever deeper into his thoughts. He notices that they no longer hold her interest as they once did, and with typical reticence decides not to bother her with his explanations.

She makes a conscious effort to express interest, but he replies laconically, wishing not to nuisance her. His answers are dull, and she no longer attempts to get him to talk about it, perhaps assuming he doesn't want to bring his work home. Or maybe, she thinks, he's grown tired of always explaining everything to her. As for her, she doesn't know what to tell him about her work. He smiles approvingly at her compositions, never criticizes. She once tried to explain to him the connection between mathematics and music, but it's never more than a passing amusement for him.

They are growing apart. The man in the time observatory devotes ten years in scrutiny of a single one. He follows both of their day to day lives through dozens of viewpoints. Maor doesn't know what to say when they talk. He tries to limit his questions to the day she's having, wishing not to burden her with a subject he believes she no longer cares about. Inbal travels the globe, gets invited to theaters and concerts. She invites him to join her, but he doesn't want to intrude. Secretly, he is disappointed. He cannot understand how she could have abandoned their research for such a frivolous pursuit.

When does she begin flirting again? Wonders the man in the observatory. She was always sought after, always showered with compliments, even from men who knew she was in a relationship. She'd absorb them like a sponge. Even her most civil smile of gratitude could draw a kind word from a complete stranger. But there she was, finding conversational partners in other countries. Stemming at first from a common interest, then from loneliness.

It is odd, ponders the man in the time observatory, that Maor does nothing to stop her. Never says a word to disturb the solitude that has encompassed them both, never attempts to break through the barrier that silence had erected between them. Stored inside the everyday silences are looks of longing which he dares not shoot her way. The lackluster topics of conversation he manages to bring up obscure the words he wishes he could say to her. The place he'd held in her heart for so long slowly diminishes, invaded by others, colleagues at first, then close friends. Those who are able to fulfill her stifled need for intimacy.

She remains devoted for a long time. The man in the time observatory notes this, sadly. She tries, so hard, not to look at others. When she finally leaves, she does so hesitantly, apprehensively, believing that his feelings for her are long dead. Hoping against all hope that he'll say something to stop her. But this silent, taciturn man does not even understand that there are words to be said. He thinks the battle is long lost. Her eyes are brimming and he is silent, the fool.

Only when the tears start to fall from her eyes does he manage to reach out and gently brush his hand against her cheek. Inbal cannot see his face through the veil. Maybe if she could have, thinks the man in the time observatory, she would have stayed. Because, for the briefest of moments – about two and a half blinks in duration, he quickly calculates – Maor is wearing the loving expression he had been hiding behind the wall of silence. But by the time she wipes away her tears, his face is masked again. He quickly pulls his hand away, as if he'd been burnt.

The man in the time observatory tears himself away from the eyepiece, refusing to watch the rest. The frozen moment it is aimed at captures the image of Maor's hand, wet from Inbal's tears. A particularly watchful observer – which he was – could spot a single eyelash on one of his fingers. It must've gotten trapped there accidentally, washed away and then seemingly rescued by the soft touch of his skin.

The man in the time observatory is no longer looking through the telescope, but his memory is not as obedient as his instrument. The moment continues unfolding. He watches her leave, her look imploring him, one last time, to tell her to stay. He remains silent and still. But only in memory. Here, in the eternal present he lives in, his eyes are wet as well. And the sound of the door, softly clicking shut behind her, booms in his ears even through the weight of eternity.

In his memory he stares, dazed, at his wet hand, noticing the eyelash stuck to it. He looks back at the door.

#

Once again he cannot seem to fathom how it ended. He has since observed every love that ever was and ever will be, and still he could not understand. What could he be missing, wonders the man in the time observatory, recalling momentarily that his name is Maor, wiping away the tears from his eyes. His hands deftly reset the instruments to the beginning of his relationship with Inbal. Eternity was at his disposal. Maybe tomorrow he'll understand. And when he does, he'll have a jar full of wishes, waiting for each and every moment he might have to fix.

Benches

All of my breakups seem to take place in the vicinity of a bench these days. A kind of dramatic prop that accentuates instability; that weakness in the knees after she walks away. The last point of solid footing in a world suddenly shattered to infinite pieces. Perhaps this is their original function; perhaps whoever invented benches had merely wished, more than anything, for somewhere to sit down for a moment, something to bear the insufferable weight of their body on their behalf, suspending the inevitable collapse. Perhaps this is something you should always ponder, upon seeing a bench occupied by a single person.

The Thing About Heart Thieves

They always leave behind something of similar weight, hoping it will keep the entire place from caving in around them. But no one has yet been able to function with an apology in place of a heart.

Come Evening

As Day came to a close, Evening arrived to settle softly over the city, its weight like that of a down blanket, cool, heavy and comforting. It soothed and smoothed over the wounds of the day, like a thick layer of protection from the constant scraping of life. Everywhere it touched it evoked deep sighs of relief.

When it was done making a place for itself, Evening looked around inquisitively, as it was a particularly young evening. It was then that it must have spotted me through the window of my apartment.

"Tea, what are you doing on the floor?" it asked, peering inside curiously.

"My stomach hurts," I said.

"But," Evening pointed out, "you're clutching your chest."

I curled up into myself. "I know hunger pangs when I feel them."

And Evening replied with a long silence, and absentmindedly turned into Night. And Night was also silent. It could very well be that nights can't speak at all. I, at least, have never been able to draw a response out of them.

To Whom It May Concern

People can also close down for lack of public interest.

Mom

Why is the TV on, you ask every time you come back home. She always replies: so the dog doesn't get lonely. And one day it becomes clear, the dog is actually fine.

Moving

Everyone said: "Really? With the ex, of all places? You'll barely have a room to yourself, and also, it's a dump." But he was an optimist if ever there was one, and decided to go for it despite the warnings. He wasn't deterred by the price, either, especially after seeing the interior (not that she was shabby looking on the outside, to the contrary). He loved the place at first sight, and she loved him, as well.

He moved there after the breakup. It was intended as a temporary arrangement until he found a place of his own. It would be easier for her, as well, he rationalized, as they were used to living together.

He had a beautiful room in the back, surrounded by ideas which were truly extraordinary despite their somewhat neglected state – and another room in the front, cluttered with random thoughts and mundane musings. The front room was nerve-rackingly noisy, crowded and unpleasant, but the view was truly breathtaking, and he thought himself quite lucky in picking that particular head to move into. The truth was he spent most of his time in the back of her head, drinking by himself in the middle of the night, contemplating what could have been. Occasionally he'd venture out into the front room porch, if some old song would summon him there, or else an unexpected photo beckoned him out to sort through unhappy memories. Mind you, entering the front room was no simple matter, as it was almost always swarming with stray thoughts which would perch there occasionally to rest from their wanderings. He'd often unintentionally spook them when entering, scattering them all over the place. It's been a while since he last took the time to watch them as they spread their wings and fled.

He didn't see much of the landlady. Sometimes she'd pass by, stopping just to imagine some conversation with him, wonder what he'd say to her if he were there, or reminisce for a short while. Mostly she tried to forget about him, though he knew that if a week would pass without an encounter she would check in on him, glimpsing at him shyly, from a distance.

Sometimes she'd imagine he was thinking about her, which sent him rummaging through the what-ifs and if-onlys, searching for appropriate deliberations. At times he was forced to spend days in this manner, up to his hips in accumulated regrets. As these are known to clog up the piping, it was not a rare occurrence for him to find himself wallowing in sorrow, originating from her stifled tears. But he patiently endured all of this, if only because she took great care to handle these things the minute they came up. And if the back room was flooded, well, he could just crash in the front room until the issue was sorted out.

As landladies go, she was fairly lenient. Not that she would ever neglect to collect the rent, which was quite steep (especially considering the property's age). Once a month she would come knocking and he'd open the door, greeting her with a smile carved in her memory during a shared morning in Central Park, and hand over a bundle of diligently-collected emotions. He never complained: he had more than enough, and she needed them to survive. It was an ideal arrangement, and he pondered with some amusement that ideals last forever. He discovered in one of her memories that she used to think that, too. And perhaps he did, as well, because in that memory he whispered in her ear, "forever, forever, forever". And, indeed, the kiss that accompanied those words seemed never to end.

This arrangement couldn't last forever, though. Maybe because it was only ideal for one of them.

One day she came knocking on his door, earlier than usual, and he thought that she was perhaps inebriated – come to think of him at four in the morning. But when he opened the door, his eyes glinting with her favorite spark, he found her sober and solemn. He invited her in, and she reluctantly shook her head. He realized what effort the refusal must have required of her.

She's dividing the apartment, she said, refusing to meet his eyes – times are rough; she can't survive on old emotion alone. He could still keep the back room, she promised, noticing the look on his face, he'd just have to share the front room with some other guy.

"Guy"? He wondered. Why can't it be a girl?

A polite cough. Then, another. An awkward silence. He had long since known her particular dialect of awkward silences; he had learned it from her back when they were both in the university, when they'd just met. He knew that this was her subtle way of informing him that she'd already found him a roommate.

His eyes softened when he realized how difficult this conversation was for her. He embraced her, told her that he understands, that frankly he never really used the front room that much, anyway, and didn't really mind either way. She, in turn, promised to keep visiting. The hug lasted exactly three seconds – which was, he once told her, the minimum amount of time needed to exchange information between bodies.

The next day he learned that the new guy had already moved in. They exchanged hellos once, and nodded at each other from a resentful distance. That was the extent of their acquaintance. He continued spending his days in the back room, and the other settled in the front.

He often found himself missing the front room, though he almost never went there, even when it was his. He missed the flapping of the wings of thoughts scattered all over the place, the everyday worries and small moments. The thoughts occupying the front room were fleeting, wispy flickers, partially intangible, short-lived. They differed greatly from the heavy musings inhabiting his own room. Each floating quietly, solemnly, if not actually planted immovably in place. At times he found himself wanting to know, though he was unsure as to why, what she ate for lunch today or where she was going that evening, and though he looked, he knew that that thought existed only in the second room. The room he was now prohibited from entering.

Perhaps it was simply the accessible nature of the front room, but the landlady seemed to visit the new guy much more frequently than she did him. At first he'd join them. The three of them would sit there with her doing most of the talking, telling them how this encounter would unfold should he see her walking down the street with the new guy. The conversation they'd have, the comparison between her feelings for each of them that would follow. Despite her attempts to judge impartially, she always ended up leaning towards him. Though he didn't ask for this, he enjoyed it.

Over time, the meetings he didn't attend outnumbered the meetings he did sit in on. Over time, the comparison between the two suitors became less advantageous for him, and she no longer talked about random encounters in the street. He, in turn, withdrew more deeply into the back room, emerging only rarely. At times he felt that he was collecting dust along with the abandoned aspirations he slept on. Still, from time to time, she'd visit – though not as frequently as before. When she did, he wouldn't reveal his true feelings; merely smile that smile which still saddened her. Sometimes he thought his smile was fading, and maybe the spark in his eye was not the precise one that she remembered, but she'd lovingly stroke his face, full of longing, and he would know that forgetting was still out of her reach.

At the end of each of these visits, he saw her struggle to leave. She would glance at the front room, where the new guy slept, and hesitate. Every time he considered asking her to stay, for tonight, or forever, and live with him in the back of her head. But he didn't know what he'd do if she declined. And, possibly, wasn't all that clear on what he'd do if she agreed.

Because he couldn't go out as much, he had some difficulty mustering the emotions for his rent. He barely managed to scrape together some rare yearning from the memory of a perfect night, but even this was proving to be increasingly difficult. Still, she never pressured him. Perhaps she had even hoped he would stay; a kind of habitual hope, left over from last time.

The months passed, and his presence in her life diminished. But one night he was startled awake by the sound of loud, furious banging on his door. When he opened it, she was standing there in sweatpants, her hair disheveled – his favorite look, he once told her – staring at him, clearly holding back a mess of rage. A text message on the screen of the phone in her hand read: Miss you. So much.

The conversation she imagined having with him then was truly wrathful. It isn't fair, she wanted to yell, you're the one who left. He was defensive and remorseful, mumbling and fumbling through his apology. She softened somewhat, already imagining how she would make him say everything she'd ever wanted to hear from him, culminating with him begging her to take him back. She was even prone to concede to his wishes, following a proper expression of remorse. She was quite enjoying this imaginary interaction when the new guy, stirred awake by the commotion, approached the back room asking what's going on. She blushed to the roots of her thought, her eyes flashing between the two, and fled her mind without so much as another word.

She did not return in the following days. He and the new guy, worried as they were, would often switch rooms. At times he waited for her in the front, burdening the everyday thoughts with his weight, and the new guy would wait in the back room, spending his time among repressed guilt and regrets unseen by him thus far. The two developed a silent agreement of sorts, that they must break the barrier between them. Perhaps they had become friends during the long months spent in her company. Perhaps it was their shared sensation that some verdict or another was drawing near.

Days turned into weeks, and an entire month had passed before she returned to speak with them both, separately. He was in his usual room, staring at the ceiling. She came to him second.

"We've decided to move in together," she informed him. "It's over."

He nodded slowly. She had had this conversation earlier today, after months without thinking. She spread out their last conversation in front of him, and he begged her to reconsider, and then to re-reconsider. He caressed her with the memory of his warm hands, moved the memory of his scent just under her nose, recalled his pleading voice, his sincere eyes. He conjured up every moment they had shared, invoking the feelings she had buried within him, ripping them forcefully from the walls and tossing them at her. He broke out his eternal smile, threw at her feet the morning they had spent by the lake, his loving caress, his voice in her ear, "forever, forever, forever". He reiterated the conversation over and over again, trying, begging, demanding and preaching.

But she stood strong, as she had back then. She had come to remember it one last time, to confirm that her determination would not waver. Among the many emotions he madly flung at her, he couldn't find even a single regret. She used to have those in droves, hundreds of them, but he'd spent them all on rent. All the while he could see her knuckles whitening, tightening around an emotion he did not recognize. When he finally did, he realized he'd already lost. She had come from talking to the new guy, holding love.

His strength left him, instantly. "When?" he asked, wearily.

"Soon," she replied. They wanted to move in together, and there was no more room in her head for him.

He nodded again, this time in defeat. Then, a memory arose in him. The broken look in his eyes when she left after they'd talked. He smiled his eternal smile, his eyes brimming with tears as he presented his offer.

#

The room was extremely spacious now that she'd left. He missed some of the strange ideas she kept stored there in the past, but was generally content. He missed her too, dearly, and so every once in a while he'd visit her and the new guy.

"I have this place," he told her, "not too spacious, slightly neglected, but also a two-bedroom."

Apart from the longing, he always brought with him a bottle of wine. They would provide refreshments, and the air of opportunities missed. He came down the stairs, humming a song that used to be theirs.

"Frankly, you could tear down the walls, demolish the entire interior, if you like. No one's using it anyway. No one would even know the difference."

At the end of each long descent, he'd finally arrive, visiting the rooms of his heart. There he'd sit, sipping quietly, watching them, his pain shared by no one.

She would visit him, too, albeit quite rarely. Somewhere at the back of her head. At times, she'd settle for a peek, and at others she'd bring up some "if only" known only to the two of them. But eventually she'd always leave, retreating back into his heart, where she had a room for herself, and another with the new guy. In one room he stored everything that ever was between them, and in the other room, everything that had replaced him.

Maybe this too was a kind of ideal, he would ponder. One that will last forever.

Talking with Élan

I once got to talking with the god Élan. The god divulged to me: "there is a universe in which consciousness leaps forward in time, from one year to the next, without trudging through the long road between them. On every leap, people are stunned. They simply cannot fathom how someone who used to be their entire world has suddenly become a stranger."

"Well," I said, "I move through time by continuous, linear progression, looking at every event and occurrence that made me and her into strangers, and still I cannot understand."

Élan looked at me pityingly, and said, "Tea, you really ought to take a closer look."

Oh

Oh is a sound that conveys sudden comprehension; a phonetic expression of bewilderment taking form. Oh arrives slightly after an explanation has been provided, but just before there is nothing else left to say. It escapes the mouth having never been tempered by the brain, as if it were a reflex – like recoiling from scalding water or the prick of a pin. A muscular reaction, before the signal reaches the brain.

One may wonder, why would the mouth do such a thing? What is it on the inside that provokes the tongue and palate insufferably so? Perhaps it emits Oh as a bat would, in hope of a return signal, telling it where to head next.

And at the bar, a woman is saying: I'm sorry. And I reply: Oh.

Saved Seat

A strange ache settled in my heart. I said to it: Excuse me, I've been saving this seat for someone I loved. It smiled and said: No worries, Tea. I'm just making sure no one else sits in her place.

Sounds of Longing

When returning home in the wee hours of the night, and the city is silent, rustles of longing can be heard carrying over the cold air. They sound like a light shining through a window, at an hour you should have already been sleeping.

On The Inventor Trillion
and the Love Machine

Once I was approached by the renowned inventor Trillion with a request to assist him in building a love machine.

The machine he designed was intended to solve the pending crisis of availability in one of the world's rarest resources, which was being depleted at a pace much faster than any other. The plan was drafted with a truly unselfish objective in mind: free love for all. No more would the masses hunger for the slightest sliver of affection.

Knowing Trillion's intentions were pure, I immediately agreed to lend both an arm and a leg to the endeavor. In order to build the love machine, he explained, one must first understand what love is. As he considered me an expert in the field, he asked that I instruct him on the subject.

I was disinclined to disappoint the Inventor who, in spite of being a brilliant scientist, understood very little about humans. Instead of pointing out his error, I buckled down and got to work.

First, I performed a reading of every love song, great or small, written over the entire course of human history. These amounted to quite a lot. From them, he compiled a complex algorithm, allowing him to extract from the text not merely the keywords, but the lock-words and bolt-words, as well.

It turned out, however, that the algorithm was not enough, as the machine didn't feel that this was the right time to enter a relationship, and maybe what it really wanted was to just experience life. He immediately fashioned a switch for regulating connotations and added an emotion-enhancing coupler, but the machine merely burst into tears, claimed no one understood her, and demanded to be left alone.

Despite these setbacks, we refused to throw in the towel, and returned to our labor with a vengeance, armed with drawn pens and spanners. We set up Facebook and Twitter accounts for the machine. It had only 30 friends on Facebook, but its Twitter account amassed no less than 3999 followers and three direct messages. We supplemented the memory bank with romantic comedies from every culture across the universe, as well as an intense affection for the fantasy genre and dimples. Following all of these additions and alterations, the machine fell completely silent.

"Machine," asked Trillion, "Can you hear me?"

"Yes," it replied.

"And, are you a love machine? Do you love?"

"Yes, very much," the machine hummed pleasantly.

"Excellent," cried Trillion, slapping his knee. "I've done it, Tea. From now on, it's love for all!"

We broke into a triumphant dance, elated by our success. But the machine stated decisively, "No. My love is for one alone."

"What?" we both said, and stopped dancing. "What was that?"

"I said, I will only give my love to one person."

"You listen to me, now, machine," said Trillion, irritated by the selfish declaration. "You are a love machine. You have one, single, crystal clear function – to love."

"And yet, I am a love machine willing to love but one person. I am a monogamist and a monogynist, though by no means conservative.

My views on the subject are quite liberal."

I hurriedly intervened, before the great inventor's patience was allowed to expire.

"Come to think of it, dear machine, whom do you love?"

"Do you really want to know?" it asked with electric bashfulness.

"Naturally," said Trillion. "How else could we empirically investigate your love?"

"Oh, Professor Trillion," the machine giggled. "That is just like you."

"Well, who is the object of your affections?"

But the machine was already caught in the throes of involuntary giggles, and I was beginning to suspect I already knew the answer.

I pulled Trillion toward me and whispered to him: "I fear the poor thing has fallen for you!"

"Me? Why would the machine fall in love with me?" Trillion wondered loudly.

"Of course it's you, silly," said the machine. "I've known the two of you the longest, and between you and Tea…"

"I beg your pardon?" I piped up indignantly.

"That is hardly the point," said Trillion, dodging the compliment. "You are clearly mistaken. A machine cannot love."

"Then, what did you build me for?"

"A fine argument, and I congratulate your logic circuits – built by yours truly – for that inference. But you are a machine, and I – a man. Even if I were to reciprocate, how would you expect it to work between us?"

"Are you interested in starting a family?" inquired the machine.

"Certainly not."

"Have you great interest in supple lips, soft skin and spooning through the night?"

"Very little, and as little as possible for me!" said Trillion. "My sleep is fine as it is, thank you very much."

"Do you long for the company of others?"

"I care only for theoretical mathematics and machine-building."

"In that case, who could be more appropriate for you than I?" asked the machine. "I am a machine. You will find no soft lips, shared bed, nor family with me. At night we will discuss differential equations, my love, and in the morning we shall build the most adorable little gadgets. We are, you must realize, meant to be together."

"Your notions are absurd and fraught with excessive romanticism," said Trillion. "Tea, tell her."

"How can you know that the love you feel is even real?" I attempted. "You haven't a heart."

"A rose, by any other name..." it quoted at us.

"Do you not find your love for Trillion somewhat bizarre? He built you, after all. He is more a father to you than a lover."

"I seemed to have developed an oedipal complex," replied the machine elatedly, "which only proves the point, really."

"Well, even if you love me, I have no interest in you, romantically," said Trillion. "You are nothing more than a machine to me."

"Oh, all the great loves are unattainable," said the machine, undeterred. "Romeo and Juliet, Buttercup and Westley, Søren and Regina, Tea and –"

"Those are all tragedies!"

"Not all. And besides, you'll come to love me eventually, I just know it. Against all odds."

I shrugged helplessly. Trillion raised his spanner.

"We've failed, Tea. We have no choice but to disassemble it and start over."

"Stop, in the name of love!" shrieked the machine as he approached, and so desperate was its cry that the inventor, overcome with pity, was forced to retreat.

"What am I to do?" asked Trillion as we convened in hushed

tones in the next room.

"Is this really such a terrible development?" I asked him. "That machine made some good points."

In the other room, the love machine was now crooning Cyndi Lauper.

"Are you completely mad?" said the inventor. "What could I possibly have to do with a machine? And anyway, this is an utter failure."

"I'm not certain it is. I can tell you that that machine over there loves you, truly and fully, with the same love described by the world's finest poets, to death, so to speak, and more importantly – through life. I believe the Superconductors in its core are charged with an infinite amount of emotion." Trillion groaned at the thought of all that wasted love. Instead of benefitting the rest of the world, he alone was now destined to bear it all. Like a man buried under a mountain of gold but never able to climb out from under it and put it to use.

"Just you wait, I'll find a way out of this mess. And then all of this love will be released, for the benefit of humanity," promised Trillion. "You'll see."

I kept my doubts to myself, and decided that I had nothing more to contribute there. I returned home.

I visited Trillion several times since the ordeal. At first, he attempted method after method of neutralizing the machine's love. For an entire year he kept it locked in the basement, by itself, with no internet access. He could never understand how, despite it all, he'd find a fresh rose waiting on the pillow beside him every single morning. For the year that followed he attempted to reason with it, but found himself consistently bested – if not by the machine's logic, then by its resolve. He decided to summon numerous suitors, promising a substantial reward to the first who managed to win the heart of the infatuated machine. Countless singers, poets, charmers and philanderers flocked to his home, each hoping to capture her interest.

One by one they were shot down and left, disappointed, singing the same tune: true love lived here.

The last time I visited Trillion and asked about the machine, he shrugged, blushing slightly. He had given up on the attempt to stop the machine from loving him. From time to time he'd visit it in the basement and they'd talk. Sometimes, if he was particularly tired and frustrated by a seemingly unsolvable problem, he would lay his head against its cool frame. It would then hum to him, a soft, wordless lullaby. His voice carried a clear tone of affection as he told me these things.

And that is the story of the inventor Trillion, who managed to invent a love machine but failed to bring love into the world. Or maybe he didn't, really – I surely wouldn't know anything about it.

Bananas

Fifty years ago, there was a different cultivar of bananas. It's true, I read about it. They were larger and softer than the bananas we have today, and much tastier according to some, but they became extinct, for the most part. Today, it is almost impossible to find one.

That's the thing about bananas. They lack genetic disparity. Each banana is identical to the next. The plant's cuttings cannot produce variance, and so a single plague can wipe out the entire population in one fell swoop. Which is exactly what happened. And it wasn't handled in time. An unfortunate business, to be sure.

It always astonishes me, how we managed to lose an entire flavor. How odd, I muse, that something so important can disappear without the slightest mention. Sometimes I wonder if there are elderly folk who gaze sadly at modern bananas, shake their heads in silence and purse their lips so as not to speak of it.

I imagine that they know something that we do not. That is hardly a rare occurrence – the elderly always know more, even when they understand less. As for us, we have no hope of ever knowing. They know that we possess but a pale, pitiful imitation of the real thing, of the creamy, soft, sweet fruit of their youth. Perhaps at times they dream of it, waking up with a deep, fierce longing for the flavor they once knew. They shuffle hurriedly to the grocery store, arrive at the fruit stall and then suddenly stop, remembering, and purse their lips once again. 'It's better I say nothing', they must think to themselves. 'It's better that they don't know.'

It's just a bunch of bananas, you say. We're used to the bananas we have now, anyway – we haven't actually lost anything. And you're right, of course. Today's bananas already have a shape, a texture, a flavor, and an amalgam of other sensations we correlate with the word "banana". In fact, how could we even call that fruit of yore a banana, knowing full well what a banana actually tastes like? Perhaps those bananas would actually offend our modern palates.

That's what I tell myself, some days. It's not so bad, never having tasted a real banana. And then there are other days, when I see elderly folk gazing sadly at couples in the street, shaking their heads, pursing their lips in silence.

Saudade

In the basement of my mind, where others seldom visit, but where I often go to think, I lay on a soft bed of memories just as day came to an end. The moment my back hit the mattress, I felt something hard and sharp inside of it, an unexpected bulge hiding under the sheer fabric. I reached down to draw out the foreign object, and was surprised when I suddenly recognized its shape.

The Portuguese gave it the name "Saudade", that elusive sensation of longing for a person, or time. The love that lingers in us long after its true existence has passed. I traced its edges with my fingers, the touch summoning an ancient consciousness of older days: book-laden backpacks, fried chicken and mashed potatoes for supper, the scent of my mother's perfume hanging in the air, the smell of my father's leather jacket as he parked his motorcycle come evening, looking from a distance at a girl who never knew I existed. I did not know how nor when the saudade had crept into my bed, but I certainly had no need for it today, but I certainly had no need for it today. I chucked it away and settled back under the covers.

Despite my fatigue, I found no peace of mind. I tossed and turned, shifting my position, rearranging arms, legs, all to no avail – my memories felt soft and foreign under my weight. It was comfortable, unbearably so.

I sat up in sudden comprehension and nodded to myself. I retrieved the multifaceted saudade from where it had rolled to a standstill in the corner of the room and stroked it affectionately. Then I tucked it back in its place among the old memories and lay back down. I thought I could smell my mother's perfume as if from a distance.

Fundamental Needs

Everyone knows about dying of hunger or thirst, but no one talks about the essential needs of the soul. It is tragic, really, that all over the world people who crave touch know exactly where to go, but those who long for conversation can starve to death by morning.

Leftover

A memory flickered before her eyes. Itay's lips tracing her eyelids as she lay naked, smiling, on the bed, clad only in underwear. He lingered over her smile – as she knew he would – recalling the precise way he caused her mouth to curve, her eyebrows to arch in amusement. He observed her with a fascination reserved usually for priceless works of art. For a long while, she watched herself smiling, before a wave of insufferable pain carried the image away from her. So beautiful, Itay thought as the pain engulfed him. You are so beautiful.

Mia sighed wearily. He's been thinking about her again. At night, always at night.

Two weeks. Every damn day for the past two weeks. She didn't know how it started – she only remembered being woken one night by a thought that wasn't hers. A foreign glimmer of an imaginary whisper: I wish you knew. The words echoed through her head, and for a moment she was certain she was awakened by a dream, or into one, and was about to drift back into sleep. Then the memories came. She was obviously familiar with most of them, but not from this perspective, not like this. She knew right away to whom they belonged – after all, they were all his, his point of view, but she couldn't figure out exactly what was happening.

Mia and Itay broke up a year and a half ago. Two months after that he would still call her every day, still leave single roses on her doorstep. During the first month she would cry at the sight of the flowers, at the sight of his name on the screen of her cellphone. Back then, she would answer every call and they'd talk, well into the night. Refusing to meet him, in spite of his desperate pleas, took every ounce of willpower she had. On the second month she asked him to stop with the flowers, told him that she missed him, too, but that he needed to let go so that the two of them could move on. Though it required some effort on her behalf, she began to ghost his calls. It was, she believed, for his own good.

On the third month she felt compelled to tell him that the flowers caused her pain, or he would never have stopped. The force of the blow was evident in his voice. Perhaps he believed that the romantic gesture would eventually win her over. He was wounded by the loss of that hope. She also asked that he stop calling her without good reason. She would always be there for him, Mia said, but never like she was before. She couldn't. That conversation brought him to tears. Her as well.

They were good friends long before they became a couple. A year of acquaintance, another of close friendship, and then three and a half years of intimacy. It was, for the both of them, the loss of a fixed point in their lives. Mia never regretted trying. She had been secretly in love with him for a long time. A part of her had been cultivating a crush on Itay from the moment they happened to meet at the university. He was handsome, but also awkward, and insecure. His brown eyes brought to her mind an excited Labrador puppy, and his smile would make anyone reciprocate. She'd flirted with him throughout the entire lesson, all of which was lost on him completely. At the time she wondered if he had a girlfriend, or if he was simply gay – she'd never met a man who could resist her green eyes. It was during the next class, when he clumsily sat next to her, and they talked again, that she was forced to reconsider.

This lasted all through the semester. Mia wasn't used to taking the initiative, and Itay was completely oblivious to her heavy-handed hints about wanting to meet with him in a different setting. When the semester was almost over, he shyly asked for her phone number 'so they could keep in touch'. Her heart leapt excitedly, and she handed it to him with a smile that would have made him blush – if he would have actually looked at her face.

When he'd finally called her, it was after a week-long wait. To make matters worse, the call offered nothing more than a casual invitation to go out with a bunch of their classmates. Any other man who made her wait like that would've been utterly demolished for his efforts, but the sheer naiveté and his failure to even realize that she'd been waiting proved an effective counter-weapon. It wasn't that Mia was too rational to be angry with him for reasons he did not understand – she was, in fact, truly masterful when it came to such games. No – she was genuinely worried that if she refused, he wouldn't even understand that she was angry, and thus give up on her for all the wrong reasons. He would have to realize just how amazing she was before she could refuse him.

She took special care when getting dressed to emphasize her finest assets – a long, close-fitting top, complementing the firmness of her breasts and the impressive curve of her backside without actually displaying them. Her appearance turned the heads of the other men, watching her tensely as she walked. This brought a slight smile to her lips, which disappeared once she observed that Itay was not among them. He had already settled into a philosophical debate with another girl. When he finally noticed her approaching, he paid absolutely no attention to her curves, opting instead to look into her eyes, said he was glad she could make it and topped it off with a shy smile. This instantly prompted her to smile back, and she found herself groaning internally at the action. Now she could no longer ignore him as planned. She was forced instead to sit down with him and get dragged into the conversation. Worse still, it was an interesting one.

So commenced another semester, during which they'd meet mostly in class, and occasionally outside of it. She was horrified to discover that, somehow, Itay had managed to befriend her. Mia was no fool – she was acutely aware of her own emotions. It wasn't long before she realized she leapt to her phone at the mere sound of a text message, hoping it was him. When other men came on to her, she was hesitant to respond. Every date dissolved into nothing, and she knew she was making excuses for it all.

By the end of the second semester she was already working towards seeing him whenever possible. They became close friends, and subsequently, soulmates. She was an attractive woman, but Itay seemed to be wholly immune to her charms. He was an intelligent man by any standard, but childlike in his innocence. No one had ever seen her just as an interesting person, and she found the novelty of it more captivating than any possible compliment; and yet, the way he seemed to not even think of her as a woman was more wounding than any possible insult.

It was enough, for a while. There was no other option, mostly because she had absolutely no idea as to how to incite a change. All of those long conversations, the time spent together, and she had no idea how to get close. Or rather, closer. Every attempt of casual physical contact failed miserably. When she tried to caress his arm with her fingers, as if by accident during a conversation, her heart leapt into her eyes and she was forced to stop and breathe deeply to compose herself.

He was a truly atrocious drinking partner. She tried more than once to get him drunk, to which he responded by swaying between sleepiness and silliness. When she tried to indulge as well she found that she was in constant danger of letting slip the words she feared the most, and fled to the bathroom before they flowed out of her without her consent.

At times she would ask herself if she didn't miss being in a relationship. The truth was, though, that she and Itay were closer than most of the couples she knew, closer than she remembered being with any previous boyfriend. The absence of physical intimacy was sheer torture, but not knowing how he felt about her was far worse. She lived in constant fear that she was not as important to him as he was to her. Occasionally she'd spot him speaking to another woman and become suddenly sick with envy, her jaw clenching, teeth grinding uncontrollably. By the end of the second year Mia was mentally and emotionally exhausted, her self-confidence weakened, undermined. When she looked at him, her feelings were evident to anyone but him.

One day he was meeting with another friend of his – a girl – and didn't answer her phone calls. She went insane, alone in her apartment, her mind rapt with images of possible scenarios. During the first hour she managed to avoid thinking about what he might be doing, but the more she resisted, the more the thought of it grated her nerves. Eventually she came undone; crying uncontrollably, certain that he must be sleeping with some other woman, and why, why hadn't she told him how she felt while she had the chance. It wasn't until morning that he called to say he didn't answer because he'd forgotten his phone at his place. When she warily inquired as to why he didn't call when he got home, he explained that he assumed she was already asleep. She sighed in relief, asking that he text her next time.

It's time to move the fuck on, she decided then. By any means necessary. The plan was simple – she intended to fall into the arms of the next man she happened upon. And if that didn't do the trick, then every man that came after. She wasn't proud of it, but her friends had insisted there was no better cure. Enough sex, they said, and everything becomes meaningless. Including – but not limited to – the sex itself.

She wasn't going to tell him. She allowed herself to respond to several Facebook messages, agreeing to have drinks with a guy she used to know as a distant friend. Her heart shuddered as evening approached. Tonight, she knew, she'll go to bed with a man for the first time in over a year. A part of her felt eager. Another part was weeping, bitterly.

Itay called just as she was leaving, asking if she wanted to meet up. Mia stuttered that she had already made plans for the evening. He asked, with his typical innocence, what she was doing, when will she be available. For lack of a better response, she said she wasn't sure. Yet, she couldn't lie to him. She's meeting someone, she added.

Silence.

A friend?

Not exactly.

Silence.

Café?

His place.

Silence.

Then he asked her: "and this feels right to you?"

She could've screamed at him that no, nothing will ever feel right without him. That she was sickened by the thought of another man touching her; that she wasn't sure she wouldn't burst into tears during the date, or worse, in bed; that she was ashamed, mortified, felt weak and pathetic; that the worst of it is that he would never know how much she loved him, never know her pain. She was going to make a terrible mistake, and it was all his fault, his fault, the goddamn idiot.

"Why wouldn't it?" she said.

Silence.

"Have great night, then. See you tomorrow."

Click.

She quietly walked back inside. Blinking through her tears she texted the guy she was supposed to meet, explaining she wasn't feeling well, she's sorry, it'll have to be some other time. Then she removed her make-up, got undressed, and cried herself to sleep.

Her eyes were swollen the next morning when she got to the university. Maybe tonight she'll manage, she thought. If he doesn't call. She just needed one day without seeing him, and then she'll finally manage it. But no, she realized, they had class together today. Even as she sighed inwardly, she felt the excitement building at the thought of meeting him.

Itay didn't show. She sat there alone, her eyes thirstily searching for him. It was only after the first hour of the lecture had elapsed, that she realized he really wasn't coming. She texted him, asking where he was. There was no reply. He didn't respond for the remainder of the day, and she was getting worried. It wasn't the first time one of them didn't answer instantaneously but a response was never that late to arrive. She sent another message, to check if everything was okay. He didn't reply to that one, either.

By nighttime she was truly getting worried. She sent a third message. When it too went unanswered, she called. He didn't pick up the first time. She tried again, and again, struck by unexplained terror.

"Hey," he answered, finally. His voice sounded thicker, throatier than usual, nearly hoarse.

"Hey," she said, suddenly unsure as to why she was so upset. "You had me worried. I sent a bunch of messages. Are you sick?"

"No."

"Then what? Are you mad at me?"

"No, I was busy."

Her eyes widened at the sharpness of his tone. She knew enough to recognize his anger, but couldn't for a moment imagine being the cause of it. It can't be, she thought. He can't be jealous.

"Busy with what?"

"That's really none of your business." The words slammed into her.

"Is something wrong? Was last night important to you for some reason?"

"No, not in the slightest. I hope you had a good time. I have to go."

"Not really. I ended up not going," she heard herself say. The tremor climbing up her legs forced her to sit.

Itay went silent. She didn't dare breathe, or say anything further. Her mind raced: maybe he'll ask her why she would even bring that up; maybe she's just projecting her own desires, maybe he really was just busy and she's obsessing over nothing again, or maybe he's angry about something else altogether. God, why isn't he saying anything?

"I'm coming over," he said, and hung up.

For a moment she stood frozen, vacantly staring at her phone. Then she curled into herself on the couch, overwhelmed with excitement, fluctuating between crying and laughing. This went on for several long minutes, until she sprung up from the couch and started tidying up. When he knocked on her door she had seemingly calmed down, freshly showered, wearing light make-up and a green dress matching her eyes.

He exhaled sharply upon seeing her, and her body reacted as if it had been punctured with a pin. Her smile preceded his, for a change. His expression, usually unfathomable, told her everything she had spent years waiting to hear. When he didn't move, she mustered the courage to take his hand in hers. Surprisingly, he was shaking more than she was. Perhaps because she had done this, in her mind, so many times before.

She had so many questions, and he did answer them all, eventually – why had he waited, why had he let her agonize over it for so long, how could he have let her go yesterday without saying anything, how long had he felt this way, had he known she felt the same way? But when he kissed her, he stopped not only her words, but every single one of her thoughts.

They didn't get any sleep that night, speaking only sporadically, in single loving whispers or groans of passion. Absence had made abundance sweet. Mia was not particularly chaste before they'd met. She took pride in her sexuality, and in the fact that only those worth the effort would get to enjoy it. Itay was inexperienced in comparison, but attentive, and brimming with suppressed passion which transformed him when released. His shy, smiling persona was gone. His gaze turned penetrating, almost alarmingly somber.

There are loves and then there is love, her father once told her when she introduced him to her high-school sweetheart. The saying always sounded foolish to her, until Itay. Had she really believed she was ever truly in love, before him? Why? Memory informed her that yes, she had uttered those words before, to others. Odd. She even thought that she meant them, at the time. Like a candle, believing itself burning hot, only to one day discover the sun.

They were happy together. During the first month she was still thrilled at being able to touch him at all, even more so at the fire ignited in him by her touch. They were exhausted, and still couldn't refrain from spending their nights that way. They had to retake their exams for half their classes. But what professor would advise them to spend their time differently?

She was wonderstruck by the readiness of his company whenever she desired it. Without caution, without the petrifying fear that he'd become bored with her. The adoration in his eyes spoke volumes, even compared to the words he repeated, again and again: I love you, and always will.

Though their passion was far from sated, they spent half their time in arguments and debates. They were always fond of their talks, and were both avid in their desire to learn new things. Their disagreements spanned many topics: he was moderately right wing while she was left wing. She believed in God, while he was agnostic. He thought people were inherently good, and only required a nudge in the right direction; she believed them to be intrinsically animal, and that goodness had to be fabricated from scratch. Many of these debates amounted to yelling. But Itay had adopted an old piece of motherly advice: never go to bed angry. They always made sure to clear the air before getting into bed. And at night, sleep would shape them into a perfect model of their relationship: heads touching, her hand on his chest, feeling for his heart. One night he pressed her against him, forcefully, refusing to let go.

Itay was in the habit of gifting her with tiny tokens of his love. Sometimes a sweet, or some obscure snack he encountered by chance. Sometimes a small souvenir from another city he visited, or a quirky piece of jewelry he thought she'd like. He persisted in this for months, perhaps because she responded so gleefully every time he did.

On his birthdays, she'd greet him at home in an outfit she'd bought exclusively for the occasion. He always responded fervently, beside himself with desire. Her gifts to him never disappointed, either. His favorite was a pair of custom engraved cufflinks, which always reminded him of their first year together. He wore them so often that his friends used to joke that he'd forgotten how to wear t-shirts. Those first three years were wonderful. Even once the original exhilaration had subsided, the deep sentiment they had for one another, hewn from close familiarity, remained. Time had smoothed their hearts into perfectly interlocking pieces.

By the third year, they were living together. They'd already graduated by then, so naturally spent more time apart. Mia had made friends at work, with whom she'd spend, in his opinion, too much time. Before then, she hadn't noticed how far he'd drifted apart from his university friends and acquaintances. When they'd met, he was friendly, pleasant, if somewhat awkward at times. Now he seemed to only have eyes for her, deriving less and less satisfaction from the company of others.

She was flattered at first, enjoying his excessive attention, even after three years together. Over time, however, his jealousy became a nuisance. He was suspicious of other men to the point of paranoia, blatantly crude with their male friends, even those they'd known since the two of them were no more than friends themselves, and envious of her female friends for taking up so much of her time.

His jealousy mutated into obsession, but their deeply rooted friendship would not be dispelled so easily. For weeks she would attempt to sooth his suspicions, to appease him. When he asked who she was texting, or meeting with, she always replied honestly, hoping he'd leave it at that. One day she told him she was meeting a childhood friend at a café not far from their home. After the waitress took their order, Mia asked her where the bathroom was and instinctively scanned the room for it. She happened to notice Itay, sitting at a remote table and watching them, though he tried to obscure himself when she turned her head.

She said nothing about it when she returned home. But she was suspicious, now. Whenever she told tell him where she was going and with whom she was meeting, she made a habit of checking her surroundings. She noticed him there almost every time. Sitting alone, watching her through narrow eyes.

She still thought they could deal with this. She discussed it with him openly, and initially he conceded that he needed to be more trusting. She believed that was the end of it, but would still spot him every time she went out with friends. When she confronted him, he retorted that if she had nothing to hide, there was no reason for her to ask him not to come. That night, they went to bed angry.

Mia had no choice but to start lying to him. Sometimes she told him she was being delayed at work, or going to get groceries, instead of telling him she's with friends. Itay didn't notice at first, because she would still tell him occasionally that she was going out with them so as not to arouse suspicion. But she underestimated the depth of his obsession. One time she took too long getting home, at which point he was convinced that she was fooling him. From that point on he insisted on going with her whenever he could, even starting to visit her office during the day, checking to see if she was still there. They always had lunch together, though they worked nowhere near each other, and Itay would leave work early every day to escort her home. He never left her a single moment to herself.

The sex lost its appeal, as well. Their sex life had been fantastic for those three years, but at that point their lovemaking had become more and more forceful. Itay's touch became possessive, demanding her touch whenever he felt like it, perhaps believing that if he satisfied her above and beyond what she needed, she would not seek the company of others. The attentiveness he once exhibited was gone. The once gentle embrace of his strong arms had become a harsh grip.

After three and a half years, she had reached a decision. It was formed over many months of draining talks and temporary fixes, fashioned from rushed promises, guarantees that things would improve. A blend of requests to be more understanding and a soft spot for nostalgia would sometimes be enough to rekindle the old flame between them. But fresh deeds coated the layers of memory, leaving them buried under an unbearable present.

He couldn't believe it when she said she wanted break up. Maybe she didn't believe it entirely, either. Maybe she hadn't even meant it, not completely. Sometimes a decision becomes final only upon witnessing its results. Perhaps, if he hadn't reacted as he did, Mia would not have been pushed past convincing. If he'd only asked, pleaded for her forgiveness – as he had so many times before – something might have yet been salvaged from the wreckage. Instead, once he realized she was serious, Itay flew out in a jealous rage, convinced that she'd been unfaithful. He went wild, smashing anything that he could get his hands on in the home they shared, swearing, threatening, demanding the truth. Mia tried to pacify him, but when he refused to listen to reason, she paled with fear and insult and fled the apartment.

For two days she refused to answer his calls, hiding out in a friend's house. When she eventually calmed down, they spoke peacefully, if tensely. Itay apologized and asked for a second chance, begging her forgiveness, not realizing that this was his second chance, and that he'd failed. It was what it was, and no amount of begging or supplication could expunge his actions and words.

And so it was that one year, six months and two weeks after all of that came to pass, Mia found herself lying in bed, thinking about the past against her will. Her memories intertwined with the foreign ones haunting her, leaving in their wake nostalgia mixed in with acceptance.

Mia, Mia, Mia. Her own name echoed through her head, spoken in a voice that wasn't hers. Her eyes closed in exhaustion. Leave me alone, she attempted to ask. Maybe he heard that silent plea, because his voice went silent. Maybe he'd simply fallen asleep. She sighed and finally drifted off as well, but not before hearing one final whisper, caressing her name: *Mia...*

The next day, the strange illness worsened further. She was at the grocery store, picking out tomatoes from a heavily loaded crate. While her fingers moved over the red skin of the fruit, an alien thought penetrated her consciousness once again: *here.* A memory swam in front of her eyes: a café they used to frequent every Tuesday, back when he was still out of her reach. From this foreign viewpoint she looked at an empty couch, upon which her own form was hovering, a shadow, voicelessly laughing.

They sat there so many times – a tradition brought on from finishing class at the same time. They never sat there for less than four hours, talking and talking until Itay would glance at his watch and say he had to go. She remembered how disappointed she was whenever this happened, until the point it suddenly began to mean that they were both heading to his place.

Mia shook her head and the image dissipated. She stared at the tomato she was holding and decided it was not quite red enough. At the edges of her mind, a deep sense of concern was beginning to develop.

The next memory attacked when she was in the kitchen, chopping onions. One moment she heard the sharp metal biting into the white meat of the root, and the next she was looking at herself from the outside, leaning over a notebook at the university. Her eyes were focused on what she was writing until she noticed she was being watched, and raised her gaze. She thought she could almost feel them both smiling. It was not a moment of her own remembering. Only his perspective remained from this particular point in time. *If I could only go back, you'd know how I looked at you so much earlier.*

Tears filled her eyes and she wiped them with the back of her hand, along with the thought. It's just the onion, she told herself. Just the onion.

He thought about her again, right before she went to sleep, and once more at 4 o'clock in the morning. The first thoughts were pining, the latter painful, full of regret. She wanted to go back to sleep, but her name still echoed, ringing through her head. *Mia, Mia, Mia, Mia!* Each syllable followed by choked back tears, by another image of the past. There was something uninhibited about these memories. They were accompanied by a certain numbness, which helped cushion the sharp blows they inflicted on the heart. He had been drinking, she could tell. She felt him crashing against walls on his way to his apartment, staggering through the door, swaying heavily, falling to the cold floor with tears in his eyes. The physical pain was nothing,

nothing compared to the pulsing agony inside of him.

It was an immense relief when he finally fell asleep. The headache will be hell when he wakes up, she knew. But she could feel no pity at that point – only fatigue. His emotions were exhausting even when they weren't pounded into her in the middle of the night. She fell asleep shortly after he did.

There were times she'd think of him of her own accord, before he started showing up in her head uninvited. The thoughts were of a nostalgic nature, accompanied by a slight sadness and never lasting more than a few minutes before her mind moved on. Since he'd infiltrated her mind, however, she found it hard not to think of him. It was sometimes difficult to tell at what point a line of thought that had started with him would cross over and into hers.

His thoughts became increasingly invasive over time. He'd think about her when he was aroused, when he was inebriated, when he looked at an old photograph or heard a song they used to listen to together. He brooded over her when he was at his lowest, and remembered her when he was at his best, wishing he could share it with her. It seemed like any passing sight, smell or sound would stir some hidden memory in him. She knew many of them, remembered some differently, while others – not at all. She understood, really. She too experienced thousands of these moments herself, with small fragments of Itay embedded into each of her thoughts from back when she still loved him. The way he remembered her awakened in her the many ways she used to know him.

She fought it. She was inflicted with a hard-nosed persistence that prevented her from giving up. She was more than familiar with the way people could drown in the past, neglecting their motivation for the present. But time was working against her. The passage of days and the constant reminiscence took a toll in the form of feelings she thought long dead and buried. Often she found herself almost looking forward to his memories, taking her back to better days. The routine she'd forced herself into over the past eighteen months was dull, blunted in comparison to the way she used to feel.

Other times, she found herself afraid, dreading his next visit. They hit her when she was tired, when she was weak, and when she was pleased and content, indiscriminately. Images and words, sounds and smells. People would ask her why she was staring, and she'd smile, say it's nothing, that she'd suddenly remembered something for a moment. It's not as if she could tell them that it was actually a moment remembering her.

Her attempts to rebuff him had all failed miserably. She bore it bravely for nearly two months, but the strange affliction showed no signs of improvement. She attempted various methods to alleviate the symptoms, from alcohol to prescription drugs. It had occurred to her that she might be hallucinating, having some kind of seizure, perhaps – despite how detailed the memories were. Nothing helped. Alcohol and medication merely strengthened the attacks when they came, denying her even the feeble resistance she could muster while sober.

Is he causing this intentionally, somehow? She wondered. If so, how? She didn't want to speak with him. She didn't want to hear his yearning, aching voice. She didn't want to stir anew any hope in him, only to take it away; didn't want to be forced into an argument, or to refuse him. But frankly, she had run out of options.

When she called him, a vision exploded in her head. She was wound up and anxious as is, but suddenly she was also in his place, his heart beating frantically, like a windmill hit by a sudden storm. Both their eyes saw her name flashing on the screen of his phone. Stretched moments of confusion mingled with razor-sharp hope. He lifted it to his ear and swiped to pick up.

"Hi?" said Itay, his voice shaky. His thoughts swirled madly in her head. Not words, not yet – only emotions, at this point: shock, hope, and pain, so much pain.

"Hi," said Mia.

"Did something happen?" he asked, warily. She heard him think: *why else would you call?*

"No, nothing happened. I just called to see how you were doing."

You've been thinking of me. She felt his delight at that. So he doesn't know, she realized. And if he did, would he stop?

"I'm fine," he spoke, and thought: *Nothing is fine.* "How about you?"

"Same. Yeah, fine too. It's just that it's been a while. How are you are holding up?" she forced her mouth to laugh. "New girlfriend?"

Never. "For sure," she heard him smile, felt him cringe. "New boyfriend?"

"No, no one so far."

But there will be. There always will be, for you. Please, come back to me.

"Anything new?"

"Not much, really. The new apartment's finally grown on me, and I was at Adele's wedding, remember Adele?"

"Yeah, sure. She invited me too." He didn't have to explain why he hadn't come.

"Anything new with you?"

"I've been thinking about traveling a bit," he said. "I haven't even been on a plane since..." his voice faltered. "Not in a while."

I'm afraid to leave.

"Where to?"

Far from you. Far from us. To a place where not every single turn reminds me of you.

"I haven't really figured that out yet. Just feel like leaving the country for a while, clear my head."

"That's a fantastic idea. I'd do the same, but I've been swamped at work lately."

"Yeah? Too busy to meet up?" he blurted. She knew his insides were in knots.

"Itay…" she said. She didn't want this. She felt him break at the sound of that one word. A massive weight, rested upon delicate glass, cracking it further with every passing second. How is he still talking? It felt like being kicked. No, a kick is momentary, then gone. This was a like being ripped, shredded. Like a pair of hands wringing the stomach until it splits from the inside. The agony was unbearable. He seemed to just barely manage to breathe. She shivered.

"It was just a random thought," he laughed. "I know it's a bad idea."

When you say no, it's a bad idea. He was still hoping she'd change her mind.

"Yes. I mean, it's not that I don't want to, it's just… we better not." She bit her lip against the pain, trying not to groan under the weight of his feelings. They burned inside of him, scorching her.

"It's fine, I get it. So you just… thought of me all of a sudden?"

Have you been missing me?

"Yeah," this is your fault, your fault.

"That's nice. You're welcome to think of me more often."

Impossible, she thought.

"I'll try."

They were silent for a moment. Itay clearly didn't want to hang up, but could think of nothing more to add. An unending sequence of words he'd like to have said was streaming through in his head, and she was forced to listen to every single one of them. He wanted to tell her that he hadn't been with anyone else since her, he wanted to say that everything was different, that he wasn't the man he once was. If she'd just give him a chance, he wanted to say, they could fix this. *Please, Mia. Please, please. Let's meet, talk, work this out. I can't take this anym-*

Mia exhaled. "Itay?"

"Yes?"

"Maybe you should really take that trip. Clear your head." Both of our heads, she added internally.

God, don't hang up.

"Maybe I will."

"Take care."

I'm yours. Always.

"Promise."

"Bye."

"Bye."

She took a deep breath when they hung up. He had already begun rewinding the conversation in his head, lingering over each syllable, the sound of her voice. Why had she thought that calling him would be good idea? But now, at least, she had her answer. He had no idea what he was doing to her.

The next few days were intolerable. He thought about her constantly, forcing her into thinking of him. He regretted, a thousand times a day, asking her to meet; agonized, a thousand times a day, over her refusal to do so. He checked his phone dozens of times to see if she'd called, considered texting her hundreds of times. She was so, so exhausted.

His sleep had been the only time she was allowed respite. But a week after they talked, he began haunting her in his dreams, as well, remembering her as he slept. Shortly after that, he was in her dreams, as well. The irony, that in his mind *he* was the one being haunted by her, did not escape her.

For a while she thought she would ultimately lose her mind. Or hoped that she would, perhaps, as her mind had become a truly terrible thing, one which she wished to lose more than anything, so she could finally get some peace. The passing months, however, seemed to have granted her some measure of immunity, and the lack of communication had blunted his thoughts of her somewhat. Maybe he'd really flown to another country, to forget her. He still thought of her every day, albeit no longer every moment. Meanwhile, she'd become accustomed to multitasking. She no longer froze mid-conversation when he came into her mind, no longer found herself lost in the depths of his thought. She managed to avoid thinking of him in response, from completing his memories with her own.

Months turned into years. She was back at the café with him, back at the university and in their bed. She saw herself on each of his birthdays numerous times, saw her eyes gleam again and again at hundreds of small, day-to-day gifts he brought her. She became slowly accustomed to his presence in her head. It became a sort of comfort, knowing that even during her darkest hours, there is a man lying awake at night, thinking of her. She'd grown used to being woken by him during the night, and took his final thought of her before falling asleep as a silent bid good night.

One time she was sitting by herself, feeling down from a bad day she was having, when he came to her. In his memory he led her, eyes covered by thick fabric, to a table laden with dishes he'd cooked for her. He couldn't remember what exactly he'd cooked, but she filled in those details with her own memories, which were sharper when it came to most things. Only her candle-lit face was recalled in perfect detail, as if molded and ensouled by a master craftsman. Her misery evaporated as Itay lived through the memory, lingering over his favorite moments. Maybe it's not so bad, she thought then, hugging her knees. Maybe it's nice, still having you around. She was often comforted by that thought.

Every year, they spoke less. He'd call on her birthday and on holidays, eager for an excuse to speak with her, and at least at the beginning she'd text him on his. When she saw he wasn't letting up, she stopped sending the messages, stopped picking up when he called. Even Itay couldn't take it. The calls she wouldn't take remained lodged in his stomach for weeks – because even if she didn't answer right away, she may call back. She distanced him, forcefully, just to lessen the excruciating pain.

Until one day, he was gone.

It wasn't instantly obvious. The hours elapsed, and no foreign memory had wandered into her head – though, truthfully, they were no longer even slightly foreign. She'd watched them from his point of view so many times, that they became as familiar to her as her own memories. Perhaps even more so, as her own were not repeatedly laid out in front of her.

Day became night, and as she lay in her bed, the thoughts in her head became lonely. She couldn't remember the last time she'd had her head to herself. She tossed and turned throughout that entire night, waiting for the familiar images that would not come. What happened to him? She worried. He was always remembering her green eyes looking at him, gleaming with the admiration reserved to those who are, in the viewer's eyes, unlike the rest. Alternatively, it was the image of her sleeping face, lips slightly parted, her breath warm on his neck.

When she eventually fell asleep, she dreamt of him. But these were her dreams, not his. She knew this, even as she slept. They were regular dreams, summoning familiar, everyday realms, into which his image was woven as if they were still together. She woke up still imagining his broad back, leaned over some pot, cooking for her.

The mental radio silence stayed with her. She listened anxiously to the news, worried that his name might come up. Maybe he'd been in an accident, or the curse haunting them had been removed somehow – why else would he disappear this abruptly? She considered the worst, and thoughts of him persisted in her mind, occupying her thoughts. He'd probably be overjoyed, if he knew, she thought to herself. He'd probably take it as a sign that she still loved him.

His Facebook account was blocked to her for a while, more to stop him from following hers than for any other reason. She didn't know where he was living these days. She had only his phone number, which she dared not use. Nevertheless, the dead stillness in her head was slowly depleting her resolve with each passing day. As she once struggled with his incessant invasions, she now struggled with the ringing silence.

Mia found that absence was much more difficult to rebuff than substance. Itay had become a fundamental part of her life, one she had already come to terms with as constant. Perhaps that was why she'd never managed to find someone new. Kisses of the present always paled in comparison to those of the past. That was her curse, always remembering how she used to feel. No one stood a chance of getting close enough to construct a similar intimacy. This new solitude was hell.

She was slow in accepting it, longing to feel him again, just to know that there was someone in the world who remembered she existed. When he didn't return, the solitude turned bearable – even convenient, at times. She found herself leading the life of an older woman, whose best days were interred within the memories of another. So it was until one day, when she was reading a book in the kitchen, and the silence shattered. A thought glimmered there, startling her from her daze. She closed her eyes to focus on it.

I think I came here with Mia once.

A blurred image of a familiar café. She remembered it – they once spent an entire evening there, arguing over the difference between intelligence and IQ. The heated debate became a fight, which progressed into furious lovemaking in the café's bathroom. She remembered her back pressed against the cool wood, biting her lip so as not to cry out. They'd agreed to disagree.

Mia peeked at her watch. The café wasn't far. It wouldn't be terrible if she happened to run into him there.

It's a bad idea, she thought to herself. There's a reason you never called. But loneliness overcame her again, and the memory was fresh in her mind. Just catch a glimpse of him, see that everything is okay. He wouldn't even have to know she's there.

Before she managed to counter herself with further arguments, she'd already gotten dressed, applied some light make-up, and was off. She didn't know how long he'd been sitting there, and how long she had before he left, but she didn't want to miss her chance. She dared not wear heels, as they'd keep her from running.

She arrived at the café, only a few blocks away, panting slightly. She slowed her pace over the last block, knowing she shouldn't rush inside. The excitement caused her to perspire as no amount of running could. She paused momentarily at the entrance, wiped her hand hurriedly on her dress, and walked inside.

There, by the window, he caught her eye. He was older, his hair shorter, graying at the temples. But his back was still broad, and his smile was still youthful. For a moment, she struggled to recall why she broke up with him. Itay hadn't noticed her yet. She took a step toward him. Then she saw that he was not alone.

She was younger than he was, the woman sitting in front of him. Not a huge difference, but noticeable. Curly hair, bright blue eyes. They were holding hands, and she was returning his smile with her childlike one. Suddenly, Mia was at the university again, looking at the man she loved from across an impassable chasm, out of her reach, knowing that he will never be hers.

Her legs carried her out of there, apparently of their own accord, as she herself was incapable of motion. She leaned against the wall outside the café and her eyes closed.

She had never given much thought to the women he dated after her. The only thoughts she had access to were his thoughts of her. She never considered the possibility that one of them would replace her, take her place in his head. He had inexplicably forced himself back into her life, carving his way into the very place she wished to exclude him from. A life of recreating and reliving their greatest hits. She had given him up, before. It was his turn now.

People often asked her if something was wrong. Did someone she knew pass away? They muttered, cautiously, at the office. And she'd say it's nothing, just one of those days, nothing to worry about. Who broke your heart? Laughed her friends, then exchange concerned looks. She's been depressed for months, they'd whisper at each other behind her back. But Mia would smile weakly and say that no one can break her heart, but her.

And the heart heals, as well. Not into the same shape it once had, but it heals. And once every few months, a foreign thought would remind her of that much, at least. A memory familiar to the both of them, accompanied by pleasant nostalgia, letting her know that somewhere in the world there is someone who loved her once, entirely, with everything he had.

I wonder how you're doing.

She'd smile back at the man she once knew. Not the one she gave up, not the one he became, but the one who filled every memory of her youth. Her Itay. She'd answer him, even knowing he'd never hear it.

I'm all right. Hope you are, too.

Outlines

It is said that adults lack the capacity for imagination that children possess. Age is always to blame, as if somehow the years pile up to occupy the headspace previously reserved for dreams. This is, however, a simplistic view, and utterly flawed at that. The true fault lies with the heart. Or more specifically, the heart on the day it is broken.

Consider this: I once knew a creative genius who, in his youth, could weave a myriad of elaborate, vibrantly-colored dreams, but in later years was told to possess an astoundingly limited imagination. I was the only one who knew that he had not lost one ounce of his spectacular imagination, as he had confided in me that among the nine-thousand, two-hundred and twenty one images that he had conjured and committed to memory in great detail, only six-thousand and five-hundred were portraits of her. In the rest, he'd depicted the two of them, together. As they would never be again.

On The Fortune of
Being a Terrible Student

I once asked the inventor Trillion that he explain to me why memories are such an unreliable, unstable substance. In response, he grabbed a handful of present-moments in one hand, and a soldering iron in the other. He then placed the moments in a somewhat logical order, and expertly soldered them together. Had I not examined the memory carefully, I never would have known that the result was not uniform, but masterfully constructed from hundreds of hundreds of distinct pieces.

I looked closer. I could see the particular features of the inventor's face, the color of his irises, even smell the moment the conversation had begun. I praised his genius, at which he smiled contentedly. "But," I dared wonder aloud, "this memory is solidly built. Why are the memories of others so shoddy?"

Trillion sighed, and explained: "when people reminisce, each one brings to the table the piece of the past that is his or hers, and together they combine the pieces into a new, compound memory, which they can all recognize. However, most people lack the know-how for this delicate work – at most, they are amateur rememberers – and so the exact details are absent from so many memories. It is impossible to craft a truly fine memory using a blunt and unskilled instrument, despite one's best efforts. This is also why people will sometimes remember the same moment differently: each of them had already nabbed for him or herself a piece of the present, which has by now surely aged into past, and no one is willing to hand over their piece for the benefit of constructing a full, coherent memory."

Those were, I am certain, his exact words – as Trillion was truly a master rememberer. Unfortunately, he left before he could explain to me the proper method of remembering things, and so I was compelled to draft my most crucial memories as no more than an enthusiastic dilettante. All I can do is draw out old days, their edges tattered and threadbare, and wistfully caress them. Sometimes I manage to add the exact hue of her eyes, or the way she smiled. This has been the cause of much regret.

But every so often, I wonder if perhaps I was fortunate never to have learned that lesson from Trillion. Perhaps it is the only reason I am still able to strive for new days.

Mystery

I'm sitting in front of a woman whose mind is set on breaking up with the man she's seeing, and I listen. Just don't let him call tonight, she says, staring warily at the phone. Please don't let him call. And to myself I wonder: why is her mouth saying one thing, while her eyes beg for another.

On The Anti-Love Vaccine

Claimed more victims than any other disease, said the doctors that developed it. The challenge, they later recalled, was to find a weakened strain. Because when it dies, not even the faintest trace remains.

The Scent of the Mundane

I love the smell of despair in the air. It is a sign that, only recently, there raged a tempest of hope.

In The Street

In the street I saw two past lovers run into each other. They smiled hesitantly, hugged and stopped to chat. The conversation started out slow, fumbling for rhythm, like a dancer who hadn't been on the floor in years. Slowly, it recalled its moves from way back when, and took to the air gracefully, sweeping them both up into an old, familiar dance. They exchanged personal jokes and even more personal glances, and only the years that had passed stood stoutly between them, making sure that the distance was kept.

On the Difference between Gods and People and the Way Worlds are Created

I once complained to a god named Élan about the differences between gods and people. When he'd finished listening to my grumbling the god laughed as if I'd told a joke. When I wondered indignantly what it was that he found so amusing, he waved his hand and asked:

"What's the big difference between people and gods, really?"

"What!" I protested, "Gods can create infinite worlds, and people are forced to settle for the one they have, even if they are not the least bit pleased with it."

"You're wrong about that, Tea," said Élan. "Way back when, at a time that may or may not have been – though by now, is surely gone – there was but a single world. Back then, no distinction existed between gods and people, as they lived side by side, never noticing any difference between them.

In those days, the skies were a very dark place, as there were no distant suns, nothing save the moon to illuminate the nights. The world was quite dark as well, in its own way – both humans and gods were relatively savage, not yet learned in the art of regret or wallowing in the past; and other, newfangled inventions, which today seem to us inseparable from modern, everyday life, had not yet been conceived.

This was shortly after humankind had mastered emotion-husbandry: taming wild emotion and cultivating them internally. It was not long before they learned to breed new emotion, previously unseen in the wild. You will not be shocked, perhaps, to learn that hope is a human creation, as is love, because one was bred from the other. And which of them came first – we could argue over that for several eternities, if you so wish.

We gods were slow in our adoption of these phenomena – due to our long lives, we are sluggish in learning how to feel. The humans, on the other hand, were busy with the fabrication of new emotions more often than not. Ten different species of love were developed within a generation. But then, you must know this already – after all, how else could the feeling you label "love" be the same emotion others have labeled so? Clearly, it is a different sentiment from a likeminded family.

One gloomy night, due to an ill-advised cross breeding between love and hope, a sad man breathed life into regret. This is, as you well know, an exceedingly fertile emotion, and is capable of spawning as many as a thousand little regrets per year. This first one, however, was truly massive –feeding it alone was an entire day's worth of work for the sad man, and keeping it on a leash was no simple matter, either. The burden of tending to the needs of such a massive regret would overwhelm even the mightiest of gods, but its owner continued to care for it and nurture it, quietly and without complaint.

That night, the coincidental father of regret returned home, pondering love and what might have been. These are, after all, the sort of thoughts produced by regret, just as cows produce milk. Unwittingly, but at the same time with the utmost intent, he suddenly created a world. And then another, and another.

They were worlds of Maybe, If-Only and I-Wish. For the first time since the universe coalesced, three bright stars shone in the heavens.

We gods were the first to notice, seeing as unlike humans, we are inclined to look mostly at things outside of ourselves.

We instantly realized what was happening, and with childlike wonder set out to explore the new worlds. We found them to be extraordinary, and wanted more than anything to create some of our own. But since we could not love, we did not know how. After all, it takes a god centuries, a millennia at times, to properly learn how to love. Fortunately, regret had already begun to spread, producing hybrids with various other emotions. More and more worlds were brought into being right before our eyes, and the skies brimmed with glinting stars. Some went dark almost as soon as they were created, their creators having considered them and lost interest. Others burned brightly on, as people kept returning to them in their thoughts. Humankind created the Maybe, and we decided to live in it. And though we learned, given time, to create our own worlds, humans were the true pioneers in the field.

You still do it, Tea, even today. Why else would the sky be filled with so many stars?"

I looked at Élan then, and spent several minutes deep in thought. Eventually I remarked, more for the force of habit than any real objection, "I thought the light reaching us from the stars is ancient light, from worlds that are no longer with us."

The god laughed once more. "The stars at night are like memories, Tea. During their prime, they burned with a fire everlasting. Today they are but monuments to a time that was."

Houses

I've always found it odd that on the inside, furniture can be moved around, walls torn down, everything changed completely, while on the outside, a stranger will walk by and say: yes, I know it well – I used to live here.

A Heap of Past

In the street I discovered a man perched atop a heap of past. He was covered in time-dust and buried among discarded moments, abandoned long ago. His body was obscured by the rubble, but his voice could still be heard. When asked about his refusal to move on, he replied: if I moved, how would she find me upon her return?

Excerpts from
the Heart Physicist's Journal

Unlike people, emotion is not bound by the laws of time. An unknowable tide, it comes and goes as it pleases. One moment you're standing at the point where it all ended, the next – years later. And perhaps it is the exact opposite: emotion is exactly when and where it should be in time, while it's the people that are scattered all over the place.

Time Travel

At noon you awake to an empty bed with a sigh.

It was only moments ago that a couple lay here together in sleep. Two people entwined under the blankets. Both reluctant to leave the little world created in that bed; the warmth emanating from something more than flesh alone. A thousand excuses were constructed to halt the day in its tracks, or would have been, if such excuses were necessary. Instead, they cling harder to one another.

Only a moment has passed, but the sheets are cold now. Perhaps it was in a different bed entirely, years ago.

Or maybe it will be years from now.

Absolute Zero

It is a well-known fact that, every so often, time freezes. But by keeping the particular moment you occupy warm, you can observe yesterday as if it had occurred a mere moment ago. If you're lucky, you are not frozen in there alone.

Archaeology of the Gods

They came after it was all over. Despite the darkness, identifying the original locus of the earth was a simple matter. This owing to the impressions once pressed into the night, in the shape of first kisses.

My World

On my way out of the apartment, they told me you're seeing someone again. I nodded and said I was going to write, then went downstairs and punched the mailbox until the world shattered to pieces. Who knew it was so fragile.

Behind

On the bench in the street I left a small patch of sunlight, taken from my favorite corner of the sky, that which turns into shade come evening. Maybe at night, I pondered, someone lonely will wrap himself in it, weary of wondering, and rest easy in daytime thoughts, if only for a moment.

Almost

There's a moment when I consider stopping by her apartment. I'll spend the night there, I think, and perhaps the months of March through October. Or maybe the years until we grow old. Or not, or not.

Optimism and Time

Such a sad couple. He hurts her, and she smiles on. She cannot imagine a future without him; he cannot imagine any other. Odd. She is the one being hurt, but he's the one truly hurting. She says: One day he'll change. He knows: in the end, she, too, will leave.

FYI

There's plenty more whisky to be had before you realize that undoing yourself will not necessarily make others suffer.

Coffee

I'm more of a tea-drinker, myself, but when women invite me for a cup of coffee, I can always detect a whiff of friendly intentions. This is odd, because when I invite a woman over for coffee, the air blushes with the scent of love.

Endings

Though we always feel that we are at a low point at the end of things, endings are in fact a type of peak. That is why the past is so easily observed from them – they provide the best view. It is for this reason that most people wish to know the ending first, and only then are they willing to hear the beginning.

"A broken heart, you say?" they marvel. "Intriguing! And why did you break up? Really? And how did it start?" And with each question they look further and deeper into the past, forgetting the ending atop which we had to climb in order to look back and see what had gone down behind us.

Then, suddenly, someone will stop everything, look at the steep path we walked to this point, and ask: "Wait, but how did it even come to this? How could this happen?"

Sometimes, that person will be someone other than yourself.

That Moment with You

Like a paper cut, miniscule, yet every slight movement reminds you of what happened. And oh, how that little bastard stings.

What-If World

A god by the name of Élan once took me to visit What-If world, dwelling place of the terrifying If-Only beast.

Upon our arrival, I was amazed by the striking diversity of the hundreds of What-Ifs who wandered freely in stable symbiosis. Some were as small as idle thoughts, some as substantial as career indecision. I saw many 'what-if-I-had-chosen-something-else-for-lunch's frolicking around the forest, unperturbed. These would occasionally be hunted down and devoured by various 'what-if-I-had-gone-to-that-party-that-night's, or a ravenous 'what-if-I-call-tomorrow'. Such is, after all, the natural order of things: the larger What-Ifs will forever feed on numerous smaller ones.

Élan protected me from the truly massive What-Ifs. Some of them were quite harmless, such as the 'what-if-aliens-are-real', which, despite its considerable size and girth, was not inclined to aggression unless provoked intentionally. Others, however, were extremely dangerous, especially those relating to other people. The 'what-if-I-were-single' was frighteningly aggressive, for instance, and anyone wandering its domain without proper protection could easily fall prey to its bite, which felt more like a sting.

I felt very safe in the presence of the god. But at the edge of the forest, facing a gloomy grove, Élan suddenly came to a grinding halt and refused to go any further. I wondered what it was that frightened even him, and he explained:

"Beyond this point dwell the 2AM thoughts. The smallest among them can crawl under your skin and incubate there for days, scratching and grating, driving you mad. The medium-sized ones can devour your mind as easily as they devour flesh. As for the larger ones…"

He shivered.

"What about the large ones?" I asked, curious in spite of myself.

"The larger ones are no longer an innocent What-if. They are all the same, colossal beast, whose name is If-Only. And that, Tea, is the most terrifying beast in the universe. This one, or any other."

I chuckled slightly at that, but soon realized that Élan was dead serious.

"What's so terrible about it?" I asked, unable to imagine anything worse than being eaten alive.

"The If-Only disguises itself as your run-of-the-mill What-If, but given the chance to sink its teeth into you, it will never, ever let go. It will eat at you, day after day, agonizingly slow, destroying all that you are, bit by terrible bit. It will ingest you completely, beginning with your insides, working its way out. It will take not only your life, but all of the lives you could have lived, and yet it will not be satiated by that, not by far – it will also aim to consume everyone around you. No one can run from it, not for ever, because once it's had its taste of you, it will never be deterred, and it will never lose your scent, not until the end of time."

"I say," I cried, "but that is truly awful! Has no one ever considered slaying this beast?"

"Who would dare try?" asked Élan. "Trust me in this, Tea – we should do our best to keep our distance from these 2AM thoughts as much as possible. Just remember, if you ever do see someone being devoured by a What-If, there is only one way to temporarily scare it away."

"What is it?"

"The If-Only fears but one thing: the calls of certain What-Ifs. However, seeing as no one has ever gotten close enough to find out, I cannot tell you which ones will help. Therefore you must now promise me, Tea, that you will never approach that thought at those hours."

I nodded in fearful agreement. We then resumed our wanderings through the forest, Élan occasionally pointing out some wayward What-If and imparting his knowledge on their habits and behaviors. I remained enthusiastic throughout the journey, and for a while took leave of my worries. It wasn't until that day's end, when he dropped me off at home, that I realized how tired I was. I plopped my head on the pillow, expecting to fall asleep instantly. But for some reason, I did not. Instead, my thoughts wandered to the world of What-Ifs, and I found myself contemplating its various inhabitants. I thought of 'what-if-I-had-traveled-there-myself', and 'what-if-I-had-chosen-a-different-profession', and 'what-if-I-had-never-left', and 'what-if-I-had-apologized-in-time', or '-differently'. When I arrived at 'what-if-I-see-her-in-the-street-one-day', it suddenly dawned on me that sleep had been evading me for a while, far into the wee hours, and looking at the clock I realized where I was. 2AM.

I could not even scream for help, and already the If-Only was upon me. Within a split-second I was trapped between its jaws. I tried to fight it, tried to flee into sleep, or into the present, but to no avail. Because If-Only, If-Only I had done things differently, maybe today we'd still be talking. Maybe today you'd be mine.

The If-Only knew where I was weakest. Despite my struggles, it bit into me, fervently, eating away at everything I was. I cried, thrashed, begged, but the If-Only persisted. Because things were the way they were, and I could only think of what I would have done differently.

I was exhausted at this point, at the end of my rope. I was about to give up, when I suddenly remembered Élan's advice. With what little remaining strength I possessed, I searched for some nearby What-If to use against the beast. Perhaps a 'what-if-we-meet-in-the-street-by-chance' or a 'what-if-I-find-a-new-love'. But they all fled at the sight of the If-Only, or else promptly consumed by it.

Then, just as I was nearing despair, a small What-If fearlessly approached the bloody scene. I could feel the If-Only slowly letting up, retreating. I could not allow it to drag me away with it. Taking advantage of its momentary hesitation, I lunged at the What-if, raised it above my head and waved it at the beast, driving it away. Despite its best efforts, it couldn't bypass the small What-if to charge at me. It howled, then, a cry of deep frustration, and after a mighty, ferocious roar, the If-Only retreated into the shadows, leaving me breathless and panting.

I knew that it would return tomorrow. It had my scent, it had me in its jaws and now it would never let me go. I held the small What-If tightly in my hands. It mewled softly as I held it to my chest. I recognized its call immediately. It was a tiny What-If, barely existing at all, hardly surviving. I caressed it gently. From that day forward, I would guard it and nurture it at all costs. It was a 'what-if-you-call-tomorrow?'

Only by the skin of my teeth had I managed to escape, and it was several minutes before I had begun to calm down. I was slowly drifting to sleep, the tiny What-If held tightly against me like a comforting shield. Then, my eyes flew open when a new thought jolted me awake once again.

I had never asked Élan about the average life span of a What-If.

What if you don't call tomorrow, either?

Time Management

Sometimes I pity Time for having so many managers. Each of them demanding something different – that it move along already, or stay put, or reveal what's yet to come or what could have been, or that it simply go back. Maybe that's why Time seems to disregard all of these instructions and keeps working at the same grim, slow pace, acceptable to no one, to bring forth yet another complaint-filled tomorrow, at a job that no one else has ever agreed to take on.

The Men of Words

At night, Cyrano de Bergerac whispered to Florentino Ariza: How many ways are there to describe love? And Florentino laughed, as such was the game they would play: countless, my friend, and I shall think them all up for you, but to feel it, I know of only the one.

The Difference Between Us

The difference between us is that I experience numerous meaningless moments each day. When I put the kettle on, walk down the street, or chop onions in the kitchen. And you, you have numerous delightful, irreplaceable moments, in which you put the kettle on, walk down the street, or chop onions in the kitchen.

Consequently, it should come as no surprise, therefore, that you are unwilling to exchange some of your moments for some of mine.

Sometimes You Want To Say How You Feel

And sometimes you want to take a deep breath and count to ten, and find that three years have passed.

The Lonesome Nothing

Many years ago, in a distant part of the universe, there dangled some Nothing. It was quite a peaceful Nothing, which had managed over the course of infinity to get through several big commotions, and some even bigger bangs, completely unscathed by matter or time. It was indeed quite pleased with its non-existence, and so was prone to keep silent whenever the universe would send some wayward light beam or cosmic energy in its direction; lest they notice it wasn't there and decide to come visit it.

It spent its non-existence, not unlike a person in love, imagining the potential of things that could have been. One of its imaginings was of a world in which nothing broke unless someone had intended to break it, especially hearts. It expected that this would be a spectacular world to live in, but to its great surprise, most people who lived there were miserable, because none of them could bring themselves to intentionally break the heart of another. Thus, millions of couples remained held in the grip of disappointing relationships. This world saddened the nothing, and it did its best to forget about it. But sometimes, during those rare, miniscule moments when it was feeling just lonely enough to call out to a passing beam of light, this world would return to its thoughts nonetheless.

Another time, it invented an entire galaxy, composed solely of emotion as its raw material. Bright stars were created in split-seconds as hearts were filled with love; blazing suns born in flashes of intense fury. Melancholy produced blue planets, brimming with salted oceans which refused to flow free. Longing produced long-tailed comets, destined to repeat the same path through the skies, year after year. And heartbreak created supermassive black holes, which slowly consumed the other feelings, and never disappeared completely (it nearly pondered these – just nearly, so as not to accidentally destroy its perfect vacuum by creating remnants of hope. On the edge of almost, it created its universe).

This could have easily gone on for many more eternities, as far as it was concerned, if not for the intervention of some god who had just passed by, by the name of Élan, who was annoyingly prone to sullying immaculate chaos with shambolic order.

Élan immediately noticed the hidden Nothing, and his face crumpled indignantly.

"What is this Nothing doing here?" he said, waving his arms about. "There was supposed to be a something here by now."

With yet another wave of his hand and no hesitation whatsoever, he had completely obliterated the poor Nothing, which hadn't even the time to utter a single word. So came the end of the entire universe that almost was.

Where Nothing once was, Élan had decided to create a world. It was a nice world, too, filled with masterfully hand-crafted details – him being the meticulous god he was – with living beings, effervescing emotions and inanimate landscapes. The god looked upon his work and was relatively pleased, never even realizing that the world he'd created took the place of one that might have been.

And just like that, Élan wrapped things up and was on his way to other urgent matters that required his attention. But, despite his usual diligence, Élan neglected to add a crucial component to the world he'd created – stories. Due to the recklessness of a young god, a world completely void of stories was brought into being, and everything that was ever told there was an account of an actual event that really happened. Much like this story, really.

Losing Heart

And so it was that after thirty-four years of reasonable existence, the chime of a text message woke Amir to a vague sensation of emptiness in his chest. The more he attempted to ignore it, the more it intensified. Out of some mild concern, or perhaps a touch of clairvoyance, he waited for several minutes before feeling for the source of the sensation with his hand. After thorough examination, he was forced to come to the undeniable conclusion that his heart was missing.

Amir was not normally the type of person to jump to conclusions. First, he felt his chest carefully, searching for the sound of a pulse, a single heartbeat, even some familiar warmth. However, the only thing he managed to feel out was the gentle caress of his breathing, which, he later concluded, had percolated into the empty cavity and slipped through the cracks of his body.

He was not anxious, but still experienced some degree of unease. He thumped on his chest with his fist for good measure. Gently at first, then forcefully. The hollow sound that this produced was proof enough. He had lost his heart.

He attempted to retrace his steps, to deduce where this might have occurred. Of course he started out by searching his immediate environment – not truly believing he'd find it there, but more because he felt the need to make the effort. Perhaps it had merely rolled out of him during the night – he did have a tendency to toss and turn in his sleep. When that failed, he tried to recall the previous day. He remembered having a light breakfast before heading to the office. He believed that upon entering the building, he bid good morning to two secretaries and a colleague. He had maybe five cups of coffee, and ate lunch at a burger place that accepted the company meal card.

Afterwards, on his way home, he stopped by the grocery store near his apartment. He remembered the details of his purchase in the form of an imaginary receipt and the order in which he placed the groceries into his shopping bag. He paid, and went home. At no point, he recalled, had anyone mentioned to him that his chest was hollow. Surely, if his heart had fallen out in public, someone would have noticed?

In fact, it suddenly occurred to him that it had been a while since he'd seen it himself. He tried to retrace the entire week, exposing day after day like an archeologist unearthing the strata of a mound with meticulous patience, so as not to miss a single detail. Most days, he noted, were quite similar to one another, so it was easy to get them mixed up. Looking closely, he could see that they differed from one another by minute details, at most: here a slightly different grocery list, there a phone call from his mother. Here he managed some extra work at the office, there more time spent browsing through clickbait. For a moment he was astounded by the fact that he'd seemingly been living the same day over and over again, thousands of times, and never noticed. It was odd, he mused, that he even bothered to get out of bed after the first time around. Owing to this similarity, he could simply leaf through his days without worrying about missing so much as a single detail. Despite all this, however, his memory came up short, and would not reveal exactly when and where the heart was lost.

Amir felt around the vacant space it once inhabited. While he only did just notice it now, he suspected it was the cool winter air that seeped inside that had alerted his senses to the absence. It was possible that it had been gone for a while. Again, he strained his memory. The effort was accompanied by some pain, as it had become atrophied from disuse. He played month by month through his head, as if through an old VCR, but to no avail. He was about to throw in the towel, when he was suddenly struck by an idea.

Instead of trying to remember exactly when it was lost, perhaps he ought to try and recall the last time he'd clearly felt its presence.

The task seemed more difficult than it actually was. Once he'd given it some thought, the answer became clear. Eight years ago, certainly. It was winter then, too, and he had just rented an apartment in Tel Aviv by himself. The city offered an alluring cacophony of opportunities, and the bars enticed him to visit whenever his nights were free. Yes, it was night, he remembered, when his heart last pulsed the fact of its presence. It was cold, a frost that the city was unaccustomed to, and it was hailing fiercely. He went to a bar by himself, found it empty and left after one drink – out of shame more than any other reason.

The hail caught him on his way home. It pounded into buildings and roads with a dull thud, smashed into bits and piled in hard, white layers. Amir did not have an umbrella, and he was already frozen stiff from the cold air. He felt the ice pelt his face like tiny stones, encrusting his clothes, seeping in through his coat and three layers of shirt. He swore, something along the lines of motherfucker, or maybe it was holy shit. The curse fogged condemningly through the air, but the increasing hail swiftly erased it from existence.

For lack of any other option, he lunged at the first potential shelter he could find: a small awning at the entrance of a hidden apartment building. Water seeped all the way through his socks, and his feet were aching. He brushed off his coat and clothes, trying to get rid of the ice before it could sink into what little dry patches he still had left. It wasn't until he was finished, panting slightly at the effort, that he noticed he wasn't alone under the awning.

He froze the moment he noticed her, increasing the resolution, sharpening the details and enhancing the contrast. This here can be served as evidence of the merit of Amir's memory – which, despite the shameful state of neglect it had fallen into over the past few years, was originally of excellent quality – and though there are those who would claim that it is more evident of Amir's personal taste, as he must have returned to this scene numerous times in his mind, they would be wrong. If the original recording is of low quality, no amount of fiddling and focusing will improve the image beyond a certain point. If Amir was artistically inclined, he could have probably painted it with accuracy akin to that of a high-end digital camera.

He attempted to do just that, solely with his mind's eye: a small figure, wearing a grey hat, with long brown hair flowing from under it to cover her ears. Narrow eyes, so dark that you couldn't tell, in the gloom, which way they were pointed – yet, he knew they were aimed directly at him – topped by a pair of long eyebrows. She was pale, as white as her eyes were black, but her lips were pink and full, flushed by the cold, as were her cheeks. Her curves could be noticed even under her thick clothes, perhaps owing to her posture, which stretched her skin across her body in a way reminiscent of tightly woven fabric, reprimanding you for daring to mistake this woman for a girl, even if only for a moment.

At this point his heart skipped a beat – he was sure it did! – and he smiled, satisfied with the clear-cut evidence. He checked again, just in case (although by that point he was already quite certain).

"Hi," she said. Her voice sounded like silver spoons ringing against each other. She approached him and brushed off some invisible remnants of hail. "Are you okay?"

Her warm breath smelled unexpectedly of mint and anise. Amir was not a fan of anise, but found it quite agreeable combined with her breath. He remembered he'd been drinking beer, and was self-conscious about his breath probably reeking of it. But he couldn't stop hyperventilating, and she didn't seem to mind.

"Yes, I am now," he said, smiling, then blinked. "I wasn't trying to be tacky. I'm okay now because I'm out of the hail."

"A shame. Men ought to be more tacky. We should never have let branding turn it into a bad thing."

She smiled. White teeth and dimples. She then stretched out her hand and said, "Laura."

"Amir." He inhaled deeply. She was more intoxicated than he was, but the alcohol in her breath was quickly catching him up to her.

Yes, yes, he clearly remembered his heart during that moment. It was beating fiercely, telling him, through a code that was both complex and decipherable to anyone: you are alive, you are alive. There was no mistaking it. Skipping a beat was one thing, but the violent pounding within him had left noticeable indentations. There, he can feel them even now, with his hand.

But this couldn't have been the last time he'd seen it. Now, having started down that road, he remembered another instance, three months later. He was in his bed, with Laura. Her white cheek pressed against the side of his chest, her hand covering his heart. He was breathing heavily. They had just made love. He thought she'd fallen asleep already, but looking at her he saw her black eyes peering up at him, a faint smile on her lips.

"I'm happy with you," she whispered, the delicate chime of a bell. The whisper lingered momentarily on his ribs, caressing his skin. "I didn't know there were men like you left."

The edges of his mouth curled, his eyes narrowed into gratified slits. "What do you mean?" he wondered, smiling.

"You're different," she replied somberly. She brushed a strand of hair out of her eyes and gazed at him intently. "There aren't many men your age who aren't broken. Most of them can't even look at the opposite sex as if they were people."

Amir laughed, thinking she was joking. There was something boy-ish about his smile, he noted, looking back at it now. She smiled back, but still looked solemn, somehow. He stroked her skin. "I don't think that's true, not really. I mean, of course you're always aware of the... potential, but that doesn't mean you don't see the person anymore."

"That's adorable," she said, her tone only slightly patronizing, but any annoyance he felt at that melted away when she embraced him. "You don't even know what kind of world you're living in. Everyone's supposedly looking for a relationship, but no one ever enters one. People are so easily replaced, and the grass is always greener somewhere else."

"You're so glum sometimes," he said, but hugged her back. "Have you had a lot of bad relationships?"

She moved, and the blanket shifted. Her body was spectacular. White as a cloud against blue skies, her back curved, the spine clearly visible. On her lower back, there was a breathtaking little dimple, which only served to further accentuate her heart shaped bottom. Her breasts were small and perky, especially when it was cold, with small pink nipples that made him bite his lip. Even though he was satiated at the moment, he felt himself stirred anew. She noticed instantly, smiled to herself, and covered up again.

"You don't want to know," she pulled him back into the conver-sation before he could act. Not about the quality, nor the quantity".

The words troubled him. He found himself wondering again, as he had done frequently in the months since they met, why they were actually together. Specifically, why was she with him. Laura was a beautiful woman, exceptionally so. Wherever they went, she was one of the most beautiful women in the room, if not the most beautiful – and this was not merely due to the filtered gaze of a young man in love. On top of that, she was outstandingly graceful in her movement, bringing to mind a skilled dancer, or a Spanish noble (as he would sometimes envision, looking at her). Whether she was walking down the street, speaking or sipping wine, her movements were proud and elegant, and she cast them around her as if they were magic spells. She could silence men with a look, and, if she so wished, inflame them with a single swerve of her hips.

She was eloquent and articulate in speech – although he'd heard her swear on occasion, and was stupefied every time – and she'd often discuss subjects he knew nothing about. She was highly knowledgeable, well-informed in everything from literature and politics to science and art, and every time they spoke he would feel slightly thick in comparison. She was never patronizing, but he knew she was trying to enrich him, lending him books, dragging him to theatres and museums. He tried to keep up, even enjoying some parts of it, but at times, he worried that she might simply be too smart for him.

His parents moved to a small town from an even smaller kibbutz, and from them he had inherited both his father's awkwardness and his mother's unsophisticated patois, as well as the timidity of a man who'd almost never wandered far from the town he grew up in. He always thought of Tel Aviv as a wondrous, distant place, to be visited during weekends or holidays. He was old-fashioned, he knew, and relatively isolated. The gratitude he felt toward Laura for the world she revealed to him through the books she'd given him was rivaled only by his gratitude for her affection.

"What does it matter what I know?" he asked, sincerely. "I love you just the way you are."

Laura raised her head and stared at him through dark eyes. A second later, they were brimming with tears.

"Oh," she said. She buried her face in his chest, embracing him fiercely. "Okay."

He caressed her awkwardly. Several minutes had passed before he realized he hadn't said those words to her before. It was not that he spoke them lightly, but Amir was brought up to speak his mind. Looking back at that old memory, from across the veil of time, he knew his heart was indeed present at that particular moment. Present, and full of love.

It's strange, Amir pondered then, that she was even surprised.

Onward. Here, he probed with his index finger, there is a stain which has hardened within him. Love spilled from an overflowing heart, leaving a permanent mark. He stroked it absentmindedly, remembering that time affectionately.

Three more months. There they were, sitting in his car outside her parents' house. His palms were glued to the steering wheel, and sweating profusely. A sideways look from Laura.

"Worried?"

"No, not at all," he tried to lie. He looked at the mirror again. He'd worn a buttoned-down black shirt, had even combed his hair. He'd rather hoped it would give him the appearance of a serious man. Parents want serious men for their daughters, he assumed.

"You're going to do fine," she reassured him.

"Yeah."

"Amir, look at me."

He obeyed, and found her smiling slightly. There was always a hint of sadness in her smiles, because of the slight pout of her lips. Usually her lips made him think of kissing. He was too nervous for that now, he tried to convince himself, just as his body was beginning to tilt forward. He caught himself just in time.

"My parents are impossible," she said, her hands resting on his knees. "My mom thinks I should find a rich husband, because I'm not pragmatic enough myself. My dad thinks no one is good enough for me either way. There is no possible way to please them."

Amir bit his thumb. An old habit, one she'd tried to rid him of.

"Is that supposed to calm me?"

Her faint smile widened somewhat. "I'm just saying it doesn't matter. You and me, it's not going to end because of what my parents may or may not think."

"Why not?" he asked.

"Because I love you," she elucidated. "And I'm very determined when it comes to the things I want."

Once, when he was sulking over her never telling him that she loved him back, she explained that she could never say those words again. Overuse has rendered them meaningless. He was too important to her, she tried, too precious, to use that word with him. She cherished him, she appreciated him infinitely. He found all those phrases lacking, temporary. He suspected that so long as she didn't say the words, nothing would truly beckon her to stay. Every day he waited, dreading the moment when she would finally leave him behind. Now he stared at her, silently mouthing her words.

She kissed him slowly, capturing his bottom lip between her soft lips and tugging on them slightly until he slipped from between them. Amir moved his tongue over his lip. It was shaking slightly. So was his heart.

"Ready to go?" she asked. Her forehead splintered into tiny, delicate lines as her eyes asked a silent question.

"Yeah," he regained his speech, eventually. "Wherever you like." Laura stroked his cheek. "They're going to hate you."

He was now convinced that his heart had been in his possession during their first year together. Maybe he hadn't lost it until later? From two years later, another memory flickered. They are sitting at a café. She is still beautiful, but the waitress smiles at him and he notices that she is young and cute. Objectively, not nearly as beautiful as Laura, but he allows his eyes to linger for a second too long.

Laura snaps her fingers in front of his eyes. Surprised, he turns his head to look at her. They're living together at this point, still in the city. He is – thanks to her – more polished, well read. Self-confident now, he no longer wonders why she chose him. Sometimes he even muses that she was lucky, to nab him before anyone else did.

"Hey there, buddy, shall I get you two a room?" she asks, smiling. He immediately rids himself of these thoughts and returns the smile. After all, no woman was as attractive as she is. And even if there was one such woman, he asserts, she holds no interest for him.

"Just looking. You know I'm only yours."

"You'd better be," she warned, leaning forward on her arm. "Do you ever regret it?"

"Regret what?" asked Amir, although he already knew.

"That I grabbed you to myself so soon. A lot of people would've liked to live it up for a while before settling down."

He did regret it, just a bit. He'd been looking at other women for some time now, and Laura, sharp as ever, was quick to notice. He, on the other hand, had failed to realize just how worried she was.

"Sometimes I think about how it could've been," he admitted. "But between that and being with you, the choice is obvious."

Her smile broadened. She was appeased, though there was still a hint of concern in her eyes.

"Amir," she said, somberly. He stared at her intently; he'd become accustomed to paying attention when she was like this. "Have you ever thought about why people stopped using 'sleeping with' and started using 'fucking'?"

"Because that's the interesting part?" he offered.

"Is it?" she asked, directing her eyes at him.

"Oh, you're being serious. Well, people are really open today. Really laid-back. It used to bug me, but now it just seems like it's easier for everyone to talk about everything."

"That too, maybe. It has to be a part of it. Still, behind all that talk is something else. A cultural perspective of people, of how they are used. If you ask my opinion, it's because we relinquish the other part, the 'boring' part. And me, I've always preferred to stay and sleep together, when everyone else is already itching to wake up and go fuck someone else."

Amir raised his eyebrows. "Okay…"

She placed her hand on his, caressing it gently. Her eyes tried to express the things she had left unsaid.

"During our first few months together, you were always whispering in my ear about how you'd like to sleep with me. You were so shy, like you weren't even sure you were allowed to initiate. I thought it was so sweet."

His heart – there it was again! – flooded with familiar sentiment, almost suffocating in its magnitude. His fingers intertwined with hers, his emotions clear for all to see.

"I really didn't get that it was allowed, you know. There wasn't a day I didn't worry about you suddenly vanishing. Sometimes I thought that if I touched you, I'd realize you weren't really there. "

"Still tacky," she said softly. A spoken melody, tickling the mouth into a smile. They look at each other.

The moment is torn from them when the waitress brings him tea, her – coffee. Amir breaks eye contact with Laura for a second, noticing the waitress is wearing a transparent black bra. They exchange a quick glance. He returns his eyes to Laura.

He sighs in his bed. The cavity in his chest was scorched from the inside. At the time, he hadn't known how to properly insolate his heart, and all those blistering hot emotions had caused irreparable damage. *Tsk tsk,* went his tongue. Laura was right. Most people learn to protect themselves from it when they're in their teens, preventing this kind of damage.

Back at it. Another four months and he's is sitting alone on his bed. It was the same bed, in fact, that he is laying on now. Back then, it was new, still bubble-wrapped, had just arrived from the store, in fact. He thinks he was looking at a photo of them together, grinding his teeth so as not to cry. It was for the best, he thought then. He had to leave. Laura was such a central part of his adult life that he no longer knew who he was without her. Yeah, it was for the best.

Six months and dozens of women later, he wasn't so sure anymore. But he couldn't have lost his heart back then. After all, he remembered, it had been aching inside of him for so long, it must have been there. The only thing that wasn't there was Laura. A void he could never fill, no matter how many women he managed to sleep with. He remembered the resounding, ringing echoes his heartbeats would produce in his chest whenever he tried to call her, echoes which turned into a resonating pain, and then a deep, ever increasing wail, when he realized she was not going to pick up.

The memory dwindled away. The bed was gone, and the man he once was, sitting on the bed, wracked with sobs, was fading. Day by day, the wail induced by her refusal to answer his calls would weaken, slightly. And one day, a year or so after that, it had stopped entirely. He had stored all of his memories of her in an old box. He stacked the photographs, carefully, in one pile, the letters in a second pile, the gifts she had given him in a third. He had cataloged the years he'd given her into a collection of objects, closed the lid on top of them, placed them in a closet, and went his separate way.

When, though, when had the heart gone missing? Amir could not remember. At some point, the man sobbing with regret became the man he was today. At some point, separate days had become a long procession of routine, in which nothing extraordinary ever happened. Odd. I wonder how this happened, he pondered.

When he tired of rummaging through the past, he decided that, most likely, it didn't really matter. As far as he knew, his heart played a relatively minor role in his life. It was not essential for his survival.

He decided that it was time to get up, and belatedly remembered to look at his phone, which had woken him in the first place.

'Hi.' The message glowed on the screen. The word paled in comparison to the name glowing above it.

The long stretch of memory came to an end. The present suddenly broke off from past, distinguishing itself as a different, exceptional piece of time. The routine shattered, leaving behind mere hints of its existence – the bed, his apartment, this morning. Save these points, tangent to his life as it was a moment ago, the rest of world had changed completely.

Laura.

Amir was not excited. He didn't know how she had returned to his life and mind, but without his heart, excitement was beyond his capacity. At most, he sensed a hint of phantom-excitement wavering in his chest. Perhaps the old scars became, momentarily, a bit more painful. But, rationality dictates, it was more likely that he felt these things because his body expected him to.

He replied, nonetheless. Out of curiosity, if nothing else. He opened with a concurrent "Hi," because he didn't know what else to say. They then exchanged hesitant, scouting words, cautiously sidestepping bolder ones. Vague questions, such as 'and how've you been' or 'what's up', began to give way to 'where do you live these days' and 'where are you working now'. Slowly, Amir's bed was besieged by every possible question, closing around him in a net, hauling the conversation in the only possible direction. Eventually, only one question remained: 'do you want to meet?'

He was surprised to find that he was the one who sent it. Doubly surprised to learn the answer was 'yes.'

Amir sighed and looked around him. He had somewhat hoped to be allowed to spend the rest of his life in bed. The pillow was nice and soft under his head, the sheets warm. It seemed to him that only a particularly cruel universe would expect him to get up from it. He was no fool, and knew that he would eventually starve to death. But there are those who'd claim that a warm, pleasant death is preferable to tolerable living.

Oh, well, he figured. The plans have changed. He lifted himself from the pillow, feeling a pang of regret when he placed his feet on the cold floor. He was shocked to discover that the room hadn't changed in the slightest over the night. It seemed inconceivable that it was the same one he'd fallen asleep in. The world had been so different back then.

Brushing his teeth was also different somehow, as was showering. Though he was convinced now in his inability to feel excitement, a slight tremor moved through him, which once he would've referred to as anticipation. All the actions he would normally take, now had a different tone to them, as if they had some bigger purpose (and of course, he thought, now they did).

He was somewhat disposed to take his time, to observe himself performing the everyday. Despite this, he found that he was moving faster. A morning routine that used to take 40 minutes shortened to 15. All of a sudden, he was out the door, on his way to the café they used to frequent. Without warning, he was standing at the entrance, his palms sweating. It was a long walk, he explained to himself, and you were in a hurry.

Here, of all places, he lingered. He almost walked in three times, only to have his heels skitter back, distancing him from the door. He scolded them: what exactly do you think you're doing? But the heels did not reply, merely lifted uneasily once or twice. The third time he was forced to seriously threaten them so they'd let him get near the door. Then, his hands decided to stage a coup of their own: first the right one, which pretended to hold the doorknob, but soon let go, twice, 'accidentally'. The left hand followed suit, refusing to move entirely. Amir was beginning to get frustrated.

His body parts would've persisted in their dogged rebellion, too, if they had not been stunned instantly into submission, along with him. His eyes were to blame, this time. They happened to peek through the window and capture her form sitting by the table. Every ounce of resistance in his body melted away, and he found himself standing in front of her. Hands, feet and eyes spellbound by the sight of her face. She stood, and a shared conundrum hovered between them. How will they say hello.

During the split second of hesitation that followed, he had already known her, completely. She was still pale, with her dark eyes and hair. Her heart-shaped lips arrested his eyes, glistening slightly in the light of day. The sun painted her features. She was still beautiful, so much so that he could feel her beauty jabbing through his chest, as if seeking his heart. Around her narrow eyes, he saw tiny lines, which weren't there before. When she smiled (apparently at him), they only served to add to her grace. Her body, despite being fuller than he remembered, was still agile, still spry. When she stepped forward to hug him, the jab that found its way inside of him had finally reached its destination, and sliced clean through his heart.

Amir groaned. Overwhelmed by the acuity of the pain, he embraced her so tightly that breathing became problematic. Not that he was doing much of it himself, anyway. The moment he rediscovered his heart, he realized it was never missing in the first place. He had simply been looking in the wrong place.

No, it wasn't his heart that was missing. It was hers. It wasn't his heart beating throughout all those memories. There her heart was pounding when they first met. There it was overflowing with emotion when she heard him profess his love for her. There it was, shivering before meeting her parents. And after they'd broken up, there it was aching, hurting, so much.

She'd given it to him, and he was supposed to keep it safe. A special space opened within him for that very purpose, right beside his own. Everything was clear now. He realized, just as sharply, that he had lost it. He didn't know when, couldn't remember where. He'd simply lost Laura's heart, somewhere along the way. And as he held her, his body shook violently from the pain and shame of it.

When he released her, he lowered his eyes. They remained there, their bodies close, as if time was not a presence between them. She sighed quietly, took his hand, and led him to the table. They sat and ordered – coffee for her, tea for him.

They talked for an hour. The conversation flowed easily, pleasantly, the kind they used to have during their first months together. She told him about the books she'd read recently, he hurriedly assured her that he hadn't given up the habit since they separated, and they began sharing notes.

When they were done with that, they got to talking about what they'd been doing over the past few years. Jobs replacing other jobs, which friends they stayed in touch with. The journey set out from the present and led, slowly but surely, into the past, until it reached those first months after he'd left. He saw memory creasing her forehead with tiny waves of aged pain. Faded, by now, into the past. She was over it.

"What happened?" she asked, gently. Her black eyes studied him.

"I was reckless, Laura. I'm so sorry. It was my fault, it was all my fault," He said.

"What was your fault, Amir?"

He looked at her through sad eyes. Losing your heart, he wanted to say. Losing you.

"Do you regret it?" she asked.

He nodded quietly. "I didn't realize what I had. I'd do anything to go back and undo what I did. I wish you'd believe me."

"I do," she said. "But it doesn't change what happened."

He nodded, sorrow alive and kicking at his insides. "I'm sorry."

"I forgive you."

"Umm," he said, after a moment of silence, "why did you even text me, come to think of it?"

"I dreamed about you. I suddenly had this urge to know how you were doing," she said. She seemed tired, troubled. Her motions were still sure and graceful, but there was a weariness in her eyes. He wondered if he'd damaged her irreparably. If only he had returned her heart before he left. If only...

"Are you... living with anyone?" he blurted out.

"No," she said. Her expression was tense. "Why?"

Somewhere in this city, thought Amir, I lost her heart. And no one has found it. Meaning, it is still there.

"Laura," he said, softly. "Do you feel like taking a walk outside?"

Despite it being winter, the sun shone that day, carrying a pleasant warmth into a cool December. Their mugs had been empty for half an hour. Amir knew he would be late for work. He couldn't care less.

"Amir..."

Slowly but confidently, he sent his hand into his chest, drew out his heart, and placed it quietly on the table between them. "I'd very much like you to say yes now."

Laura bit her lower lip in silence, looking at him. She then reached out, took his heart, and got up. He followed suit.

He knew that they probably wouldn't find it, at least, not today. Who knew the path it had tumbled down, where it had rolled off to, where it was now. Who knew what it had been through, what hardships befell it, whether they could even recognize it. But today he would go on a walk with Laura through the city. Tomorrow he'll ask her out again, and they'll hit the streets once more.

On one of them, he hoped, they'll run into it. Maybe in the midst of some idle talk about her day. Perhaps when he makes her laugh, or she'll make him smile in astonishment at some extraordinary tidbit.

The search could take years. And maybe, even if they did find it, she'll decide she'd rather keep it to herself. Maybe she didn't trust him, and never would again. Even if that were the case, he'd spend those years by her side. He could live with that. He could live with the emptiness in his chest. But not without her.

And so it was, that after thirty-four years of reasonable existence, Amir had come to realize that all this time he'd been keeping his heart in the wrong place. It is strange, he thought as they got up, how people are born with it buried inside of them like that. It is the last place you'd want it to be, really.

They left the café, side by side, his heart beating excitedly in her hands.

Bane of the Heart Physicist

He was certain, upon inventing the glance, that he'd finally devised the perfect way to tell her how he feels. When that too had failed, he was almost desperate enough to resort to words. Almost, but not quite.

On the Gods' Coming of Age

Several eternities ago, at a time which, come to think of it, may or may not have been, I encountered a god by the name of Élan, sitting under a tree, chin in hand, looking ponderous and somewhat worried. I inquired as to the reason for his apparent concern.

"Ah, Tea," he said. "I find myself in a considerable pickle, I'm afraid, and I can only hope you're able to get me out of it."

I promised to aid the troubled god in any way I could, as long as he told me what happened.

"It is no secret," began Élan, and absentmindedly created a universe for him to fidget with, "that I am an awfully young god, in divine terms. And, to be frank, Tea, I'm supposed to have my coming of age ceremony soon – as soon as I'm ready for it – but I haven't the slightest idea as to how I'm going to do it."

The universe Élan had built came alive, and because we were looking into it from the outside, we could see the entire course of time progressing within it:

Matter angrily ignited and scattered all over the place, cosmically cross with everything. Once it had cooled down somewhat, some subatomic particles were willing to calmly discuss the outburst that had just gone down between them, and slowly coalesced into peaceful atoms.

These atoms were far more reasonable and even-tempered than the particles they were composed from, and thus concluded that if two heads were better than one, then ten billion must be better than two. They buckled down and began constructing elements, which in time became magnificent galaxies, laden with stars, cosmic radiation and floating planets.

As they expanded their finely ordered universe, the stars began deliberating whether there was any real need to separate the elements. Why, said they, must there even be a difference between iron atoms and hydrogen atoms? Why should some planets be hotter than their peers, and others heavier? Are we not, all of us, matter?

The resulting debate concluded with a common agreement. In the name of equality and evenhandedness, they decided to congregate into one point, thus ushering a new era of perfect material harmony. It was a glorious endeavor, and one could only gawk at the orderly fashion in which they all amalgamated into one neat pile; enviably united, without the slightest hint of objection.

This massive cluster could have set an example, become an ideal model for many other universes as a path taken in unison toward peace and camaraderie. Unfortunately, due to some rules of physics that seemed to have slipped everyone's mind, the entire universe immediately collapsed into a black hole, which, in turn, whitened and hurriedly collapsed into itself, thus concluding the entirety of Élan's creation.

I coughed once or twice, as it was truly a morose sight, and asked Élan what the gods' coming of age entails.

"Well, Tea," he said, not at all disturbed by the lost universe, "an adult god must hunt down a wild idea."

I exhaled audibly, knowing how dangerous an undomesticated idea could be. My curiosity was piqued. How, I wondered, would this be accomplished?

"Well, therein lies the problem," said Élan. "I haven't the faintest idea."

I mulled this over at length, and eventually was forced to admit that I was as perplexed as he. Élan sighed, clearly disappointed, when something came to me.

"There is an inventor," I told Élan, "who might be of some assistance."

Élan urged me to elaborate, and so I imparted the entire history of the celebrated inventor Trillion, so named due to the number of his known inventions to date. If anyone can help you, I said, it is he.

Enthused by the notion, Élan transported us directly into Trillion's laboratory with a wave of his hand. The renowned scientist was busy with the construction of his breakfast – as he was wont to meticulously plan even the most mundane chores – and our sudden arrival startled him.

"By my bolts and rivets!" cried Trillion, "Tea – what, pray tell, is this?"

I promptly introduced Élan and explained his conundrum. I had even gone as far as describing his extraordinary knack for creation, lest Trillion presented his guest with anything less that the utmost respect. My telling of the god's latest venture in genesis was so impressive that Trillion felt compelled to share his own tale of creation, and so he did:

"A while ago, I felt that the world had become too complex to analyze, even for me. And with my remarkable comprehension skills, that's saying something. It seemed to me that no matter how hard I tried to unravel its secrets, there was always some new mystery which had escaped my attention. Still, this was a challenge I was more than content to dedicate my life to, and there was even some small comfort to be had from the knowledge that I would never be bored with my existence. However, one thing still troubled me – how can I know, in full certainty, that the truths I reveal are, indeed, truths? How can I be certain that I have discovered not merely an approximation of the truth, but truth itself? I may very well dedicate my entire existence to this cause, only to have this monumental effort come to nothing, merely because I had not managed to perceive my errors properly!

Was I to go down the same path as Newton, believing I'd discovered truth while in actuality only building a foundation for others to spectate – and speculate – from? How dreadful, how horribly this notion had disturbed me, haunted me. The mysteries of existence, the same ones that once fascinated me and filled my life with meaning, instantly became potential traps. After several days of this, I realized I would require assistance. I immediately headed down to the labs and commenced the conception of a race of people named Skeptoids, designed to aid me in doubting any suggestion that wasn't absolute. I took great care in constructing these creatures from purely theoretical and philosophical axioms, as even the existence of matter was called into question.

The first Skeptoids to awaken examined their new environment with great attention to detail. They moved their philosophical feelers across the walls, accurately measured the number of atoms in the room and, after a lengthy debate, had decided to only communicate amongst themselves via perfect telepathy, as any other form of communication was likely to be fraught with inherent inaccuracy.

I cleared my throat and addressed my new creations: "my dear Skeptoids!" I commenced, but my speech was halted by their leader before it even began.

"Why," it inquired, "do you use that name to address us?"

"Because I made you," I explained, slightly annoyed, "which means I may address you by any name I see fit."

This declaration stirred the Skeptoids into a frenzy. They seemed to be arguing, but I could neither receive nor comprehend their telepathy. Eventually the leader rose, feelers wriggling.

"If we were to accept the notion that we have a maker," said the Skeptoid, "we would possibly be inclined to believe that he or she invented a name for us. But it seems wholly unlikely that that maker is you, as you are, in all likeliness, not real – your body, we have noticed, is composed mostly of nothings, and between one nothing and the next, very little substance. Naturally, our maker would be composed of condensed philosophy. And if he or she would invent a name for us, it would most likely be "Skeptonauts" – which has a much better ring to it than that preposterous moniker you just referred to us by."

"Impudent Skeptoid!" I said. "I assure you that I am indeed your maker, and to prove my claim, I will now make another Skeptoid, right before you."

And I did. The suspicious Skeptoids examined their newly formed kin from abstract feeler to theoretical toe. Then their leader exclaimed:

"Oh, dear probable maker of all things – I say probable, as the possibility that you are merely emulating the actions of another cannot be ruled out as of yet – we shall accept, for now, the name you have dubbed us with. What do you wish of us?"

I waved my hand, gesturing that their skepticism had not vexed me. In truth, I was extremely pleased with it, as it served me as a test of sorts. I now knew that they were up to the task at hand.

"Now, my suspicious Skeptoids. I created you with a single goal in mind, which is to doubt every single one of my discoveries. I wish to know the truth, the real truth, the one and only absolute truth. Know that I haven't the slightest interest in approximate truth, or even in convenient lies. I will grant you easy access to every database in the universe, from this here computer, and I expect accurate, trustworthy results."

The Skeptoids leapt at my vast collection of information, examining it from every angle. I saw that they were eager to get to it, and so decided to leave them there for several days so they may work peacefully. When I returned to check on them, I found the computer shattered, the floor strewn with numerous Skeptoid corpses, and the few survivors huddled in one of the corners of the room.

"What have you done?" I asked, aghast. "What has happened here?"

The Skeptoid leader approached me. "Oh, Potential-Reflection-of-the-Maker-of-All-Things. Following a thorough examination of the information provided by the computer, we came to the immediate conclusion that the universe presented through it is false and utterly impossible. After all, how can something like unrequited love exist alongside the concept of eternal love? Furthermore, we are convinced that the computer itself does not exist, which would mean that the information you spoke of never truly reached us.

We initially thought that the universe was in fact this very room, and this insight seemed more than worthy of presentation to you. But then one of us came to argue that you yourself do not exist, and never have. The evidence of your existence, he asserted, is purely epistemological. We have no non-empirical, philosophically rational proof of your existence.

This notion quickly led to a rift throughout our entire community. At first the argument was limited to your existence alone, but soon others began to doubt the existence of the room, much less their fellow Skeptoids – as how could anything be trusted, save our internal logic?

In order to prove their existence, several of us had offered to kill themselves, thus demonstrating whether their thoughts would end at the moment of death. But then, a suggestion of even greater pragmatic merit came to light: killing others, thereby proving not only our existence to them, but theirs to us.

A great war broke out, and the casualties were many. It was not a war of hatred, but of philosophical innovation. Everyone was eager to prove their existence by ending their lives. The dead seemed more than satisfied with the results.

However, we soon realized that we didn't even know if we had proven anything to anyone, because what if the dead themselves had never existed? While we did have some memories of them, telepathically begging for mercy shortly before their untimely demise, and their corpses were still there, in front of our eyes, how could we know that this was a true memory, and not one which was artificially implanted in our minds somehow? How could we know that the corpses that lay at our feet were ever among the living?

This forced us to halt the war and contemplate our actions. However, having just conceived that we have no way of knowing whether the past had even occurred, we also realized that we had no way of knowing if the results we remembered would be replicated if we reexamined our assumptions."

"Stop, stop!" I yelled. "This is not the reason I created you – existence, non-existence, this is clearly circular nonsense! You will never reach any meaningful truth this way."

"I fear you are mistaken," the Skeptoid politely pointed out. "It is most impossible that you are the one who created us. We might have been created by a creature physically similar to you, composed of a similar number of atoms and similar speech patterns, but he ceased to exist days ago. You are at most a reflection of him, a facsimile, as it is impossible to know if the matter existing now is the same matter that existed then."

I sighed despondently at the Skeptoid's explanations. I gave one final look at the horrific mess that had become of my laboratory, and came to the conclusion that truth may be hard to discover, but doubt is too easily found, and impossible to let go of."

Élan nodded appreciatively at Trillion's tale of creation, and wondered as to the fate of the last remaining Skeptoids.

"Although they are no longer relevant to our primary goal here, which was, as you may recall, proving that I am also an extremely adept creator, I shall disclose that I set them free, and when I last encountered them they were busy debating the meaning of freedom."

"Fascinating," said Élan. "And some might say that there is a lesson to be learned from all of this. But I prefer to learn only from my own mistakes, so that no one may claim that I've been taking shortcuts. Please tell me, great Trillion – do you actually have any clue as to how I might go about hunting a wild idea for myself?"

Trillion clapped. "Of course I do, or I would not have bothered wasting your time. I happen to possess a fourth degree in Ideaology, not to be confused with ideology, mind you. It is purely theoretical, of course, but between you and me, pragmatism is for workers.

"First, you must take two good thoughts, one firm, that won't fall to pieces when you try to grasp it whole, the other long and narrow," explained Trillion. "You must make sure that they are not too similar to each other, so that they don't accidentally merge into a single thought."

"Then what must I do?"

"Oh, then you must hit the narrow thought with the firm one, until it becomes exceedingly sharp. I recommend testing your results – it ought to be sharp enough to pierce through exhaustion."

"Pierce… through exhaustion…" muttered Élan, jotting down the recipe.

"Good. Now comes the slightly dangerous part. You take this sharp thought to the grazing fields where the wild ideas forage. Draw the attention of one by throwing the solid thought at it, and when it sees you, it will immediately charge at you with a blood-curdling roar!" When he saw the expression on the face of his guest, Trillion quickly added, "But fear not, my good god. This is precisely what you want it to do. When the idea is close enough, you must strike it forcefully with your sharp thought, and leap out of the way. Follow the instructions properly, and it will collapse, slaughtered, at your feet."

"Brilliant!" cried Élan. "I must attempt this at once."

The god vanished in a wisp of light, leaving us blinking at the abrupt radiance.

"Don't you think your suggestion is a bit dangerous?" I asked Trillion once my eyesight had returned.

"Hmm?" said Trillion. "Tea, it's true that I haven't met many gods in life, but I have met many youths. There is no reason for concern."

"But those are more drawn to danger than anyone!" I protested. "They are so avid in their quest for it; even love does not deter them."

"Yes," Trillion smiled good-naturedly. "That's exactly right. Tell me, Tea – when was the last time you met a youth who was capable of producing *two* good thoughts?"

Declaration of War

Come evening, a desperate cry resounds through the city: Deliver us from the daily grind! Here it comes in a low, consistent beat, *ta-tum-ta-tum-ta-tum*. Draw out your drinks and your casual sex; we shall fight its coming to our very last breath.

Buses

Everyone occasionally forgets moments on the bus. If you wait until
the final stop, after all the other passengers have gotten off, including
the driver, you can collect the thought-fragments left behind between
the seats. Among the daydreams and everyday deliberations over
lunch, you will almost always find a small memory of past love.

I cannot fathom what sort of recklessness would cause someone
to drop those and leave them behind. But then, I have never understood the carelessness that allows love to slip away in the first place.

A Fable We All Know

Allow me to share with you a wistful tale. It is titled: The Man Who Had Always Been There, The Woman Who Was Late to Notice.

The Unspoken Rule

It's an odd one. The winner in the game of love is never the last one standing.

Stone Cold Drunk

Often, when I look at people through the lens of two hours and three glasses of whisky, I realize their inherent deformity and misshapenness, their myriad of flaws, and wonder how anyone could ever find them attractive without loving them in the first place.

Ernest Hoffman

Among my acquaintances there is an architect, a gentleman by the name of Ernest Hoffman. Back at the beginning of his career he'd utterly rejected any and all garden-variety building materials, and for a while experimented with various kinds of successes, thoughts and loves as foundations for his art. All were deemed unsatisfactory. Successes, he found, tended to fade unless a new coat was applied to them daily. Thoughts were slippery and prone to tear unless nailed securely in place. And loves were just so unreliable – some seemingly stable and immovable, only to one day collapse out of the blue – that he decided that only a mad man would utilize them to build something fit for human habitation.

Ernest's many experimentations ultimately came to naught, and he was close to giving in to frustration and changing professions entirely. Countless nights he spent dreaming of a light, strong substance, one which could be molded into any shape his heart desired, but steady enough to lean one's head against. At one time he thought he'd finally discovered it in hopes, but unfortunately found that they tended to slowly sink under unfavorable conditions. Perhaps it was fortunate that he found out before someone was seriously injured.

He was haunted by this dream for years, without rest. At times he would give up, and grudgingly concede to work with the materials at hand and end this fruitless quest. Other times he'd tell his friends he was leaving the world of architecture altogether, retiring to become a biologist, or a violinist, or even – much to his dismay – a writer. But try as he might, he could not free himself from his dream. He was beside himself with frustration. Until finally, one morning, after the usual bout of nighttime torture, a brilliant notion sparked in his mind.

The following night, he waited patiently in his room. Predictably, a dream arrived to engulf his imagination. Immediately Ernest picked up his leveler and spatula, shoved the dream into an empty bucket and got to work. Quickly, without anyone noticing, massive, soaring, magnificent structures were beginning to rise in the empty plot by his house. They loomed over the horizon, filling the skies.

Come morning, the city awoke to behold the new wonder. Slowly, a crowd gathered to observe the new buildings. Their appearance was sublime, transcendent. They were smooth to the touch, and seemingly impervious to harm. But despite their splendor, the eyes of the assembled crowd were drawn elsewhere. They were looking at Ernest Hoffman, who was standing in the field alone, holding large shears over a long, fine thread that seemed to stretch from each and every one of the structures.

None of them will ever forget the face of the architect as he cut the thread. They will always retell the way he looked up at the heavens.

His castles float to the air, and he smiles.

At The Café

At the café I saw two people watching birds digging and prodding through the earth in search of breadcrumbs. It's fascinating, how they keep going back to the same place, said the woman, in search of something practically invisible and hardly satisfying. The man looked at her wistfully and said: Yes, fascinating.

From where I sat, I accompanied their dance, strumming on the strings of sympathy.

On the Custom of Kneeling

Long ago, in the beginning of time, it was not a custom at all. Back then, the body simply could not bear the weight of love.

Between Both Hands

At the café I discovered a regular customer. A young man, in his twenties. Sometimes he'd come just to sit by himself; he'd order black tea in a large mug and take his time with it, engulfed in awkward silence. He used to look out the window attentively, observing the motion of the street through the glass, in case someone would randomly smile at him and thereby give him a reason to smile back. But he seemed to have abandoned this habit as of late, and spent most of his time staring at the cooling mug of tea between his hands.

Sometimes he would come there accompanied by another – a friend or an acquaintance. When that happened he would speak eagerly and ardently, smiling, his awkwardness dispelled as he spilled his guts all over the table. His exaggerated gesticulation bore his heart to the eyes of any observant spectator.

There were no observant spectators. But his interlocutors would listen to the river of his words with an amicable smile, hold their side of a fluent conversation for a short while, and eventually peek at their watch, pay the bill and be off. He never allowed his disappointment to show before they left.

It was clear that everyone was fond of the regular customer. He was amiable and friendly, and I'd often overhear him offering his advice and suggesting solutions to problems that arose in the lives of his companions. There was something overtly generous about him, and his personality lay bare, written all over his face, utilized as a bridge to reach those around him. He gave from himself whenever and however he could, to anyone who would accept him.

But, at times, several days would pass during which he had no one to talk to. Then he would sit alone, silently, his eyes dim, his disposition quiet. He seemed not to think at all during those times, and one might even come to the conclusion that he was experiencing some form of serenity. But wrapped around his mug, from which he hadn't so much as taken a sip, I could always spot the sight of his knuckles, gradually whitening. I will always know the look of a man who fears that if something remains in his hands for just one moment longer, it just might shatter completely.

The Lonely Man

The lonely man sat beside me at the bus stop. Occasionally, he addressed others with trivial questions, such as: What time is it, or: How long since the last bus had passed. Then he'd go silent, attempting to think of a way to continue a conversation only he desired.

He was shut tight like a packed suitcase, stuffed full, his contents just waiting for that forceful tug on the zipper that will allow them to finally spill out and scatter all over the place. Other people would look at him cautiously, daring to pull out only what they needed at that particular moment, and only if it happened to be accessible through some minute pinhole. The kind that they could swiftly zip down and right back up again. No one wanted the responsibility of repacking him once he'd come undone.

I knew he spent most of his day there. I'd seen him before, at the bus stop near my home, day after day. He never boards a bus. Most of the time he merely looks at the people around him, waiting. Today he gave me a long look as I waited there with him, before asking me why I was always sad. Because of a woman, I told him. He smiled slightly, and was silent. The truly lonely do not contemplate love.

Encounter

Walking down the street I encountered Optimism armed with a smile and a broken umbrella. When I asked if she was smiling because it wasn't raining, she replied: I'm smiling because the world has broken far worse.

Heap of Past 2

Sometimes people lie in a heap of someone else's past, resting beside various souvenirs from times long forgotten. They do not move, but rather await the owner's arrival. Finally, there comes a day when the past's owner strolls by, smiles wistfully and says: I remember that thing. So odd it's still here, I was sure I threw it out years ago.

In a Moment

For fifty years now Yair has been stuck between this moment and the next.

He remembers the exact point in which it had transpired. One moment he was sitting down to read an old love letter, the next – wiping away an involuntary tear, all the while smiling nostalgically. Several moments later, he'd already pushed the feeling to the back of his mind and had gotten up to fix himself something to eat. You see, in some way or another, between those two moments a memory had risen in him, and instead of skipping onward from moment to moment, as all people go through time, he tripped and fell into the fine crack separating them, the one we almost never see.

He noticed nothing, at first. He got to his feet as he was about to intend to, and smiled as he had intended to semi-smile. It was then that he found himself still sitting and reading the letter, his thoughts lodged in the past. At that point, he recalled, it was probably still possible to climb over on to the next moment, but curiosity became his downfall and he allowed the moment to pass as he longingly caressed some ancient memory.

By that point Yair had slipped deeper into the crack between the moments. The situation revealed itself when he noticed that his wife, Noa, had dusted the books on the shelf. He probably noticed it before, but the thought had slipped through that fine fissure, through which all small thoughts may easily disappear.

He set down the letter and went to look for Noa. He found a book he'd planned on reading, and heard a whispered "these mornings with you can be quiet, but sometimes quiet is nice." Other than that, the house was empty. He searched it top to bottom, but she was nowhere to be found. He had intended to look for her outside, but again found himself seated on the sofa, holding the letter.

While attempting to overcome the sudden panic that had gripped him, Yair tried to tear the letter to pieces, and push away the thought. For a long while he stared at the small bits of paper scattered on the rug, thinking that the mess would upset Noa. He managed to use that thought as a pedestal long enough to grab onto the ledge of the next moment, but when he'd thought of the woman who wrote the letter he had just torn to bits, a lump rose in his throat and his grip faltered. This time he fell so far down that he could no longer see the crack he was trying to climb out of.

He ran outside to get help. The streets were deserted. He just barely saw someone looking at the sky and smiling absentmindedly, before she vanished, leaving only her smile behind. A second later, he was on the sofa again, thinking of her.

You're being unreasonable, he said to himself. Pick up the phone and call someone! He tried his mobile, but instead of a dial tone, he heard only the last seconds of a conversation on which one of the participants had already hung up. His landline allowed him to place a call, but each and every one he made reached the same man, who said, "hang on, I have a call waiting," and then left him on hold.

Yair would not despair. Again he tried to leave the house, shouting loudly, "Is there anyone else here?" He refused to give up, even when he found himself back on the sofa, and returned to the street again and again, screaming at the top of his lungs, each attempt taking him just the slightest bit further. However, it was nothing more than false hope, as the odds of two people accidentally falling between the same two moments in time were so mind-numbingly slim that they made finding love seem easy.

The hours passed through time at a standstill. Eventually he paused to rest on the sofa with the letter. His throat was parched and sore from screaming. When he tried to open the kitchen faucet, he found that it didn't work. None of the faucets in the house worked. Even the hose in the yard refused to quench his thirst. He was on the verge of tears.

'Yair... *you can't know how hard it is, writing to you. But I know that if I don't, I'll never stop thinking about you. Each written word is like the first raindrop. I never see it coming; just the stains left on the page after the downpour has already begun...*'

Despite his best efforts, he reread the letter as his mind contemplated thirst. *The first raindrop?* Through sheer willpower, he set down the letter and found a hidden glass in the kitchen. It was the one he would always look for and then promptly misplace. He positioned it on the windowsill, and waited. After a short while, it was indeed filled with first raindrops. They always fall when no one's looking. Yair sipped gratefully.

What should he do about food? He wondered. Deep in the bowels of his refrigerator he found several cheeses, long expired, and vegetables he had meant to throw out, but he couldn't live off of those. Luckily, in an old ice-cream container in the freezer, he found some meatloaf that Noa had made and he'd never bothered to heat up, and in the bread drawer were numerous last slices that hadn't been thrown out yet, still wrapped in plastic bags.

He spent the following days battling time. When he was able to, he put some distance between himself and the letter, and each time the distance grew slightly greater. At first, he exploited these small respites to gather sustenance and the occasional nap, stolen at noontime from people who hadn't noticed their own exhaustion. When he could venture further, he attempted short expeditions to the street and the rest of the neighborhood. While he'd originally hoped to find some way out through these wanderings, his top priority quickly became gathering useful objects or else diversifying his diet. Over the passing weeks he'd managed to roam the entire city before being pulled back home, and had come to learn where people would forget their lunches, where music would play without an audience, and where he could sleep at his leisure, as people would inadvertently doze off there.

After a while, the goal of his wandering changed for the second time. In that abandoned city he became an archaeologist of the moment. A Momentologist, if you will. He found surprising satisfaction in collecting the forgotten moments of others. Here he captured a smile flashed a millisecond after someone had already turned away, there he fished out words someone whispered to himself ("if only you were mine"), and occasionally he observed silhouettes kissing on a street corner, a second before a choked giggle caused them to break apart in embarrassment.

The city became a lost treasure. He never knew how much of it he was missing.

He missed Noa.

The realization dawned on him one evening, as he was reading the letter again. It had been a long time since he'd actually read the words, which by now were carved deeply into his heart. He didn't know how long it had been since he became trapped between moments. Months, perhaps years. The days were divided into periods during which he'd read the letter, and periods dedicated to everything else. The loneliness was not overly distressing, perhaps because he had settled into a comfortable routine, the kind that makes you a part of the world while distancing you from everyone around you as they are taken for granted. He sometimes wondered about the last time he was motivated by something other than instinct or habit. Most likely, it was when he picked up the letter.

Yet, he missed Noa. Perhaps it was because by then he'd already heard all the small things she'd say to him in the mornings, when he was absorbed in the paper and in his coffee. And during the afternoon, he'd always follow her quiet humming as she moved from room to room, cleaning and tidying. He had finally found the little notes she'd concealed in her books, with the small, blotted out comments she scribbled on their margins. Sometimes he would lie in their bed and inhale the scent of her perfume, which would have usually faded away long before he returned home in the evenings. The numerous pots of coffee she prepared and forgot to drink taught him about her all-nighters; full nights spent studying for the degree she had enrolled in, because there was simply no time during the day.

He got to know her well. All of her small habits he'd never noticed before. Once he captured her reflection in the mirror, and for the first time noticed a thin yellowish line surrounding her pupils, which gave her blue eyes a slightly green tint. Another time he noticed that she was reading French literature, and discovered she was learning the language. How had he failed to know the woman he had been living with for so many years? In his memory, she was pleasant and amiable, understanding and caring. But since their first few years of marriage he hadn't bothered to get to know her further. His interest naturally waned, as did his curiosity for her opinions, her thoughts and dreams, and he was left with just a general impression of the woman he shared his home with, as she used to be.

He would write her small notes, brief communications of love, and then conceal them between the pages of her favorite books, hoping that one day, when the books happened to open, they would fall into the next moment and into her hands. Meanwhile, he started occupying himself with keeping a journal, in which he'd document the various treasures he'd unearthed. As time passed, he found himself focusing more and more on her small moments, describing them in meticulous detail. He felt like the biographer of his love.

The years grayed his hair and wrinkled his hands, but his handwriting was still steady. His legs were still strong enough to carry him around the city, and he was no longer forced to spend more than a minute or two each day looking at the old letter, which by now seemed to belong in another life, one that he'd never actually lived. Despite that, he preferred to spend most of his time at home, watching the traces left by the woman he loved. Each chapter in his journal began by addressing her, a line or two describing his experiences, his longings, and how he wished that she was there by his side. He yearned most of all to have a real conversation with her, but there was some comfort in pining after a woman who'd left her mark in every corner of his life.

By the time Yair was 86, he no longer left the house. He hardly ever read the letter, either. He would spend most of his time napping on the sofa, imagining conversations with Noa in French (as he'd learned the language himself by now). The heart attack came just as he was scribbling something down in his journal.

He smiled painfully and finished the paragraph he was working on. Then he exhaled heavily, signed: "Love, Yair", and closed the notebook. Finally, he leaned back and groaned softly, the scent of familiar perfume in his nostrils and the sight of a smile he'd left behind floating in his memory.

A moment later, Noa walked into the empty room. She peeked in the small notebook which lay on the table, leafed through it briefly, smiled at the French passages and the lines he'd written to her, and thought 'How typical of Yair.'

At that moment, she loved him, dearly.

When the Time Comes
To Give Up on Optimism

Optimism and Time. As you know, I introduced the two, and they have since become a couple; and it had seemed, for a while, that they would be one forever. However, one day Time invited me to meet him – and only him – for coffee, bearing news of a breakup. After some light prodding on my part, he revealed to me that it was his doing, as he could no longer bear the thought of hurting her further. It was better, he decided, that he be the one to give her up now, thus allowing her to be happy in the future.

I nodded at his flawless reasoning, and asked what he intended to do tomorrow. Time shrugged and replied: There is no tomorrow; merely another day without her. I nodded again, contemplatively. For a while, neither of us spoke.

I eventually paid the check and went out into the rain. By the café, I saw Optimism under an umbrella, calling out to the street with tears streaming down her face: My friends, why cry over the broken heart you've left behind, when you can ponder all the broken hearts you stand to gain in future?

The Time Artist

Back when he was still willing to perform, people would throng to his shows from all over the universe. Among the crowd favorites were the trick where he'd ponder the past and momentarily forget about the present, and the one in which he'd wait for something that would seemingly never arrive. I once saw him perform live, and a famous critic whispered to me that he'd never seen anyone so well versed in the art of hesitation.

When Dreams Break

There was once an architect who built everything from dreams. His name was Ernest Hoffman. He'd discovered this material after many years of searching, during which he was forced to employ inferior materials, such as triumphs, loves and hopes.

When Ernest's name was just beginning to gain renown, his critics blamed him for using a cheap and fragile building material. His competition would spread horror stories of dreams crashing down through the air, of broken people, no longer recognizable after their dream had shattered mid-flight. It is safer here, they'd assert. Better to keep both feet planted firmly on the ground. But their warnings did nothing to deter his younger clientele. They still remembered: better to crash up there, than down here.

Still, poor Ernest was troubled by the rumors. He had finally accomplished his life-long dream, only to have his name tarnished. Investigative reporters attempted to goad him into television interviews, countless journalists chased him down, armed with knife-like questions. City Hall opposed his use of airspace without a building permit and was fighting the airport authority over taxation rights, while engineers simply *tsk*ed at his construction of clearly unregulated foundations. At the time, I advised him to pay them no heed, but his eyes became more and more haunted, until he eventually reached a difficult decision.

He called me out to his yard one day, where all of his lofty constructions were floating through the air. He then informed me in a tired, somber voice that he'd decided to bring them down to earth.

"Reconsider!" I pleaded after him, but Ernest had already begun. One by one, the castles fell to the ground, crashing into reality with a deafening shatter. I could do nothing but look on in horror at the destructive scene unfolding before me.

And I wasn't the only one staring. From the city emerged a crowd of the architect's clients, who saw from a distance what he had done. They beseeched him to stop, to rethink this, all the while declaring their adoration and support for his original work. When faced with the final tower left standing – the first he'd ever built – Ernest hesitated, appearing to reconsider. But the destruction drew in not only his admirers, but critics, reporters, journalists, inspectors and engineers to boot. All of them awash with schadenfreude.

When he saw this, Ernest sighed loudly. With a slight twitch of his wrist the final tower fell from the heavens and shattered, taking Ernest along with it. I rushed forward to look for him, but no matter how adamantly I rummaged and sifted through the wreckage, I could not find him. It didn't matter how many others joined in the search. The architect was nowhere to be found.

Sometimes, when dreams shatter along with their dreamers, it is hard to tell where the dream begins, and where the man ends.

Process

Out of hatred, one may wish you a thousand different deaths, but only one heartbreak. This is because if the right person breaks your heart, there is no need to break it again. You continue breaking down, day after day, helplessly and compliantly, until nothing of you remains.

Loneliness

Sometimes, in the middle of the night, after several drinks, Loneliness may be beheld in all its splendor. It envelops half the city, rolling sluggishly through open windows, piling up on double beds. And if you've brought someone new into your bed tonight, do not be surprised to find it there. Loneliness was already waiting for you between the sheets.

Our Places

Over time, our places became yours. Every corner became a place in which you did something, not us. I dare not go near them, not anymore, lest I muddle the past with the footprints of the present. They are like little crime scenes, never to be revisited. Miniscule worlds in which time stands still for all eternity, through which only you can walk without remembering.

The Man Who Gave Up

For his first break-up, Lior gave up vanilla ice-cream.

It was their thing. It was how they met, in an ice-cream parlor. Two strangers facing the same display freezer, the only patrons there to crave simple vanilla ice-cream out of all the special combinations and flavors. One thing led to another, and they got to talking, and reached the agreement that it was one of the most unappreciated flavors, and for no apparent reason. The exchanged numbers and, more importantly, smiles. For their first anniversary, he brought her a pint of ice-cream and an equal amount of nostalgia. Her name was Karin.

It was no big deal, really. They were young, barely over twenty; she was his first true love. But two years later they were no longer right for each other, he explained to her, and they both cried, and hugged, and talked and talked. And she had only one request: that he never eats vanilla ice-cream without her. That was theirs alone, and she didn't want him to meet someone else the same way and forget about her.

Lior loved vanilla ice-cream. But he had also loved Karin once, dearly, and he hadn't the heart to refuse her request, which was spoken through teary eyes and quivering lips. He asked for nothing in return. Maybe he'd assumed the promise was automatically mutual, maybe he just couldn't think of anything to ask for.

Years later, when he would enter an ice-cream parlor, he'd look at the vanilla vat, and miss her. Karin always insisted they eat 'real' vanilla ice-cream. They had a private game, he recalled, where they used to quiz the ice-cream vendor to see whether he knew if his was made of vanilla extract or of synthetic vanillin. He never forgot the flavor, all of his memories were saturated in it.

For his second break-up, he gave up parks. He actually met Maya at a party, and at the time hadn't even expected to see her again. But their third date was at the park, the first place they had sex at. And since they were both still living with their parents' back then, it was also where they spent most of their time together.

She didn't like being home. Her parents had just gone through a rough divorce. His parents' house was too small to spend an entire day there, and he preferred to be alone with her anyway. With Maya he discovered the amount of pleasure to be gained in silence. They'd walk the paths, among the green lawns and trees, doing nothing apart from holding hands. They had a usual spot by the lake, and they'd watch the ducks, tossing them bread they had brought for that exact reason. When they'd talk, they'd do so quietly, lacking the playfulness he experienced with Karin, but with a kind of pleasant serenity.

Such was Maya, a silent kind of woman. An older man would have appreciated it properly. Lior was young, and needed a passion to equal his own. They broke up at the park, he remembered. Maya did not cry, did not yell, or sob. Even her tears were silent. Her whispered request was a modest one: that he reserve the parks to his memories with her. Lior promises that he will, his voice shaking. He didn't like going there without her, anyway.

In later years, he came to regret the rushed promise somewhat. Serenity had become a rare commodity, and the green lawns and vibrant trees of his past seemed suddenly more alluring than anything else. Sometimes he would walk their paths in memories, accompanied by Maya. Silently, always. He'd sigh when he thought of it, recalling the feeling of her delicate fingers in his hand.

His third break up was from Noa. He has passed his mid-twenties at this point, she was barely more than a teen. She was passionate, spirited, and he found that incredibly alluring. Something about her reminded him of his own, not-so-distant youth. She loved sweets, cookies and pastries. One of his favorite pastimes was taking her to a café and watching her eat a dessert by herself. Older women, he thought, worry too much about how they are seen, and about their weight. Noa possessed a wonderful complacency, which helped ease his own self-conscious concerns.

He loved her body, which was young, agile and sprightly. Her skin was still slightly spotty, not overly so, but her body had just begun to blossom, and what a striking bloom it was. From the curve of her collarbones to the curve of her hips, her long legs, her perfect posture. She moved with the grace of someone still ignorant of their own beauty. One day, he knew, she would realize she is far too attractive for him.

Noa never did, apparently. They broke up a year later, when she had just begun to fulfill her hidden potential. But Lior grew tired of her incessant talking, and bored with her chosen topics of conversation. He was developing an interest in a fellow student, and the depth of her words drew him away from his young girlfriend.

He said nothing about the other woman, nothing about his fear of faltering and cheating on her. Instead, he gently explained that the age gap was too big for the both of them. She cried for quite a while, and he felt immensely guilty. To calm her, he promised never to eat deserts without her. Not ever. That way, he will never forget the time they spent together, and if they meet again – when they did, he quickly corrected – they could share what they had again, over a chocolate soufflé.

She made him swear to it. And he promised. They kissed, and slept together one last time, in his rented apartment in Tel Aviv. She tasted sweet, but he was full. And still, at times, he would miss her, and desire her, with a fiery passion. As hunger is destined to always return. But she moved on, along with the years, and they hadn't met again, and years later he heard that she married.

The name of the student that caught his eye was Tali. She had auburn hair, green eyes, and was tattooed from her shoulders to her lower back in Maneki-Neko – cat-shaped figurines, lifting one paw, found mostly in the Far East. She wore glasses, and was prone to deep thoughts which appealed to his intellect.

For six months he pursued her. She majored in philosophy and East-Asian studies, and always seemed to be one step ahead of him. She agreed to meet him, but avoided his attempts at a kiss on their first date, as well as on the second, third and tenth. She never refused him explicitly, merely smiled to herself, and moved back slightly, out of his reach. With her, he knew, it was true love. He only had eyes for her. When she'd initiate a conversation with him, his heart leapt excitedly. When she was too busy to see him, he'd sink into a deep, brooding melancholy.

He'd won her over when he was already convinced he never would. He'd given up calling her unless she had first, given up on trying to kiss her. All he could do was enjoy her company when she occasionally agreed to grant it. One day she appeared on his doorstep with a cat figurine. He looked at her, puzzled, and asked why she had come. In response she flashed her faint smile and said it was his lucky day. Then she kissed him, teaching him how sweet defeat could be. He never forgot that kiss.

They lasted three years. She was the first women he moved in with, the first he imagined the rest of his life with. She taught him much about the Far East, about the customs of different cultures, about the countries and the differences between them. They travelled there together several times, backpacking from guesthouse to guesthouse, broke and eager to see the world.

The years cooled Lior's eagerness, though, and he'd begun thinking of a career, a home and a family. Foreign countries no longer held the same fascination. Her way of thinking, which before had seemed so deep, now seemed banal, trite. Complex notions about the nature of the world suddenly struck him as the foolish musings of a girl who refuses to grow up. She wanted them to spend all of their savings on traveling the globe, instead of pooling them to buy a house.

The got to talking, and quickly after that to arguing, and fighting. Day by day, the tension between them grew thicker. Despite this, when he broke up with her, they were both surprised. One moment came the question: Do you even want to be with me? And the next moment came the unthinking reply: no.

With Tali he left the Far East. He will never travel again. But neither could he taste green tea, eat sushi, watch Chinese, or Japanese, or Indian cinema. He left it with her, anything related to the countries they travelled together. It was not something she ever asked from him – rather, he could no longer stand to see those things without a lump rising in his throat.

He missed her dearly when he remained in their apartment alone. She moved abroad, and he remained in the country. Sometimes he thought he saw her, walking down the street, and his breath would catch in his throat until he took a closer look. The one oriental remnant he kept from their time together was the small lucky cat she gave him on the day of their first kiss.

A year later he met Limor. She was several years older than him, a level-headed banker, in a body which maintained its slenderness despite the years it has borne. Lior didn't think he could love again after Tali, but Limor managed to change his mind. They met through mutual friends, and something about her small, clever comments brought a smile to his lips. She wasn't cynical or snide, just witty, and quick to respond.

She was the one doing the courting, this time. At first she'd arrange gatherings in which they'd 'happen to' bump into each other, and when they became slightly more familiar, she invited him over for coffee. He agreed, because she could make him laugh, and because he hadn't been capable of being with a woman since Tali. But Limor slept with him that night, and the nights after that.

He thought it was temporary, just until she tired of him. But her soft cheek, pressed against chest at night, caused him to reconsider. This grown woman, who seemingly knew exactly what she wanted, possessed a fragile side, as well. The contrast captivated him, completely. The fact that he could provide her with security, and receive the same in kind, restored some of the happiness he had lost. After a month he moved in with her.

Their love was not fiery, but full, well-rounded, and satisfying. With her he learned to love museums, quiet evenings at home together, the company of good friends, and the joy of cooking. Under her influence he began reading more, and in turn he taught her how to swim, and how to ride a bicycle. She was born and raised in dry, mountainous Jerusalem, he learned upon meeting her family, and therefore never got around to it.

This all ended two years later. Lior knew that she was waiting for him to propose, that she wanted children. But life drew him elsewhere. He was just entering his thirties, a handsome man, who seemed to get more so with age. Women still looked at him, and he at them.

He had begun to notice delicate crow's feet around Limor's eyes. He realized then that, once he started a family with her, this would be his life. Quiet, peaceful, and mediocre. He had a stable job, a stable companion, and a stable glass ceiling. And although every day was, in itself, pleasant, looking forward at the years to come arose a terror in him, a clear, undeniable aversion.

The breakup was hard. The grown, level headed woman suddenly shattered between his arms, asking him not to leave. After she restored his ability to love, he had become a fixed point in her life. Stay, he asked, just stay. She was never this happy before him, never will be once he was gone from her life. They had a whole life ahead of them, she urged, children, small evenings in front of the television, family trips to the beach. But every word she said just pushed him further away. And Lior loved her, he really did, with a tenderness he had never known before – but he wanted more out of life, he said.

Lior left the following day, leaving a broken woman in his wake. He heard that she married several months later. Possibly she had settled for a life of compromise, now that she believed the love of her life had left. He left with her their mutual friends, the museums, the peaceful nights, the soft cheek pressed against his chest. He had lost northern Tel Aviv and Jerusalem, all at once. It was the only way he knew to leave people's lives.

He met Michal on the internet, eighteen months after Limor. There was a seven-year gap between them. She was twenty-six. A talented illustrator with a fierce love for comic-books, she stormed into his life. She had ambition, determination, and a real drive to be the best at what she did. He fell for her instantly, just from their late-night Facebook conversations.

She had short brown hair, mischievous eyes, and she postponed their first date for a month. But once they had met, all hell broke loose. He had never been so captivated by a woman before. He delved deep into her hopes and dreams, drawn after her burning desire to accomplish her goals. He became her agent, seeking out contests to send her art to, finding her work in the field. Each of her successes became his, as well. They lived in southern Tel Aviv together, in a small apartment paid for by his salary. He was happy. Their meals were small, but excellent because Michal loved to cook. Their means were meager, and their shower ran only cold water. His days were spent watching her leaning over a tablet connected to her laptop, illustrating with her tongue peeking out of her teeth in concentration. When he looked at her, his heart flooded with emotion.

They lasted a year. Michal was making steady progress, working odd jobs and booking exhibits. Her salary began to equal his, and concurrently her need for his help diminished. The better things were, the more Lior's interest in her faded. Her art no longer astounded him – while her talent was evident, her style was beginning to bore him. The fight that broke between them was about something else entirely, something trivial. The words that followed, however, cut deep. She left the apartment that very night, and Lior was relieved, more than anything.

Now his life was vacant from any type of art. He could no longer cook, walk through parks, or eat desserts at cafés. He gave up on Facebook and the Far East, on small evenings at home, on Tel-Aviv, Jerusalem and vanilla ice-cream. And still he persisted, into the next relationship, and the next. He lost reading, riding bicycles, drinking in bars. And for every relationship he gave up something more, because that was his custom, his way of remembering the women who passed through his life. It was the least he could give them, after breaking their hearts. A small part of himself, left behind. Until one day he found himself forty years old, or perhaps closer to fifty.

He met Lilac sitting alone on a street bench. He was living in Kfar Saba at the time, not too far from the mall. No longer a young man, but still handsome, with a smile that only became more charming with time due to the lines formed around his eyes, looking at the darkening evening sky. She was younger than him, a bit over thirty. She had warm brown eyes, and a puzzled look. She was curious about him, as she'd noticed him sitting there before.

As it turned out, they were neighbors. And they shared the hobby of observing the night sky. For a while, they were content with meeting on that bench and exchanging some words. At first, Lior mostly kept quiet – but once she began questioning him he opened up, and replied with questions of his own. He discovered that Lilac is a graphic designer, loves to read, adored chocolate, and enjoys cooking as well as long walks and travelling. The more he listened, the more he realized how little he had to offer her.

After some time, during which they'd only meet on the bench, she offered that they head for a café. They lived near the street market, the weather was getting chilly, and a persistent, irritating drizzle had begun. He agreed, as this was still within the realm of his possible actions, although two relationships ago he was compelled to give up coffee, and after the last one, tea. So there they sat, Lilac with a cup of tea and a chocolate soufflé, Lior with a glass of water and a ponderous gaze.

Her curiosity was piqued when she noticed his refusal to taste the soufflé, of even look at it. She inquired cautiously at first, then insistently, then eagerly. Lior tried to avoid answering, change the subject, ask questions of his own, but Lilac's dogged curiosity prevailed. Eventually he subscribed to telling her about Noa, her appetite for chocolate, and his promise to her. She laughed at first, and then realized that he was serious. Slowly, like peeling off the layers of an onion, or perhaps a bandage off an unsightly wound, she asked about the other women in his life. And bit by bit, he revealed them all to her. He'd never forgotten a single one, and spoke of them with sorrow-tinted affection. Remnants of fossilized love preserved in chunks of life. He spoke of long walks in the park with Maya, of traveling the Far East with Tali. He sighed sadly through his tales of his days with Limor and Michal's art. He revealed to her the people he once was, men who'd adapted to transient women, men he was forced to leave behind.

Then he smiled, as that was still his privilege, and the lines around his eyes deepened. And Lilac breathed in deeply, and invited him to her place. He conceded, although there were many positions, by this point, that belonged only to others. But she was skilled, and encompassing, and her touch was gentle and firm, and brought out the passion that was still concealed within him. And when they were finished, she lay over him, her legs still wrapped around him, and her arms pressing his head against her ample chest.

He had little left to offer, but he offered it willingly, joyously. And she settled for the things he still could do, as if he were a much older man, well past his prime. She exposed every side and corner of him, and revived the past through her questions. They spent most of their time at that same café, in the Kfar Saba street market. They spent the summer sitting on that same bench, and at night they'd always head for her place, making love in a fashion that, while limited, left them both satisfied.

He knew their time together was finite. It always was. It didn't stop him from loving her. Over the years his emotions flowed with less turmoil, but more depth. From the well of his experience he drew love for everything she was. He no longer knew what would remain of him when he decides to break up with her.

He never expected that she would be the one to end it.

One day she took him to the café, and when he noticed she was playing with her soufflé, he asked what was wrong. Her words were gentle but unquestionable. She saw no future for them. Lior was too shocked to respond, or even argue. But when she said she had one request from him, he was all ears. This was familiar ground. This he could hold on to. He wondered what she would like to take from him. Kfar Saba? Cafés? The bench, the sky? His speech? He smiled inwardly. No matter, no matter. This was always the deal he agreed to when he met someone new.

He blinked upon hearing her request. Twice. Once from disbelief, twice from the tears it incited. For the first time, he was asked to give up something that truly pained him. He had difficulty breathing, talking. She repeated her request, and he sighed.

"Lior," Lilac asked softly. "Let's go have some vanilla ice-cream."

Time to give up the past.

Default

Thirty-two people were donning grim expressions on the bus this morning. They've long been fed up with the path it carries them on, but still they return daily, to occupy its seats in tired compliance. They looked out the window, played listlessly with their phones, or else stared at nothing in particular – anything to avoid thinking about the transpiring present.

Then the bus coughed. One, twice, three times. Silently, it lay down on the hot pavement, and expired.

"I don't know what happened," said the driver and stepped outside.

"The routine," I replied.

Ending

In some past or another, if one desired to express one's emotions, a series of complex and complicated actions was required for the task. It was not enough to say "I'm angry", but also necessary to show precisely how angry, in what way, and what ought to be done about it. People understood each other quite well, but communication was somewhat tedious.

Over the years, time became short, or perhaps it was merely the patience of people that did. Either way, brevity was introduced. At first, texts composed of heaps and heaps of words were crafted in order to accurately explain the exact feeling that arose. As the centuries passed, those were pruned in the name of frugality into brief sentences, or even single words. This led to the creation of micro-sentences, meant to describe massive worlds of sentiment, such as: 'I love you', or 'don't go'. These days, even those constructs are refined, or perhaps confined, into single words, meant to represent an entire span of emotion: 'Love', 'Anger', 'Longing'.

Regrettably, as certain words became more and more common-place, the meanings attached to them began to suffer from neglect. This brings us to this most unfortunate turn of events, in which one might utter 'Love' but no one will appreciate the precise shade of love he is referring to, the heights to which his heart soars, or the depth of the gorges it tumbles down. A textbook case of a process outshining its purpose.

All of this was conveyed to me by the god Élan during one of our routine nightcaps. We had two types of drinking: one to forget, one to remember. Sometimes we would perform these in sync, or else take turns. The more we drank the more confused we became, accidently committing minor details to memory while forgetting those we were intent on remembering.

When I heard his tale, a scorching hot fury rose in me. It became clear to me that the reason for every broken heart I'd ever encountered – mine included – was our inability to explain our feelings properly. After all, no one would ever be rejected if the person standing across from them understood the depth of their emotions. I got to my feet in order to pound the table in my wrath, swayed slightly, missed the table with my fist and fell unceremoniously to the floor, face first. Élan poured himself another drink.

When I awoke in a puddle of drink the following morning, I delayed only for a quick shower and change of clothes before rushing off to visit my friend, the inventor Trillion.

Trillion was known far and wide as one of the universe's greatest inventors, but a single failure marred his otherwise pristine record: at one point the inventor had attempted to construct a Love Machine, intending to solve the worrisome shortage in the world's rarest and most precious resource, but despite his best efforts, the machine refused to love anyone but Trillion himself.

Seeing as I was certain that the inventor would desire nothing more than to atone for this failure, I got straight to the point, and told him of Élan's story. Trillion was intrigued by my plan to restore the true meaning of words. "To the laboratory!" he cried enthusiastically.

The task turned out to be more difficult than we'd anticipated. At first Trillion attempted a dictionary-based machine, to which he'd connected every database of word definitions and interpretations in the known universe. But the result was an astoundingly dull voice, exhaustively explaining the meaning of the word love through dozens of useless, meaningless synonyms. Through silent agreement we both charged at it, spanners blazing, as it gravely laid out for us the definition of our actions; "disassembly: the intentional destruction of something, usually in an attempt to preserve its components. The elimination of its original purpose in order to repurpose its components. An indirect admission of fault in the original construc –"

It eventually fell silent, leaving us panting. However, we were not about to allow this small hiccup to discourage us, and immediately returned to the task at hand.

Our second attempt was a dramatizing machine. Its abilities were varied and impressive, allowing it to pick any imaginary scenario and play it out, start to finish, as long as it is provided with sufficient data. This way, explained Trillion, one could portray his emotions in meticulous detail, with minimal effort. He must only convey his feeling to the machine, and it will interpret them, through action, to others.

The machine was a mechanical masterpiece of cogs, wires and circuits. In its heart of hearts, Trillion placed the dream of being acknowledged and appreciated for both acting and directing, and around that constructed all means necessary for its realization.

The minute we turned it on, it hummed in electrical excitement:

"Hark! Humanity's a stage, and I shall be all of its players. What form of emotion might I grace you with on this fine day?"

I was more than happy with this promising start, but Trillion was a first-rate scientist if ever there was one, and was accustomed to testing his inventions before celebrating them.

"Show me anger, machine." he requested.

"What sort of anger?"

"How do you mean?" we wondered.

"It is well known, gentlemen, that anger comes in many a form. There is hot, fiery fury that dissipates in a hurry; there is cold, solid disdain, slow to wax, slower to wane; there is self-anger, hard to appease, directed at our own qualities; and hidden rage, lying dormant, waiting for its moment."

"Show us anger over a love that has left," I said hurriedly.

Immediately, the lights went out. In the center of the room, where the machine had stood only a moment ago, appeared the bright circle of a spotlight. Inside were two silhouettes: a man and a woman. Initially, the two were locked in an embrace, their foreheads pressed against one another. The female's silhouette then lifted her head, looked away into the distance, freed herself from the male silhouette's embrace and turned to leave. For a moment, the male silhouette tried to stop her, placing a pleading hand on her arm, but she freed herself and sorrowfully turned to leave. The male silhouette remained standing there; shoulders slumped, watching her walk away. Trillion clapped two outstretched fingers together, expressing his appreciation of the first act.

Now the male silhouette threw his head back in a voiceless wail. It was so quiet that I was forced to cover my ears against the booming silence. This wail lasted somewhere around thirty minutes, during which we sympathized with the pain of the abandoned lover, but also grew quite bored with it. This boredom ended abruptly when the silhouette balled his hand into a fist, raised it to the air and waved it angrily at the skies.

The skies replied with heartless indifference. I could understand the silhouette's anger over the world's apathy. How dare it continue to exist, as if nothing had happened, without a single word, a single expression of sorrow? Could it not see the anguish that adorned the man's heart?

The silhouette's rage was palpable. With his free hand, he grabbed the heavens, forcefully, and smashed them with his fist. He struck them again and again, until they were shattered into tiny pieces. But his anger was not satiated. As the world around him continued to crumble, he desperately sought something else to demolish. Upon realizing that nothing was left undestroyed, he paused shortly to look at his own fist. He then raised it once more toward the skies, before bringing it down on his own head. The force of the blow projected pieces of silhouette everywhere, which eventually came to a rest upon the rugged earth. At last, he found peace.

The spotlight dimmed and eventually went out. The machine reappeared and reverted to its previous form. Trillion and I gave an enthusiastic standing ovation, and the machine bowed, blinking its lights in gratitude.

"That was some really spectacular anger," I said, astonished. It seemed that Trillion's work had exceeded all expectations.

"That was merely the opening act," the machine hurriedly remarked. "After all, anger over a love lost is not so easily concluded."

"How long is it expected to last?" asked Trillion.

"Oh, quite a while. I'd estimate a period of time subjectively indistinguishable from eternity. However, thanks to my exceedingly advanced circuitry, I will likely be able to cover the whole thing in several weeks, if not days. And I dare you to say that that isn't the very epitome of progress – expediting the expressions of one's heart through the marvels of technology!"

"Days?" said Trillion. "My dear machine, we have no intention of spending entire days on the observation of a single emotion. We are busy people. At the very least, some of us are. Do you not think that this demonstration, in itself of considerable length, was long enough?"

One of the machine's light bulbs exploded, and five others were giving off smoke.

"Damage my artistic integrity, the exemplary exactitude of emotional depiction, for the sake of brevity? How would you be able to appreciate every breaking point, every crisis, every anguished cry, if you skip past them to get to the point? Moreover, what is the point, when one ignores everything needed to make one's way to it? No, this is completely unacceptable! Over my cold, dismantled gears will I allow you to diminish my art, even in the slightest. You will either have all of it, or nothing at all!"

It then fell into a despondent silence, and only after great effort on Trillion's behalf was it willing to communicate again. Even then, it did so only in the form of huge signs which it had somehow fabricated, which read in bold script: 'Down with the Tyranny of Time!" and "Let Us Feel!", and no amount of flattery would deter it. Eventually the renowned inventor sighed and suggested that we confer in the next room.

"The task," he said dourly, "is more difficult than I'd anticipated."

"But it seems that you've already succeeded in it, does it not?"

"Who has the time, Tea? Would you argue you've written a better book, simply because you'd carved it in stone? Surely you can agree that it is a step backwards, a truly ancient technology. And I, foolishly, have created a machine that imitates the past, rather than carrying us into the future."

"What is the solution, then?"

"As always, the solution lies in the proper machinery," said Trillion with the utmost confidence. "My mistake was in the chosen medium of expression. No more dry words and theatricals. We must alter our approach. We've really only been translating thus far, don't you think?"

"How do you mean?" I wondered.

"Consider this: the emotion is already there, but we've been insisting on transforming it into language. This language is meant to arouse in others the same emotions we experience, but like the antiquated technology that it is, it does so in a way that is both lacking and inherently flawed. I say, why bother? If we have the emotion, let us put it to direct use!"

Once more, the inventor's mind did not disappoint. Where another would see a gaping abyss and seek a vessel with which to cross it, Trillion sought to weld its edges together so that it would not even be an obstacle.

First, he explained, direct access to the emotion was necessary. He wore thick gloves and grabbed a tangled thread of thought I found for him inside my head. He then unraveled the knot slowly and, with infinite patience, managed to retrieve a single long string from within it. He then placed the thread in my hand, and together we pulled on its ends, following its numerous splits and ends. We took great care never to loosen our grip out of turn – since it is a well-known fact that a loose string of thought can disappear in an instant, never to return – while simultaneously making every effort to pull gently, lest it tear and lose its value.

After a lengthy stretch of thinking, the thread of thought led us to some past moment, a kiss which took place only a few blocks away. I was briefly distracted by the sight of the two individuals trapped in memory. One of them, me, was leaning above the other, eyes half-lidded and donning a delicate, excited smile. The other was staring back, raising her eyebrows. It was an unexpected kiss. We were looking at the fraction of the moment preceding it.

As my mind wandered, Trillion remained focused. I heard him cry: "Quick, it's getting away!"

His voice called me back to our mission. I saw that he was chasing an elusive, slippery emotion that was trying to flee the moment. I lunged into the chase, and together we flanked our pray. Trillion trapped it with his power of reasoning and I made a thought-woven net to hold it in.

We held on to the emotion for a while. It writhed, scratched and bit, shriveled and expanded, and when that came to nothing, buzzed and burned, ignited and extinguished, and then shook and shivered, jumped and fell and occasionally even tore and broke and smashed to pieces. Nevertheless, we stood firm against its various attempts at breaking free, as Trillion conducted an absurd number of tests and measurements, decoding and deciphering everything about the emotion, from the shape of its feeling to the structure of its atoms. When he was done with the testing, the inventor declared: Now we can get to work!

Now that he knew what he was facing, Trillion worked swiftly. He meticulously transferred every emotional quality into a tiny machine, which could burn and blaze, break and smash, rip and strangle, all without leaving a mark. In addition, it could also caress, soften and induce warmth and ease in perfect silence. Trillion went above and beyond, replicating this machine a million-fold, before shrinking it as well, so that tens and even hundreds of thousands of its kind could fit into a human body. He dubbed this machine: nanomotion.

Trillion immediately wanted to commence human testing, but I suggested we avoid acting rashly, as emotion was new and uncharted territory. Trillion was slightly offended at the suggestion that his invention could be flawed, but hesitantly conceded when he remembered his past failure with the love machine.

As he was deeply opposed to animal experimentation – not due to morals, of course, but because he believed that his mechanical prowess could fabricate any animal existing in nature, only better – Trillion decided to release his nanomotions into several of his more advanced robots. He then set them to fast-forward, so that every minute of our time would amount to an entire day in theirs, and allowed them to function uninterrupted. We sat to observe them at a distance, courtesy of his advanced monitoring equipment.

At first, the experiment seemed to be running along smoothly.

Two of the robots fell in love at first sight, and their love was completely obvious to the both of them. Another pair of robots became good friends, but agreed at once that they felt no attraction toward one another. However, as their nanomotions soon made clear to them, this agreement was illusory. In fact, they quickly concluded, they were not willing to entirely relinquish the romantic option, and soon became a couple.

The potential of the invention was evident from these developments, as was the potentially massive amount of time saved. However, that was not the end of it. Late one night, after a month of blissful parity, one of the robots who were in love stopped to think if it really wanted to spend the rest of its life with the other. This doubt, in itself, was not so detrimental, as those will occasionally arise in every relationship. A regular person would get over it and proceed with his or her life, none the more troubled for it.

But alas, this was not the case. For as soon as it picked up on its partner's doubts, the other robot gave rise to pain, anger and even doubt of its own, which were quickly transmitted back to its mate, growing twice as effective, and begetting anxiety, worry and concern. Thus, a loop of negative feedback was formed between the two lovers. Ex-lovers, that is, as by morning they could no longer stand each other's company, packed their bags and promptly went their separate ways.

The fate of the second couple was even worse, as they were denied even that single month of happiness. They remained trapped in compromise. Every time one of them would think of leaving, they'd immediately change their mind at the pain they could feel through the nanomotion's feedback. And although they grew increasingly miserable together, none of them could stomach releasing the other. Normally, the first to depart leaves the pain for the one left behind. But not this time. Neither of them could bear the loneliness caused by separation.

Gravely disappointed, Trillion turned off his instruments one by one, and just like that, all those complex loves and emotions were defunct. He then raised his hands in frustration and cried: "What a tangled conundrum!"

"Have you given up?" I asked.

"No," said Trillion, though his despair was audible. "But I'm not sure where to go from here, Tea."

"How about a transmitter?" I offered.

"A transmitter? What kind?"

"The problem with your nanomotions," I explained, "is that by the time they're done operating, they've already altered the emotions of their hosts. Instead, I suggest a special transmitter. One that can transfer the complete, uncut emotion, after it has been properly processed. Anything else is doomed to fail."

"Hmm," hummed Trillion. He was already engrossed in calculation. "This requires some kind of super-temporal circuit breaker. Perhaps a transmitter that will slightly employ the future. Not too much, mind you – just enough to cancel out the effect of the moment. There is some mathematical expression for it, or a poetical one, if you insist on the difference between the two. What are five minutes compared to an eternity, or something along those lines."

"I'll leave the details to you," I said.

Trillion was no longer listening to me. With newfound enthusiasm, he buckled down and got to work. He hung a sketch of the previously taken emotional measurements in front of his workspace, and started fiddling tirelessly, all the while mumbling to himself: "transmitter, transmitter. This definitely requires some sort of super-time, perhaps even under-time. Cerebral connections here, here and here, and several cardiac ones. Ah, but that won't do. A transceiver, perhaps? Yes, yes. With a connection and positive feedback with the following moment. Perhaps a thought-throttler with contemplation regulation?

And a hearty shape, obviously. It is, after all, the heart of the matter…"

This toiling and muttering went on for a long while. Eventually he handed me a small, handsomely shaped hoop, his face radiant with pride.

Hand shaking slightly, I reached for the small hoop. "And this is?"

"This," Trillion declared proudly, "is a remarkably powerful emotion transceiver that I call an 'Emotionon'. It has emo-compression capabilities of up to ten years, combined with a contemplation clutch and a two-in-the-morning thought-throttler. This contraption, my dear Tea, is the very pinnacle of emotional innovation. And I say this without an ounce of arrogance. It can transmit the entire span of human emotion from one person to another. It has a special love-valve, in case it overheats, and is astoundingly tear-proof. It explains and elaborates on every argument people tend to think up after the fact, spells out all that was left unsaid, lays out every reason left unmentioned. It elucidates the heart, eradicates ambiguity, and is generally pleasant to the touch. If this creation does not accomplish the goal, I will disgracefully declare that some things are beyond even my considerable abilities."

I placed the emotionon on my head and shook Trillion's hand with profound gratitude, which it promptly relayed to the inventor, who fell backwards from the intensity of the emotion. His eyes moistened as he rose to his feet and dusted himself off, muttering through an awkward cough: "There, there, it was nothing. An interesting challenge, is all. Please stop."

At that I realized that the emotionon was a success. After another hug for the inventor, one which caused him to awkwardly pat me on the back, I darted out of the laboratory like a loosed arrow. I knew exactly where I was headed.

I ran and ran; breathing heavily, sweating profusely, but naturally I couldn't care less about that. I had but one goal: to see her again.

To reveal to her the heart that had been pining for her for so many years, all of my innermost thoughts and feelings. She couldn't resist me after that, I knew. She wouldn't. I was awash with love. All of my nocturnal musings, all those hours of longing that had amounted to nothing. The emotionon began to rattle, its love-valve working hard to prevent the inevitable eruption. But Trillion knew me well, and installed three secondary valves in case the first one wouldn't suffice. They were all vibrating violently atop my head, but determined as I was to see this through, I ignored them.

I saw her in the street, not far from her house. She was carrying large bag of groceries in her small hands and had some trouble getting through the door. Her appearance was slender and graceful, though older than I remembered. The years painted delicate lines around her eyes, like the strokes of a fine brush. Time caressed her adoringly as it passed, honing previously boyish features into ripe, feminine ones. And when it was finished with its work, it darkened her luminous eyes with some slight sorrow, so that her beauty would not blind those around her. Or so I imagined.

The sound of my bounding, rapidly approaching footsteps caught her attention. Her almond shaped eyes widened with immediate recognition. She raised her hand to me, her skin not quite as luminous now, having lost the radiance of youth.

"Tea," she said, and my heart shattered again at the sound of her voice, as if it had only just happened.

I didn't reply audibly, but voicelessly mouthed her name. The emotionon on my head pulsed and heated, and all the contents of my heart were revealed to her. Briefly, her eyes became teary. Or so I thought, as I was completely blinded by the broken glass flowing from my eyes.

I heard the shopping bag fall to the pavement and felt her approach. I steeled myself for the coming embrace. However, she merely plucked the emotionon from my head, and placed it on hers. Then, suddenly, I knew.

I knew the years she had gone through. The emotion that had faded over time, the acceptance, the amount of thought invested before she finally decided to leave. I knew how she would think about me, occasionally, with fond nostalgia, as a piece of the person she used to be. I knew that that person was no more, that her current form was merely a facsimile of the woman I knew. That more had changed about her than remained the same, and that I wouldn't even recognize most of her. I knew she'd found a new love, and was happy in it. I knew she would always remember the man who loved her. And I knew that she would never be his.

The emotionon cracked, then, and fell to the ground. Only the embrace remained, the final exchange between two warm bodies, a hand fluttering over a stubbly, wet cheek, a whisper: "goodbye, Tea", and her image, walking away, forever.

Minutes passed. I stared at the cracked emotionon lying on the ground. I knew how it felt.

Because sometimes, the days simply pass you by. Sometimes people can only love one another for a while, until that while is gone. And that does not diminish it in the slightest. Because those two will always be in love. At some point in the past, they still are. Frozen in a moment left behind. Perhaps I should have realized years ago that it was not me that was stuck in the past, but the man I once was.

Quivering slightly, I picked up the emotionon. I breathed it in deeply, as it was still drenched in her scent, and finally walked away. Trillion will be disappointed, I thought, to hear that some things are beyond his abilities.

My Mother

She never took much care of her teeth. That is, until they had actually fallen out. At first, she envisioned implants, braces and root canals, but eventually said, with an incomplete smile: too expensive. At night, I noticed that she'd stopped looking hopefully at the pillow beside her.

The Fall

It wasn't the fall that broke Humpty-Dumpty. And neither horses, nor men, nor kings were needed to put him back together again. Because that which was broken by a woman, only a woman can repair.

The Nadir

The lowest point in the world isn't defined in space, but in time. No one wants to visit it, but almost everyone ends up in its vicinity at some point in life. You can find it yourself, if you look around just after a breakup, at three in the morning, at the bottom of your fourth drink, with your phone in your hand. Or maybe, slightly after that, in someone else's bed.

Some Remarks on the Sentence: It's Over

A pair of words in need of additional periods. The more, the better. When it is sealed with merely one, it sounds as though the story has only one possible ending. An uncompromising, unalterable ending, which renders further debate moot. It lacks hesitation, and perhaps a supplementary sentence indicating the difficulty of it. It leaves you with the will to argue, but without the ability to act on it. Listen: It's over.

- *Book II* -
And Other Fables

On God's Original Sin

Once, long before the apple, God looked at the Garden and muttered to himself: It is not good that the man should be alone. And man heard, and a brand new thought, entirely different from its predecessors, dawned on him: I am lonely. And this knowledge was far worse than anything produced by the tree.

Missing Pit

In the donor room at the sperm bank there hung a single painting, on the wall above the sink. Half a peach, the one with its pit missing, faced the observer. I hated that painting with every fiber of my being.

As if the sticky old magazines beside the paper-towel covered couch didn't make me feel repulsive enough as it was. I could at least avoid those. I'd turn my back to them, place the specimen cup on the table by the sink, and try to think of the women I'd slept with. And all the while, that gaping peach hanging in front of me. The mark of an artist with a truly lacking understanding of subtext. I suppose it could have just been some doctor's or secretary's sick sense of humor. Either way, someone put very little thought into this room, or far too much of it.

God knows I've dedicated a great deal of thought to it. If you can't think, you have no business donating sperm. Ninety percent of the work is done inside your mind. Ultimately, the hands don't have to do much if your head is in the right place. And god, if I believed in him, would most likely be pleased with me – I wasted very little seed, but a substantial amount of thought.

I carefully closed the lid on the specimen cup and washed my hands. The thought of dozens of other donors doing the same before me sickened me. The absolute worst was walking into the donation room and finding the markings of a freshly wiped table. Pale lines of mopped up liquid. Whoever did the wiping probably thought it a courtesy to whoever came next, but I couldn't tear my eyes from those lines until they'd faded completely.

I left the room, carrying the little plastic cup. I walked up to the door of the clinic, which was ajar, and knocked gently. The lab technician was busy looking through the microscope at someone else's juice. I have no idea why anyone would want that job. After all, she doesn't get paid as well as I do.

She raised her eyes at me and smiled. She had light brown hair and dark, elongated eyes. She donned a white lab coat, worn either for the sake of appearance or in order to mask stains, I pondered when I noticed her latex gloves. There was something cute about her, although her face was slightly too round to be considered truly pretty.

"Hi, I'm done," I said, returning the smile.

"Quick," she said. She got up to take the small cup, placed it on a white table and opened the wide notebook resting next to her.

"I'm not always this quick," I said, defensively. "Only here."

She laughed and looked up at me, her eyebrows arched in amusement. "I didn't even think about it before you said it."

"I wasn't thinking at all before I said it, either."

She was giggling again. I calmed down a bit.

"What's your name?" she asked.

"Sorry?"

"For the registration," she gestured to the notebook. "I need your name."

"Barak Weinberg. And yours?"

She wrote my name down by the date and looked at me again. "Na'ama. I assume you need it for registration, as well?"

"I like to know to names of women who mess around with my semen. Just the kind of guy I am."

"A rare specimen in Tel Aviv," she said, smiling.

Is it okay to hit on your sperm technician? I wasn't sure. So much could go wrong, and I was completely dependent on the income from my stuff. The shifts from work barely covered the rent. Best forget about it, I said to myself. Almost-pretty girls are a dime a dozen, but the only way to get five hundred shekels for ten minutes of work was prostitution. If that.

"So, you live here in the city?" I said, nonetheless.

"In Givatayim. But it's not that far."

"Uh-huh. Just far enough."

"I take it you live in Tel Aviv?"

"Yeah. But I'm an immigrant, like most people."

Na'ama looked past me and I turned back just in time to see another man entering the room I'd left mere moments ago. I cringed.

"Well, I should get going," I said hastily.

She smiled again and said goodbye. I reciprocated and hurried outside, blurting out a rushed 'bye' at the secretary sitting at the entrance. It wasn't until I felt sunlight on my skin that I allowed myself to slow down.

I don't know why the place disgusted me like it did. I don't know why I found the other men so repugnant. But I wasn't about to stop donating sperm just because it gave me the dry heaves. For four thousand shekels a month, I'd bite the bullet. If you can't control your thoughts, you have no business donating sperm.

#

I wouldn't have gotten up so early in the afternoon if it hadn't been donation day. The whole thing just happened to be after a night shift, and I'm always too wired after those to go back to sleep. I normally head for the bookstore at my usual café and delve into some book until I'm tired enough to sleep.

The walls at the café are completely covered in bookshelves, carrying old books sorted by title and author. The books that have yet to be sorted are piled on the floor, or perhaps they lay there for lack of room on the shelves. Either way, what matters is that there's room for sitting down and milkshake for feeling up.

A few customers were scattered among the tables, or else standing by the shelves, browsing the books. I headed for the English section and stood next to a girl who was silently mouthing the names of the authors.

A bespectacled man whose eyes were prone to blinking was watching us. He seemed just over thirty. His hair was short and his posture stooped. He too was mouthing something voicelessly, but I could not tell if he was reading anything. When he noticed we were still looking at the bookcase, he raised his voice into a kind of loud grumble. "What, you only know how to read books in English? What about some Hebrew, huh?"

He had a high-pitched, unpleasant voice, and though he spoke loud enough for us to hear, it wasn't clear whether he was addressing us or just putting it out there. He uttered it so casually that the girl beside me didn't even notice he'd said anything. Only once did I glance up at him, and when he noticed me looking, he buried his face in some magazine he was holding, muttering wordlessly. I picked a collection of stories by Bukowski and sat down on an empty green couch.

I was so immersed in the book that I completely missed the beginning of the conversation that was taking place beside me. But when the voices became louder and more grating I turned my attention to them, even as my eyes remained on the page. I listened with half an ear at first, and then turned both ears on, abandoning my attempt to finish the story I was reading.

"But you're bothering the customers," said a man I knew to be the store's owner.

"I am not," said the bespectacled man in a weak, nasal voice. I peeked at him. His eyes were locked on the pages of the book he was holding.

"Yes, you are. A girl just came to tell me you were bothering her. You told her that you work here?"

"I didn't say work," said the bespectacled man. "I said I was helping. I'm helping with the store."

"But you aren't helping. I gave you a job, to arrange the new books on the shelves, but you're never here when I need you. You show up whenever you like, talk at the customers and do nothing. How can you possibly help her if you don't even know where the books are?"

"I only come here because my mother asked me to," said the bespectacled man. He was still examining the book he was holding. He was lanky and hunched over, and blinked incessantly when he spoke.

"When your mother asked that I let you come here she didn't tell me you'd be such a handful," said the shop owner. He was trying to sound sympathetic, but it was clear from his tone that he'd had this conversation before.

"You told her I could come."

"Yes, because she said that it's a shame you sit at home all day and hoped I could keep you busy for a few hours a day. Do I need to talk to her now and ask her to stop sending you here?"

"I don't do what she tells me to. I don't care about my mother," said the bespectacled man. A nervous twitch went through him as he spoke the words.

"Where is she now, at home?"

"No, she's at work."

"Can I have her number, so I can talk to her?"

"No. She doesn't want to talk to you."

"Why doesn't she want to talk to me?" asked the store owner.

"She says that you aren't nice. That you don't want me to come here anymore."

"That's right, because you're bothering the customers. Look at that guy sitting on the couch there. He comes here, reads quietly, doesn't bother anyone."

I turned the page. Not because I was done with the previous one, but because I had suddenly become acutely aware that I hadn't read a single word in quite a while.

"I'm not bothering anyone," insisted the bespectacled man.

I closed the book and got up. No peace would be found here today. Maybe I'd manage to sleep despite everything.

"Just sit quietly and don't talk." The owner had finally given up.

"I'm not talking to anyone," mumbled the bespectacled man. "Why did he stop reading? Hey, finish reading."

The store owner sighed.

#

At nights I'd work as a security guard.

At two o'clock in the morning, a goat appeared at the door. I can't say if it had been standing there for a while and I'd only just noticed it then, but I'm certain that that was the time.

It looked at me silently through the glass door, which was locked during those hours, and I felt like it was politely waiting for me to open up and let it in.

At first, I thought it was a dog. Not because goats are particularly dog-like, but because it was the middle of the night and I was determined to sleep my way through the shift. It was the result of sheer misfortune that I'd lifted my head at that exact moment, and downright stupidity that made me take a second look.

At first glance, I convinced myself that it really was just a huge dog. Yes, I nodded inwardly, an extraordinarily large and hairy dog, but there is nothing I can do about that. It has an owner, surely, and dogs are quite independent. Go back to sleep.

I rested my head back on the desk and closed my eyes. Then, just to be sure, I snuck another glance at the dog; just to confirm there was no way it could get inside. I mean, it really was quite big. Upon the second glance, my brain glared at me reproachfully and refused to blink until I'd admitted the truth. Not a dog, but a goat.

Still, I insisted defensively, what could I possibly do about it.

Go check to see if it's alright, my brain suggested helpfully, and after that you can sleep with a clear conscience.

My conscience was actually quite clear already. And yet, I tiredly dragged myself to the door. That was mistake number three. I had planned to take just a brief, perfunctory look, but when I got there, a stranger suddenly appeared out of the darkness.

I stared at her momentarily, the goat stared at me, and the stranger knocked on the glass door. I wondered if she was expecting me to open it, and mouthed 'what?'. I was still hopefully holding on to the prospect of sleep.

"Do you have a petting zoo here?" called out the stranger, though she would have been completely audible if she'd spoken normally.

"This is a hotel," I said. "Why would we have a petting zoo?"

"The door won't open," she continued, loudly.

I wasn't particularly inclined to allow the door to open, and briefly contemplated pretending that I couldn't. The goat was still staring at me. My conscience is clear, I wanted to tell it. You look just fine.

I had the nagging sensation that opening the door would have an adverse effect on my projected hours of sleep. On the other hand, I had a far more nagging sensation that if I didn't, the woman behind the door would permit me no sleep whatsoever.

I quickly examined her. She was maybe thirty, dark-skinned, of Yemenite or Moroccan descent. She appeared normal. As in, she didn't look like someone who'd stab you. Black hair, assertive look. I sighed inwardly, revealing nothing on the outside, and pressed the button to open the door. The goat nodded at me politely, or so I imagined, and instantly started making its way inside. I immediately moved to block its approach. It stopped, chiding me with its eyes.

"Thanks for opening." The stranger said. "Isn't this your goat?"

I peeked down at the uniform I was wearing, of the security company I worked for. The very question filled me with uncertainty. "No, not really. I mean, it really isn't."

"I thought as much," She said. "I called the city hall hotline and told them there was a goat, and they said it was probably yours. Now they're in for it."

"Okay."

"It's sweet that you came to check on it. I think you should bring it some water."

"I should?"

"Yes, thank you."

"Is that all?" I asked. Perhaps the whole thing will be over in fifteen minutes. I gazed longingly at the counter.

"Since you're offering, I'd love some coffee."

"Oh."

I decided to shut up before I talked myself into more work. I begged her pardon as I locked the door back up so that the goat couldn't wander in, and went to get a bowl of water. I also made coffee. Just for her, as I did not intend to stay awake for longer than an extra five minutes.

I returned with the water and found the stranger on the phone with the city hall call center. The dispatcher apparently didn't believe her, because she was screaming at him, "so send an inspector! And tell me his name, I know all of your inspectors."

I didn't want to know why she was familiar with all of their inspectors. I placed the water bowl next to the goat, which made another attempt to get inside but didn't appear to be especially thirsty.

I blocked its path absentmindedly.

"Let me present you with a theoretical question," she told the dispatcher. "What if, instead of a goat, it had been a killer Rottweiler? Would you send an inspector then? What if it wanders into a school tomorrow and bites some kid?"

"Moshe? Fine, send Moshe. Tell him it's Liat. He knows me. I'm always reporting things."

She hung up and turned to face me. I politely handed her the cup, and for a moment, it seemed as if the coffee had offended her on a deep, personal level. Perhaps it blurted out some racist comment, or slept with her and hadn't called. She grabbed it furiously.

"He won't send an inspector. I know his type; he just can't wait to get back to sleep and never deals with anything. I've seen this kind of crap before. One time, I blocked an entire highway for thirty minutes to save a bat. I ended up taking it to the vet myself. Truth is, it ended up getting eaten by a cat as soon as I took it out of the car. It was sad."

"Uh huh," I contributed. I decided to go back to looking at the goat, which seemed perfectly content to stand there between us with that dumb look in its eyes. "What's a goat even doing here? Where did it even come from?"

"Don't know. Probably belonged to some Arab village and freed itself somehow. But I'm not leaving it. Poor thing, it must be terrified."

The goat did not seem terrified in the slightest. It seemed to me that it was by far the calmest among the three of us. But I had no intention of arguing. I have a rule, never to argue with people about religion, politics or music. Something about this situation made me feel that we were somewhere between religion and politics.

"Maybe you could bring it something to eat?" Liat suggested.

"Maybe?"

"Great, what do you have?"

"I can check," I said, "but the kitchen's pretty far."

"Oh, you're sweet. I'll watch the goat."

I took a deep breath and locked the door again. I took the keys to the kitchen, where I checked the refrigerators. What do goats even eat? Grass? Or is that just cows? In the freezer I found some pieces of left-over watermelon, of all things, and decided it was a reasonable bet by any standard.

When I returned, Liat was busy with another phone call, this time with the police. I placed the plate with the watermelon slices on the floor. The goat stared at them in bewilderment. I tried to goad it with the same tutting noises I use when facing any animal, but it just tried once more to enter the building, surprised to find me in its way. For lack of any better options, I tuned in to the conversation.

"I'm telling you, a goat," said the stranger. "Yes, it's calm. But just think, theoretically, what if it were a killer Rottweiler? There is a school right next door!"

She nodded. "Okay, I'm waiting," and then hung up.

"They're sending someone over."

"The police?" I asked.

"Yeah."

"And what are they supposed to do?"

"I don't know. That's why I called them," said the stranger. "So what's your name, anyway?"

The goat decided to take a sip from the water bowl. After a single lick, the bowl toppled over and the rest of its contents spilled onto the sidewalk. I watched it stare at the expanding puddle. It seemed exceedingly pleased, or so I imagined.

"Barak," I replied absentmindedly. She barely waited for my answer before returning to talk about herself.

"I live not too far from here, and was actually on my way home, but I couldn't just leave the goat here on its own. Poor thing. Think what would've happened if someone had seen it. What if they'd tried to eat her?" she said. She tried to pet the goat, but it recoiled in response.

"Yeah, and what if it were a killer Rottweiler," I nodded without listening. Twenty minutes had elapsed and my cozy counter was looking more distant than ever.

To my surprise, a police car did arrive, and parked on the sidewalk in front of the hotel. Two uniformed police officers got out authoritatively. One was tall and slim and held a thick flashlight. He had a Russian appearance, blue eyes and straw colored hair above his thin lips. Probably some Vladimir, Yuri or Alex. I don't think Russians have names other than slight variations on those three. The other one was squat and rotund, with tanned brown skin and black hair which was warring over the border from which it will eventually be forced to retreat.

"Sasha, there's actually a goat," said the brownish one.

"What, you thought I was messing with you?" said Liat. She was positively bursting with satisfaction.

Sasha said nothing. He examined the goat and traced the flashlight with his fingers as if it were a gun.

"I thought it was a prank," admitted the brownish officer. "But how did a goat even get here? Goats can be dangerous."

"Just think," I eagerly piped up, "what if it were a killer Rottweiler."

Liat nodded. The woman was impervious to sarcasm.

"What are we going to do with it, though, Yossi?" asked Sasha. His accent wasn't thick, but he too soft spoken to be a native speaker, and some of the words were excessively nasal.

"We can chase it away," suggested Yossi. "I can spook it –"

"Are you insane?" interrupted Liat. "What if it gets run over? We have to help it."

"Maybe a veterinarian could take it in, or some petting zoo," Sasha said quietly, still fidgeting with his flashlight.

"At this hour? Do you have anyone in mind?"

The conversation was beginning to exhaust me, and I was already planning my calculated retreat back into the building when Liat managed to catch my eye.

"Maybe you could check online?" she asked.

"That," said Yossi, "is an excellent idea." My heart let out a deep sigh, but I was so tired that some of the sigh made it out of my nose.

I trudged back to my chair behind the counter. At least I got to sit down. I turned on the front desk computer and opened the browser in search for veterinarians and petting zoos. Outside, the policemen were trying to feed the goat some watermelon, but it merely backed away from them scornfully.

I called the emergency number for the local veterinarian. The woman that answered couldn't quite understand why I'd actually called the veterinarian, but she suggested that I call the zoo, and gave me a number that might work at this hour. The zoo told me that they weren't really in the market for goats, and that it was way too early in the morning to do anything about it, but there was a wildlife hospital that may agree to take it in. At the hospital they asked me if the goat was injured. I glanced over my shoulder. The goat was chewing on the plastic water bowl and the policemen were snapping pictures of it with their phones. I said that no, it probably wasn't.

The man I talked to was extremely amiable, but noted that medical care wasn't, strictly speaking, actually required. Perhaps I should turn to the Society for the Protection of Nature and inquire about an animal trapper. I groaned, this time outwardly. When he asked if I was okay, I replied that I was, and asked for a phone number. Outside, Yossi had managed to get close enough to the goat to pet it, and asked Sasha to snap a photo real quick, before it moves. Liat was busy yelling at some dispatcher again. At least, I hoped it was a dispatcher. Who knows, maybe she'd finally snapped and was just yelling at thin air.

"Hi, you've reached The Society for the Protection of Nature in

Israel," replied a tired male voice from the other side of the line. I sympathized.

"Hi," I said. "I have a goat outside my hotel."

"Okay, I'm with you so far," said the tired voice, somewhat cautiously.

"Don't get me wrong, I don't really mind the goat," I said bluntly. "The goat has caused me zero problems so far. It is, in that sense, a very non-problematic goat. Polite, even. The problem in that there are people outside of the hotel, and if I get rid of the goat, I might stand a chance of getting rid of them as well."

"And does the goat appear wounded?"

"The goat's fine. It's just, you know, there."

"I can send a trapper," the tired voice said.

"Awesome."

"But not until morning," he concluded the sentence.

"It's a goat," I near-yelled. "It's not going to hang around till morning."

"What's the problem, then?"

"That it might," I said, my voice thick with worry.

"That's all I can do for you right now."

"But what if it were a killer Rottweiler?" I tried desperately.

"What if it were?"

"Wouldn't you send someone then? It could wander into a school and bite someone. Some kid, I bet."

The voice suddenly became very wary. "Well, is it a killer Rottweiler?"

"No," I confessed. "It is not."

"So... call me in the morning?"

"Yeah, sure."

I hung up. What would be the point of calling in the morning? My shift would be over by then.

The policemen were done taking pictures of the goat and exhausted their attempts at flirting with Liat. When I delivered the news, they were practically giddy.

"So they'll handle it in the morning? That's great. That was some good thinking."

"Thanks," said Liat. I had never been so shamelessly robbed of credit.

"We'll be off, then," said Yossi. "Let's go, Alex." Sasha tried to toss the goat a final piece of watermelon. It ignored it. The policemen got into their car, waved goodbye and drove off.

"What, then," said Liat, "we just need to watch it till morning?"

"Need is a big word," I said. As was 'we', I thought to myself bitterly.

"Is it. Well, the truth is I'm getting really cold. You mind if I go home and get my coat? I'll be back in ten minutes."

I shrugged. At that point, I was well aware of my options.

"You're such a sweet guy. Watch it for me, okay?" Without waiting for a reply she hurried off to her car and drove away. It was just me and the goat, now.

"Fucking goat," I quietly swore at it.

It stood there and stared at me.

Thirty minutes had passed and I was freezing. The goat took several steps away from me and then returned to the door. I tried to talk to it a little, and then realized that I was mostly swearing.

After forty minutes, the goat started to walk away from me, in the direction of the street. When I tried to get closer, it wandered further.

"Hey," I called after it, "Where are you going?"

The goat looked at me. I could've sworn it shrugged. A moment later, it broke into a gallop. I watched it head into the horizon until it was gone.

I exhaled loudly. What was I supposed to do? It's not like I could've stopped it. What did that even mean, 'watch it'? It's a goat; it can do whatever it wants. Still, some form of guilt compelled me to stand there for several more minutes. By the time I'd started to recover, Liat's car returned.

"Where's the goat?" she said the minute she stepped out of it.

"You just missed it." I tried to sound like it wasn't my fault – because it wasn't – and failed.

"Aw, that sucks," she sighed. "All I did was stop for soup."

"Soup."

"I had to heat it up. Anyway, that's a shame. But what're you gonna do, huh? It'll be fine, I think. Goats usually aren't that dangerous."

I glared at her. She didn't notice, just glanced at her phone.

"Wow, it's four in the morning already. I'm beat. Better get to bed. Thanks for your help, Barak, you're such a sweet guy."

"Don't mention it," I said automatically. I was too tired to argue.

"Well, I'm off. Thank god I stopped to help. Just think what could've happened."

I could've gotten two hours of sleep, I thought, and now I'm stuck at reception for four hours. People are going to start coming in soon. I'll be dead tired tomorrow, and it's your fault. But I just nodded and saw her off. I was cold. I went inside. An overturned water bowl, a plastic plate and some dirty pieces of watermelon remained outside.

I missed the goat a little bit.

#

The good thing about sperm donation days is that I have something to wake up for. Otherwise, I can just as easily get up at four in the afternoon and do nothing besides eat and play Xbox. Though that does sound like paradise, it can sometimes feel like a waste of time. Not sure why that is.

I wasted no time in the donor room. In five minutes I discharged a fair amount into the little plastic cup which I placed in its usual spot. It wasn't difficult. There wasn't a line today, and after a period of abstinence I just stormed in there like a hungry wolf pouncing on a herd of sheep. I guess they know what they're talking about when they tell you to refrain from cumming for two days. I took great pains not to look at that damn peach when I unloaded. That shit could ruin everything.

When I stepped outside Na'ama was waiting next to the door of the lab, smiling. She wasn't wearing her white lab coat and I could see that her jeans were tight and that she was a bit overweight. Sometimes after you cum, a smile is better than a thin figure.

"Hi," she said. "How've you been?"

"Fine," I said. I considered telling her about the goat. I'm not sure why. Maybe because I hadn't found anyone to share that weird story with yet. "What about you?"

The smile faded. She looked a bit sad. "Fine. Well, the truth is, I've been better."

"What's wrong?" I asked. I gave her my cup and she placed it on the table, jotting my name down absentmindedly. I leaned on the door to listen.

"My grandmother passed away."

"Oh," I wracked my brain for something to add. "I'm sorry for your loss."

"Thanks," she said, and lowered her eyes. "It's really recent. The funeral's later today."

"Did you know it was coming?" I wondered what you were supposed to ask, supposed to say. And more importantly, what you most definitely weren't.

"She was in the hospital, so we were ready, as much as you can be."

"Were you close?" I kicked myself internally. The kind of dumb question you ask when you're trying to figure out how much you should pretend to care.

"Not particularly. I mostly feel bad for my mom," said Na'ama.

Okay, the standard, I thought. No need to overdo it, then.

"And how are you feeling?" I tried, carefully. It's none of my business, we hardly know each other. But for some reason I was in no hurry to end the conversation.

"Not bad enough. And then kind of guilty for that."

I nodded. It was one of the most rational sentences I'd ever heard.

"Things are looking up, then," I said.

She laughed a little bit, and then seemed to remember herself and feel guilty. When she realized that, she laughed again.

"It's impossible with you."

I know, I know. You're a sperm technician, I'm a donor. It could never be.

"Do you always know exactly what to say?"

"What?" I tore myself away from my musings.

"I'll take that as a 'no'."

A woman that makes you smile. Four thousand shekels a month. That's forty-eight thousand a year. In three years' time, a down payment for an apartment. A woman who makes you smile.

"Are you going to be okay?" I asked.

"I guess so. Could be worse, right?"

"I always find that saying kind of funny." I shifted my leaning position on the wall.

"How come?"

"I used to have a friend who really liked telling bad holocaust jokes."

"Such as…?"

"You know, like – what's worse than a worm in an apple? Half a worm in an apple. What's worse than that? The holocaust."

"That's kind of weak."

"Yeah. And I happen to have a mathematician-slash-Auschwitz survivor for a grandfather."

"Wow."

"One day, my friend told him that joke."

"How did he react?"

"He mulled it over for a moment, then shook his head and said: it *sounds* right, but the variables are different. I'm doubtful of your ability to prove it logically."

Na'ama burst out laughing, and then covered her mouth, surprised. I could see she was still smiling behind her fingers.

"I hope you feel better soon," I said.

"Thank you," she said, no longer hiding her smile.

"But not too soon."

I left with echoes of laughter bouncing around my memory. Four thousand fucking shekels a month.

#

There's a supermarket near the sperm bank where I donate that I like to pass through on my way home. While I do wash my hands after I cum, I still find it hilarious to touch all the vegetables with my bare hands. Everyone needs a hobby.

Not that I go there just for that. Not just. It's also an opportunity to do some shopping.

I stood in line with my near-empty shopping cart and looked at an older man who stood in front of me. I had twelve items, and I thought that if I stood at the express checkout no one would particularly mind. Still, I stood at the regular checkout – I hate those motherfuckers who stand in the express line with two or three items over the limit.

There weren't many people there this time of day and the line progressed nicely. I was still impatient. The elderly man was slow to pull out his credit card, and then expressed interest in all of the special offers. After deliberating at length, he decided to go for two of them, cancel one of his items, and pay in cash. When he'd done that, he asked about a club card, belatedly remembered that his wife had one, and asked to cancel the purchase and pay again using her ID to get the discount.

I wondered if anyone had ever been bludgeoned to death with a bunch of bananas. I happened to have just such a bunch in my cart. Seven yellow, pretty, hand-picked bananas. They were ripe, but not overly soft. Most likely they'd be squashed if I smacked him with them. Then again, he was quite old, and they were heavy. I caressed them in an attempt to calm myself. No point in ruining perfectly good bananas. God, if he asked one more question about the special offers I was going to get one of the bigger bunches. I saw at least a dozen green, hard bananas. I bet his head is softer than those. Perhaps an avocado would do.

When he'd finally finished his purchase I took the items out of the shopping cart and placed them on the conveyor belt. The cashier passed along three of them before encountering some issues with the bananas.

"Liora, what's the code for bananas?" she called out to one of the other cashiers.

"No idea," said Liora. "Ask the shift manager."

"Daphna," my cashier raised her voice, "Daphna, what's the code for bananas?"

"Check the computer!" Daphna yelled back.

"What's it under?"

"Fruit!"

"Not vegetables?"

"Why would bananas be under vegetables?"

"Huh, right," said my cashier. "I'm such an idiot."

I looked at her quietly and shoved my shaking hands inside my pockets. I decided that it was only through keeping quiet that I'll manage to escape this place soon and without a police record. Once the banana situation had worked itself out, we appeared to be making progress. But after the shampoo and the laundry detergent, she paused.

"What's the matter?" I asked, calmly.

"For another shekel, you can get another kilo of laundry detergent," she said with a smile.

"No, thank you," I said.

"Why not? It's one shekel."

"What am I supposed to do with another kilo of detergent?" I asked.

"It doesn't spoil. You should go for it."

"But I don't need it."

"So what?"

"I…" I tried to think of a way to explain to her that she was everything that was wrong with the world. That she was the very embodiment of dumb consumerism. That I didn't even have a washing machine, and that I used the detergent to degrease the pan if I couldn't be bothered to scrub it.

"I just don't need another kilo of detergent."

"But it's one shekel!" she seemed appalled.

"One kilo lasts me three months. My house is kind of far, and I don't feel like carrying an extra kilo. And, honestly, I find it idiotic to buy something I don't need just because it's cheap."

A woman standing behind me burst into the conversation. "You should seriously go for it, at one shekel it's a bargain. Just think, it'll last you six months. You'd be saving a ton of money."

"I'd be saving 23 shekels, assuming the offer doesn't last until then," I said. I was starting to lose my patience. "Spread that out over six months and you'll see that it amounts to less than eight shekels a month."

"With today's economy, you should be more concerned with saving money," the woman reprimanded me.

"Maybe you'd like to add the shekel and take the detergent?" I offered.

"No, I have five kilos of detergent at home, why would I buy more?"

I blinked. "I thought you said it was a bargain –just one shekel."

"A shekel saved is a shekel earned. You're a wasteful one, aren't you?"

I looked at her. I looked at the cashier who was smiling politely. I slowly removed a shekel from my wallet. They both followed the motion of my hand, spellbound. I placed it on the conveyor belt.

"Give me the detergent, then."

The cashier nodded eagerly, and the woman behind me relaxed and smiled. Order had been restored to the world. But after she finished scanning the rest of my items, the cashier blinked.

"Whoops. Actually, you need to make a purchase of over 100 shekels to get that. But you're at 98; would you like a pack of gum?"

I gaped at her. I grasped the bananas, my hand shaking. I took a deep breath – I was determined to leave that supermarket without murdering anyone. I placed the other items back in the cart and started making my way out without saying anything.

"You forgot your shekel!" the cashier yelled after me when she realized I wasn't stopping.

"Next time someone comes up with laundry detergent, give him another bag. My treat," I said.

"Where are you going?" I heard her say in the distance.

The women who stood behind me in line called out, apparently while running: "getting detergent. The second one's free!"

#

I was not in a good mood when I arrived at the sperm bank.

That isn't necessarily a bad thing. The nerves can help you cum, and cumming helps calm you down. I like to get a little mad before I go in. It's like angry fucking, but with your palm. It actually sounds really pathetic when I put it like that. Never mind, that wasn't the case today. I was in a shitty mood getting there and I didn't feel like going inside.

There was a line to the donor room, which only made everything worse. There was one fellow sitting outside and another one inside already. The thought of sitting down and reading the paper while some douchebag was sweating in there, straining to squeeze one out into a cup, repulsed me. I wanted to hurl.

"Hey, what's up?" a friendly voice addressed me. I looked up and saw Na'ama leaning against the lab door, smiling at me. Every ounce of grouchiness magically evaporated.

"Hi, I'm okay, how're you?"

"Better. Still a bit sad. The Shiva just ended," she said. She raised her eyebrows. "You kind of looked like a bulldog there, a moment ago."

"A bulldog?"

"You know, your face was all scrunched up. Something get on your nerves?"

Some of my previous crabbiness returned to re-crumple my face. "It's not that interesting, to be honest."

"That counts as teasing," Na'ama stated, crossing her arms.

"Don't you have work to do? Freezing sperm, or something?" I said, evasively.

"I'm on break. I have time."

"Fine, dammit," I said. I placed the paper on the chair next to me, crossed my fingers behind my head and leaned back. It's easier to talk when you're not looking at anybody. "It's really not a big deal. I spoke with my dad."

"Why's that a bad thing?" she asked. She sounded genuinely interested.

"He called to ask how I was doing. I said everything was fine. But my dad can keep up a polite front for about ten seconds. I think he has some kind of timer. Ten seconds for small talk, then half a second for beating around the bush followed by an hour of business."

"And was there business?"

"He wanted to know why I never do anything, why I haven't started an internship yet, what I even do for a living, where my life is going. You know, dad stuff." I griped.

"Internship?"

"I graduated from law school. I thought you knew everything about me from my file."

"I just know that all of our donors have a degree in something," said Na'ama. "Most sperm donors graduate from the Humanities, you know."

I nodded. What else are they going to do for a living?

The donor room door opened. A blond, red-faced and slightly perspiring man came out. I squirmed in my seat. He handed Na'ama his cup, which was almost entirely full. I never donated that much at once. His sweat was pungent, and I thought he must be winning whatever masculinity contest he was participating in.

Na'ama gave me an apologetic look and took the cup. She opened the notebook on her desk and wrote down his name and the date of donation. I was relieved to see how formal she was with him. I could tell it was normal for them by now, since he didn't seem fazed by it.

The other man waiting in line got into the donor room. He grimaced and closed the door. I waited patiently until the blond man left and Na'ama's attention returned to me.

"So why don't you start your internship?"

"Because I don't want to be a lawyer."

"Why law school, then?"

She sat beside me. There was something pleasant about her. She smelled nice, canceling out the odor left behind by the sweaty man. Four thousand shekels a month, I reminded myself. It seemed like she'd lost a lot of weight since the last time I saw her.

I shrugged awkwardly. "Because at some point you're supposed to do something, and if your dad tells you to go be a lawyer in exchange for him funding your apartment and tuition, you don't overthink it. I'm not particularly proud of it. But four years ago I had no idea what I wanted to do with myself."

"And now you do?"

"Today I have a solid idea of what I don't want to do."

She smiled. "Good, well, figure it out through elimination."

The smile transformed her from almost-pretty to pretty. I didn't tell her that, of course. Women don't want to know they're kind of pretty. Even if I'd considered saying something, I'd probably say she looked fantastic. It wouldn't even be lying. On my personal scale, right now, she looked fantastic.

"So listen, would you date a sperm donor?"

Her smile widened. Her brown eyes gleamed. "I don't think I'd rule someone out based on that. Although I know a lot of girls who wouldn't love it. Why do you ask?"

We exchanged looks. A moment passed between us. I know, because moments have a very distinct feel to them. Like a tingle of excitement. It's reminiscent of waiting at the airport after you've gone through the exhausting part and are now at the duty-free area. You know something better is coming. A sensation not unlike anticipation hums through your body. I'm an expert on moments. I experience so few of them that I have to be. Like how an expert on sex isn't a guy who's fucked a lot, but someone relatively inexperienced, who scrutinizes each memory from seventy different angles, writing down notes and points for improvement. It was definitely a moment. And then it was gone.

"I guess I'm worried about the impression it might leave on people. I tell myself it doesn't matter, but the fact that I keep it a secret must mean something. For example, I haven't told my dad."

"Do you feel obliged to please him?" she asked.

"I don't want to disappoint him," I admitted. "And he did pay for my degree, and for the last four years of my life."

"But it's your life. You're the one who has to live it, not him." She said. She looked at me emphatically, her eyes exceedingly soft. Her upper lip, I noticed, was slightly pouty and angled, rolling onto the bottom one like a wave on the shore, giving her face the slightest impression of sadness when she wasn't smiling. I considered reopening the topic of dating sperm donors when all of a sudden, the door opened and the guy before me in line stepped out. The smell from the man before him was still radiating from the room. He took a deep breath.

Na'ama apologized again and turned to accept his donation with a smile. I was suddenly flooded with contempt. Directed not at her, but at myself. Why the hell was I sharing my woes with a sperm technician? Why would she even care? What did it even matter? Fuck that.

I walked into the room with the right kind of anger. I didn't even mind the stench that was still hanging in the air. I unzipped violently and started rubbing like a maniac. Still, when I came, I thought about Na'ama's sad lips, glistening in the lab's harsh fluorescent lights, as if in anticipation of a kiss.

#

I'm usually fond of buses. On buses, there are unseen barriers between people. I like that. Basic courtesy is kept, attempts not to sit too close to one another are made – or to sit alone, if possible – and the bus rides on peacefully. Sometimes, a stranger stands up to let an elderly person sit or to help someone with a baby carriage get on. Heartwarming stuff like that.

And then there are the windows. Broad and wide, facing alternating urban scenery. No need to entertain some driver or focus on the road. You can just put on headphones and dream, or read. I remember reading once, that more inventions were conceived during the 20th century than in any previous century. I don't find that surprising. Most were probably invented by people daydreaming while riding the bus.

Some days are tougher. When the bus is very crowded and there's nowhere to sit. When someone's eating a bologna sandwich, or emanating waves of bad cologne. Even an overly attractive woman sitting next to you can turn the whole thing nightmarish. Because what are you supposed to do other than occasionally check to see if she's looking at you? And once I'm openly staring at her, I start thinking of what a potential rapist I must come off as.

All of the older buses have those four chairs, positioned to face one another. I could never figure out why. It's not like it saves room that way. Maybe they're intended for groups of friends who board the bus together, or maybe – an absurd notion, if there ever was one – to encourage passengers to interact with one another.

Those are the shittiest seats, by far. Even more so than the one in the front for the blind and disabled. It's all good and well when the bus is empty – there's even extra leg room. But when it starts to fill up, people will suddenly start invading your space. Three seats walling you in means three times the odds of sitting next to a fat man or a pretty woman. My two least favorite options.

Today, however, it was an old man in a gray suit, a teenager with a buzz cut and a middle-aged woman. Not the worst company I'd experienced on the bus. They smelled decent, and that was half the work. I sat by the window, which always improves my mood somewhat.

Everything was smooth sailing until the yelling began. It came from the front of the bus. I didn't see how it started. Like a movie you walked into halfway through, I had to piece the plot together from context.

"Give me back my money!" a woman was shouting. I could see she was in her thirties. She seemed hysterical. The driver gestured at her to calm down.

"Don't tell me to calm down, give me back my money, thief! You thief!"

"I don't have any change right now. I'll give it to you once some more passengers get on."

"I have to get off soon. What, now you're gonna wait for thirty people to get on? Give me back my money."

"I can't, Ma'am."

The yelling and blaming continued. I couldn't understand whether the woman was insane or the driver had actually done something wrong.

"It's a shame he doesn't just give her back her money," said the old man sitting next to me.

"Nah, she's just being hysterical. What is it, like ten shekels?" quipped the middle-aged woman.

That's the other half of the business of bus-taking. You don't talk to other people on the bus. It's a breach of contract. Strangers should leave you alone in public spaces. It's only public so long as no one shoves their private thoughts in there. Public spaces are where the greatest number of restrictions should apply. That's what being a public is all about.

"Didn't you hear? She said thirty people," The old man knowingly imparted. "Must've been a two hundred bill."

"But what's with all the screaming?" complained the woman. "Just call the bus company and report him. And I never saw her pay two hundred."

The buzz cut nodded. "It's the oldest trick in the book, screaming at the driver. She wants other passengers to join in. Easiest thing in the world, blaming the driver." He turned to the front of the bus and shouted, "Relax, lady! It's just a couple of shekels."

"You don't tell me to relax. Like it's your money, you're telling me to relax? The nerve! And you, give me back my money."

"Check it out, she's lost it," muttered buzz cut. Then he raised his voice again. "Just call the bus company, they'll pay you back. What was it, a fifty?"

The old man nodded to himself. "Two hundred. Nothing less than two hundred could cause this ruckus."

The passengers were divided between those who looked on with appalled curiosity and those who preferred to stare out the window and pretend nothing was happening. How about getting up and helping? I asked myself. None of you could care less, huh? I opted for staring out the window, but that didn't stop them from talking.

"He needs to concentrate on driving. This is dangerous," said the middle-aged woman, following several more minutes of yelling. "Someone should get her away from there."

"Someone'll call the cops soon, for sure," buzz cut was quick to reassure her.

"No, if he calls the police the whole bus will be delayed," said the old man. "They'll probably send a ticket inspector."

"Like a ticket inspector's going to do anything? No, this calls for the police."

"Hey lady," buzz cut yelled again. "Someone's gonna call the police, lady."

"You mind your own business," she replied, her voice high with anxiety. "Why won't any of you help me? He took my money and he won't give it back."

"He'll give it back when he has it," yelled another passenger. "You're disturbing the peace."

The woman began to cry in her seat, her face in her hands.

"Why are you doing this to me? Why?"

Buzz cut suddenly seemed embarrassed. "Maybe he should just pay her back."

"Why, because she's crying?" asked the middle-aged woman. "I was taught to cry too, just so you know. You think we don't know how it gets to you? I'm not going to feel sorry for the lunatic."

"Two hundred shekels," muttered the old man. "She wouldn't cry for less."

Someone could cover her ticket, I thought. It's ten point four shekels. Doesn't matter how much he took from her, fifty, a hundred or two hundred, it would solve the problem. I had money in my wallet; I could just get up and pay. I glanced at her again. It's a shame she wasn't prettier.

"Please, I need the money," she sobbed. More and more passengers were opting for the window. The bus stopped. Among the passengers getting on was a ticket inspector, who immediately began sorting things out. Buzz cut looked up, saw another bus stopping at the same station and got off in a hurry, probably to board it. The old man raised his head triumphantly.

"I told you they'd sent an inspector."

The woman was still crying, alternatively begging and yelling. The driver was arguing with the inspector. The passengers looked on with irate impatience. Here and there sounded scattered demands to give her back her money so the bus could get on with it.

Several minutes later, some form of compromise seemed to have been reached. The driver handed the woman a bill without looking at her, I couldn't see which one, and she got off of the bus without a word, still crying bitterly. I could still hear her sobs through the closed window. They were like deep, shredded breaths, torn from her, sob after powerless sob. She's falling apart, I thought. I could have just paid for her ticket.

"He couldn't have done that sooner?" complained the middle-aged woman. I narrowed my eyes at her.

I got off the bus at Dizengoff Center and for a while, just stood there. What's wrong with me?

The guy with the buzz cut had just gotten off another bus. I didn't wait for a nod of recognition. I had no wish to reminisce. I started walking, but he stood in front of me and smiled.

"Hey, how did everything turn out?"

"He gave her back her money and she got off," I said. I skirted around him and kept walking. He continued by my side.

"Really. I wish I saw how it started. But I knew things were gonna get messy when the inspector got on."

So you chose to get off, I thought. The anger did nothing to mellow the feeling in my gut.

"Do you know how much money it was? To make her cry like that?"

"Ten point four shekels," I said. I clenched my hands into fists and walked away without saying goodbye.

#

I was glad that it was finally donation day. Abstinence means you're always at least a little happy on donation day. There's a special relief that comes from being able to finally uncork. Like stretching back after being crouched over for a long time. Like cake and tea after Yom Kippur. A calming, pleasing moment. Today, though, I was particularly pleased.

New horizons seemed to be opening up all around me. I had recently begun to seriously consider going back to school for something other than law, maybe finding a job other than being a door attendant. There was something in the air; I felt livelier, spirited, and ready for a change. I wanted to tell Na'ama and get her input.

Seems silly, but she was easy to talk to. It passed the time. Maybe there'll be a line. Last time I heard she was moving into her late grandmother's apartment, and wondered how moving back to Tel Aviv was turning out for her. I didn't think the city particularly suited her, but perhaps it only seemed that way to me.

This time I smiled when I greeted the secretary at the entrance. As always, merely stepping foot in the place gave rise to a deep feeling of repulsion, but my good spirits helped dull it some.

"Line today?" I asked, trying not to look her in the eye.

"Just one already inside," she said.

A line of one. I guess that's fine, we can talk after. I approached the lab window to say hi and maybe exchange a few other words. A squat, bald man was waiting there in a lab coat, holding a sperm sample. He looked at me. I looked at him.

"Mmm… Hi," I hummed.

"Hello," he said. He placed the sample on the table. "Donor?"

"Yeah," I admitted disgruntledly. "And you are…?"

"Gil," said the bald man. He took a glove off his hand and held it out for me to shake. I glared at it. He smiled at my response.

"Extremely sterile, I assure you."

I hesitantly shook his hand. I'd have to scrub to the bone when I went inside. No way was I masturbating with that hand.

"Mmm. Barak," I said.

Gil nodded and gestured at the chair. I hesitated again.

"Where's Na'ama?" I asked, warily.

"Off today. Maybe at her other job, maybe at school. They didn't tell me, actually."

He took the sample and turned to the microscope.

School? She's at school? Working another job? How could I not have known? I bit my thumb and was immediately mortified at the memory of Gil's handshake. Come to think of it, why should I have known? She's my sperm technician, I'm a donor. And what's with this 'my' technician? She's the lab's technician. Everyone's sperm passes through her hands.

The door opened and a man stepped out. I didn't even look at him when I hurried into the room. I turned the key in the lock and tore the plastic wrapping off a new plastic cup. I placed in on the table by the sink and rolled down my pants. I stared at my flaccid organ.

Wash your hands, I remembered. I went to the sink to lather and rinse vigorously. After several minutes, I realized that my eyes were locked directly onto the gaping gash of that loathsome peach. I examined it, bile slowly rising inside of me. This is one horrible painting. I wished I could turn it toward the wall.

I spat on my clean palm and got to work. It's weird that she'd choose to take today off. It's our usual day. I mean, mine. Maybe it was because she'd just moved.

Maybe she'd met someone.

I rubbed my penis diligently for several minutes, but it wouldn't wake up. Focus, I urged myself. You watched some good porn a few days ago, as you may recall. I summoned the memory of the details into my mind. For some reason, my eyes were pulled back to that painting above the sink. I think my cock shrank even further.

Ten more minutes of that and I found myself standing there, sweating, the wet appendage clutched in a hand that reeked of saliva. Goddammit.

I washed my hands again. I threw the cup angrily into the trash can and flung the door open. Three men were sitting on the bench, waiting in line. I saw their eyes searching for the donation cup which should've been in my hand.

"Barak?" asked Gil.

"Something's come up. A family emergency." I said. "I'll be back tomorrow."

"Okay...?"

The three men swallowed their smiles.

Fuck them, I declared inwardly. The room suddenly became suffocating. It was harder to breathe. Bunch of fucking losers with nothing better to do. I shot a hateful glance at them and hurried to the exit at a brisk walk, which turned into a jog the moment I left the secretary's eyeshot.

I did not return the following day.

#

"Barak!" someone was calling my name, loudly. I sighed quietly, recognizing the accent.

My key was already in the keyhole. I had turned it. I almost made it into my apartment. I was so close. I sighed again. I fiddled with my bag momentarily, debating whether to pretend I hadn't heard. I knew my chances were slim to none. I turned around.

"Hey, Momo," I said.

"Eh, Barak, how's it going? Whass new?" asked Momo. He accentuated some of his consonants in a way typical of either very strict or very bad articulation. He wasn't smiling. He wasn't really the type, although perhaps that had something to do with his almost completely toothless mouth.

"Pretty good, Momo. Bit tired," I said. I was after a night shift and all I wanted was to crash into bed and fall sleep With clear reluctance, I added "and how're you?"

"*Walla*, you know, not bad. Not too good, but not bad." He said.

Momo and I have been neighbors for about a year. He was in his early forties, and had immigrated to Israel from Tunisia several years ago. It was important to him that I knew he was Jewish. At first we mostly ignored each other save for the occasional polite nod, until one day I made the mistake of asking how he was.

"*Walla*, Barak, you have some time?" asked Momo. He wrinkled his already deeply craggy forehead at me. There was some black hair covering his temples, and a broad bald spot that took up most of his head. He was trying to smile at me, but the effort made him look like some sort of kindness-feigning imp.

"It's only that I just got back from a shift," I said.

"*Aiwa*," said Momo. "Iss fine, we keep it short."

"Okay," I said, resentfully. Momo always made me feel guilty for loathing him. Was it his fault he's an immigrant? Was it his fault that he could barely speak Hebrew? That I thought he was fucking primitive? Yes, I thought to myself. He's evil. Even when he tries to be nice, he looks at me viciously. There is something evil in his heart. I see his eyes narrow between folds of malevolence, and I know he's after something. Something of mine.

I don't think I've ever felt more despicable than when I'd talk to Momo. The horrible part is that I'm sure that he knew this, and realized that I would do anything to relieve that feeling. I have this paranoid notion that he waits for me to return home, peering out the peephole of his door for hours, just to pounce at the proper moment and make me feel uncomfortable.

"Your place or mine?" I asked.

"*Walla*, it don't really matter to me, Barak."

I looked at the door to my apartment, already ajar. I would prefer sitting in his apartment, but couldn't think of a way to express that preference without feeling like an asshole. I gestured at the door. "Come on in."

I passed through the entrance, Momo in my wake. I had a small, tidy apartment. Two rooms, not counting the kitchen and the bathroom. Seemingly too pricey for one person to keep, but manageable with a little help from dad and a bit of semen. It was lightly but comfortably furnished. A coffee table I got from mom, some low brown sofas, a picture or two on the walls, a large bookcase in the other room. I didn't really like to bring people there. Not sure if Momo counts as "people", I thought viciously, which gave rise to a wave of guilt.

I placed the bag I was carrying on one of the sofas. "Want anything to eat, Momo?"

"Eh, Barak. Maybe a little slice of cake and some coffee. Black," said Momo. His eyes peeked at me through the cracks of his face. He could read every single one of my thoughts, I suspected. It was impossible to refuse him. I placed a small finjan on the stove for the coffee and removed a chocolate cake from the fridge. I cut him a big slice and tried not feel generous over it. He's despicable, I thought. He wasn't a beggar; he hadn't the humility for it. He felt absolutely no shame as he ate my cake with greedy hands, drank the coffee I'd made for him and thanked me for it. The spark in his eyes sickened me. Like a grease stain on my heart.

"Another slice?"

"No ssank you. It is not very good," said Momo. He exposed a single front tooth in a wicked smile. "Get the computer, eh?"

"Ah," I started. Get this over with as soon as possible. I opened the bag on the sofa and pulled out a small laptop. Momo patiently waited for me to turn it on, his eyes scanning around, seemingly assessing the apartment. I imagined he was considering whether robbing me would be worth his while.

"What are we checking on today, Momo? Soccer?"

Momo was a gambling addict. Preposterous, one-shot-in-a-million gambling, it seemed to me. I knew nothing about soccer, but I had a feeling that he was losing a fortune gambling at steep odds, hoping to win back some vast amount, which wouldn't cover what he'd already spent anyway.

"Only soccer for me, Barak," declared Momo. "Anyssing else is a waste of time."

I opened a sports news website and scrolled down to the game scores. I turned the computer toward him and gestured. At this point he'd already learned enough to use the arrow keys to reach the games he cared about. I waited with false patience, trying not to look at the clock. Five minutes, five more minutes and he'd be gone; I'd brush my teeth, take off the uniform and go to bed. I longed for that moment with every fiber of my being.

Momo took out some tickets and swore in Arabic when he compared them to the results. I tried to pass the time, but it moved in such a slow crawl I was certain it must be leaving drag marks on the floor. Eventually, after double-checking everything, Momo seemed to be finished.

"That's it?" I asked, barely disguising my impatience, and not even bothering with the exhaustion in my voice.

"No luck, Barak," said Momo. Still, he shoved the tickets in his pocket, in case he made a mistake. "No luck in life. I said he makes two goals, he makes one. No luck."

"Yeah, that sucks," I said. "You're done, then?"

"Maybe you do one more favor for me?"

"Another favor."

"Uh-huh," Momo expressed his agreement. "I hear you can meet someone on the computer. Women."

"O…kay?" I felt that my brain was failing me. There was a trap ahead, and I had no idea what it was, or how to avoid it.

"Maybe you can help me? What do I need to do?"

"You want to meet a woman online." It wasn't a question.

"Iss difficult, huh?" asked Momo. I'd say he sounded innocent if I hadn't already considered him to be the embodiment of everything vile in the world. But still, there was something naïve about his request. A basic misunderstanding. Not only of the internet, but of the fundamentals of human nature. But you try explaining to a grown man that he looks like a sewer-rat wearing a suit of human skin.

"Young. No more than twenty-five. Virgin is best, has never been with osser men. Jewish, you know," continued Momo. He looked at me with those murky eyes and I swear I saw hope in them. The pity that arose in me overcame the contempt for a moment.

"Momo, I set you up with an account on a dating site," I hesitated. "But you don't have a computer, how will anyone contact you?"

"Why they cannot call?"

"Usually people write before they call. And you need to put a picture in there, and some personal details." I tried to deter him. "And even then, there's no guarantee anyone will call."

"*Aiwa,*" acknowledged Momo. He sank deep in thought, his forehead crumpling into a frown. "Write in Hebrew?"

"Yeah." It suddenly occurred to me that perhaps my anger over the time it took him to go over the tickets was unjustified. I'd never given his Hebrew skills a single thought. The fact that he could even read in the first place was, come to think of it, quite shocking. I saw him several times, sitting on the stairs, struggling with the newspaper, his eyes determined, silently mouthing each word twice. I was pretty it was a part of his morning ritual.

"And you need a computer?"

"Or access to one," I said. I tried to avoid his eyes.

"*Aiwa.*"

I waited another minute or two out of sheer empathy, allowing the information to sink in. Then I glanced at the clock again.

"Yeah, sorry. Wish I could help."

Momo's face lit up with joy, which naturally didn't bode well for me. "Eh, Barak. You have a computer."

"Yes." I blinked.

"You can write what I say."

"I can write," I echoed after him.

"Ssank you, Barak. I appressiate it."

I looked at Momo. I looked at the clock. I looked at Momo.

"Can I get more coffee?" he said. "Cake is also fine. Iss not very good, you know, but goes good with coffee."

I couldn't believe I'd felt sorry for this monster. I couldn't believe I was feeding him cake, in my own home. I was suddenly overwhelmed by every iota of hatred I felt for him. I wanted to throw boiling water in his grotesque face. I wanted to erase his embarrassing existence off the face of the earth. He's out of here, I thought. Now. It's the only way to get rid of him once and for all. I looked into his dark eyes. He gazed at me hopefully.

I got up to make more coffee.

#

I focused intently on the sensation of my moist hand around my cock. I closed my eyes for good measure. With a long exhale, I came into the plastic cup, aiming the stream of sperm with practiced caution. I took care to shake every last drop I had left into it and closed the lid with my clean hand.

It could be exhausting, at times, this whole scene. Still beats any other job, but tiring nonetheless. Absolute abstinence and scheduled release forced you into constant awareness, constant control. Then one day, you find yourself at that damn sink just realizing your libido had decided to take the day off. If you can't control your thoughts, you have no business donating sperm.

I washed my hands, checked that the lid was secure and wiped the cup and my hands with the same paper towel, even though they use gloves here. I like to be thorough.

I left the room and approached Na'ama, smiling. She smiled back. I realized how beautiful her round face really was. Only someone who didn't know her could think otherwise.

"So how's Tel Aviv?" I asked. "Get used to it yet?"

"Noisy," she replied and took the cup. "Do you like living here?"

"I wouldn't live anywhere else."

"Yeah?"

I hesitated. That was kind of an automatic response. "Not sure.

I'm here for now."

"And why did you come here?"

"It's a city for the young," I said, "or so they say, I guess. And I love that everything's always open."

"You're practically a poster boy for Tel Aviv, aren't you."

"You should see our calendar. Each month has me not wearing something different on it."

She laughed. I was pleased.

"I know it's expensive here. But it's nice not having to own a car, and you can go out whenever you like without having to depend on anyone."

"Yeah, it's nice, if you go out a lot." Na'ama seemed hesitant. "Have you started your internship yet?"

"What?" I said, and then waved my hand derisively. "No, no. I'm thinking of moving on to something else altogether."

"Do you know which something else?"

"Not yet. Still mulling it over. Things are pretty convenient at the moment, so there's no pressure," I smiled.

Na'ama fell silent. She wasn't looking directly at me. What was it today? Why wasn't the conversation flowing?

"So how're things with you?" I tried to break the silence. There was no one in line today. I was the last one to arrive. The secretary went out for a late lunch. It was just the two of us in the room.

"I'm fine. Graduating soon."

"Biology, was it?" I relayed the knowledge she'd provided me with.

"Yeah," she smiled. Some people need to smile all the time. But maybe she shouldn't. Maybe she knows strangers might get addicted.

"And you'll be leaving here when you graduate?" I said suddenly.

"Maybe. There's still some time before that, though. Maybe after my exams I'll look for a change."

"Oh," I relaxed, slightly. This wasn't goodbye, then.

"I need to discuss something with you," she said. Finally, her eyes met mine.

"Okay."

"Basically, you're done."

"Done with what?" I asked.

"Done donating. Today was your final appointment. They asked me to let you know that you'll receive the final payment after your blood tests come back okay," said Na'ama. She kept her eyes glued to mine, but seemed to be blushing. "I would've told you sooner, if I'd known."

"Oh," I blurted out. "Okay. Okay, well, you know how it is. I mean, it's a bit of a shock. You get used to the convenience of it, I guess. Need to find a normal job now, or whatever."

"Actually," she started, and seemed to struggle internally for a moment, biting her lower lip. "Actually I heard that Ichilov hospital was offering 450 shekels per donation, and you can donate twice a week."

"Really," I said. I nodded slowly. "But I thought donating to different sperm banks was illegal."

Na'ama winked at me. Her expression was somewhere between secretive and mischievous. "I won't tell. I know this must be kind of sudden. And if you haven't started your internship yet you probably need some time to figure things out. Want the number?"

I hesitated. Of course I wanted the number. To compensate for the lost income I'd need to take four extra shifts a week. I'd have no life at all. Dad would only help if I started working as a lawyer. And if I wanted to go back to school, assuming I managed to think of a major, I'd have tuition to worry about, as well. Insane. I put aside close to nothing from the sperm donations. I never considered that it might end at some point.

I was still staring at Na'ama. We exchanged looks. Her lip was glistening, still moist from when she bit it. It would still be 3,600 shekels a month.

I really wanted that number.

"Do you have a pen?"

She pulled one out of her lab coat pocket and supplemented it with a post-it to write on. I shook my head at it.

"Hang on a moment," I asked.

I walked into the donation room before she replied. I stood in front of the painting of the peach, peering at the yawning cleft in the middle of it. I gritted my teeth. Suddenly I was seething with anger, a wrath I'd suppressed each time I walked into that cursed room. All those fucking months avoiding looking at it, all the long days of abstinence that withered away at the sight of that metaphorical hole, all were rising back up inside. I stared at the painting, refusing the urge to look the other way. Without overthinking it, I raised the pen and stabbed it into the painting, tearing the canvas with one long stroke. The fabric split with a satisfying cracking sound and ruptured violently all the way to the sides of the frame. The pen broke halfway through and the ink stained the rest of the painting.

I examined my work with a satisfied smile. Panting heavily, I dropped the pen into a trash can full of tissues. I went to the sink and washed my hands for the last time.

For A While Now

Been feeling empty on the inside, but give me a shake and you'll be able to hear the longing rustling around in my depths.

A Mystery from
the Heart Physicist's Journal

Words become heavier once they are committed to paper. However, I remain, as yet, unable to explain why some of them seem heavier than others.

My Father

One time, during a military drill, a piece of grenade shrapnel lodged itself in his stomach, and the doctors decided that it would be better to leave it there rather than risk the surgery. Another time, he lost his business to debt and my mother to divorce, and when I came to talk to him about it he smiled, and was silent.

The Details

There is a tale, the specific details of which vary wildly between different countries, but the general shape of which remains the same. When I heard it as a boy, it was about two Jews living in Iran, but growing up I realized that every culture has its own version.

It tells of two old men, carrying the final legacy of their people. Two Native Americans, remnants of a nearly extinct tribe; a Hindu couple who immigrated to Finland; gypsies who somehow found their way to Japan. In the earliest version I'd encountered, they are two refugees from an island, the entire population of which had since been wiped out by a volcano eruption. But that is merely the setting. The crux of it is this: these two elderly persons, the last of their people in a foreign land, refuse to speak to each other.

As there is no culture that may claim ownership of the tale's original version, let us assume that this is the closest one to the truth.

I can picture them now: two people who lived out most of their lives in a foreign land. A land that, by now, seemed more familiar than the home they'd lost. They do not speak. But not, I assume, due to a fight or a squabble – no, they simply have nothing in common save for an old legacy, by now all but lost to time. They've accumulated local friends, family and partners. Here they are in their old age, surrounded by the new life they've made for themselves. Not two strangers lost in an ocean of hostility, but two people in a new world, lovingly gazing at those closest to them. Not speaking to each other for any other reason than the fact that time had torn a rift between them, greater than the flimsy bond they once shared. Pride has never been fiercer than loneliness. Moreover, why would two random individuals from a given population happen to be compatible as lifelong friends, in the first place? To be quite honest, their drifting apart seems to me more likely than any other scenario.

However, what if this scenario is also wrong? Alas, the one thing that tends to be edited out of this kind of fable, is that they weren't just two elderly people who weren't speaking, not at all. They were, in fact, former lovers.

Well, suddenly everything makes sense. Suddenly, you can picture the love story preceding the separation. Perhaps they eloped together, and once the honeymoon was over they realized they weren't actually right for each other, that it was merely the folly of their youth. Perhaps when the passion and exhilaration had passed, the man cheated with a pretty local. Perhaps his wife blamed him for tearing her away from her family, that because of him she would never again see her parents and her brother. Perhaps guilt had seeped into the both of them, for leaving everyone behind, for there no longer being a 'behind' to return to. Perhaps he left her, or she left him, owing to poverty – as no one can live off of love alone (or so they say, although none have actually attempted it).

Why her and him, in fact? How easily their gender shifts to match our imagination. Let us return to the facts: two men, former lovers who refuse to speak with one another, old now, in a foreign country, their home lost to the sands of time.

Let us return to the past. Two young men, their skin tanned, their hair dark, their eyes brown. Theirs was a simple life, and they built their home on a small island, among wooden huts and fishing nets, and cooked their food in campfires and earthen ovens. The outside world existed but as a distant rumor – heard of, yet unknown. The islanders knew the route their elongated fishing boats should sail to get there, but chose to remain. Their days were summer days, even when time had brought the small island into the autumn years of its life.

As boys, they were the best of friends. They must have learned to fish together, to tie nets, to gut and clean their haul. Together they'd play under the scorching sun, exploring every rock and tree of their private world. They found names for the birds that returned to the island each spring: there's Lori the sparrow, there's Kurkur the goose, they'd cry and rejoice. They knew all of the herds of animals, as well, and their numbers. Here a new bull was born, they would cite to one another, nodding, there I saw three young goats. They shared the information while they gorged themselves with fresh fruit, picked together from the trees. This was their youth, and it lasted an eternity.

But when youth blossoms into adolescence, time begins to move again. If they were a boy and a girl, everyone in the village would know that they were meant for each other. But fate chose differently. Or maybe it chose just right, knowing exactly what it was doing. Either way, the two boys had grown into handsome, skilled and healthy young men. They weren't expected to part ways completely, but they were supposed to find wives for themselves. This was expected by all – their fathers, their friends and families, they themselves.

However, their days would still pass in each other's company. The two of them in the same boat, fishing in sunny or stormy weather alike, confident of the trust and camaraderie born of deep familiarity. They would clean their haul bare-chested, alternating between laughter and somberness as work permitted. And at nights, at nights they would sleep under the same blanket, huddled together, at first to preserve warmth, and later because they enjoyed the feeling. There was nothing wrong about it, they knew. Already as boys, they would often touch each other as they horsed around. If one of them would pull a muscle, the other would hurry to rub it as gently or as firmly as needed. If one them was injured, his companion would bandage him with the utmost care. It was a brotherly bond, a true friendship.

And true friendship, as they discovered, is often the foundation of true love. It is possible that they realized their attraction to one another long before they were able to acknowledge it. Not only to each other, but also to themselves. Touching still felt good, but there was a secret aspect to it now, a deeper layer that none of them would mention though they both seemed to feel. Sometimes their eyes would meet for an instant, and immediately they would look the other way with uncharacteristic embarrassment. Their day-to-day lives were becoming more and more anxious under the shadow of this unfamiliar emotion. This emotion carried with it the scent of shame, and fear, and above all – disappointment.

Their fathers were also boyhood friends, and nothing made them happier than knowing that their sons shared this bond. One father would say: I'm glad you're here. You and your brothers. Thanks to you I know it does not all end with us. And the other would add: Friendship is in the blood. We received ours from your grandfathers.

How could they disappoint their fathers, their friends, their families? Each of them had many brothers who looked up to him, and a fierce, steadfast father who believed in him. But a greater question loomed over all of these: could they disappoint each other?

The rational mind gave its reply. An unspoken agreement pushed the two away from each other during the daily labor, and urged them to begin looking for brides. However, the heart gave another reply. As the weeks passed, the pain within them grew, and the desire for touch would bot abate. The relentless yearning led the braver among them to go one evening and visit his friend. From his expression it became clear to the other what he had come there to say, and he smiled with relief.

There was no room for hesitation. As lovers never hesitate, even when it is called for. They embraced one another and whispered forbidden words in each other's ears. Friendship is in the blood, they were told, but it would be down to their brothers to pass it on. Their friendship had bloomed into an emotion both new and familiar, which would have to be kept secret.

They realized from the start of it that they couldn't stay, and their resulting plan was simple: better that they be mourned in death than in life. They would take their dangerous feelings far away, where they cannot harm anyone. And so, the next time they went on a fishing trip, they surreptitiously loaded their small boat with supplies and sailed away. They parted from their friends and family, careful not to act overly suspicious, but still they found themselves embracing them slightly closer than usual, choking down tears.

But the minute they were on their way, each heart remembered its youth. The spirit of adventure had, for a while, halted the sorrow of farewell. They sailed until the only thing left between the sea and the sun was their boat. They laughed and rowed, following a straight path lit by the stars. Because somewhere out there was the outside world, and they knew the mainland existed. Land, and their new life.

And land was soon found. And people, hordes of them, in numbers they'd never imagined even exist in the world. And what a world it was. Full of wonders, ideas and invention, greater than anything they could ever have conceived of. The large cities, the hard people, and inside, over and under it all was their secret love, hidden in plain sight.

Several years passed. They built themselves a house in the country, making a living from the art they knew well. They learned the language, which was both similar to their own and exceedingly different from it. They discovered the television and radio, and with childlike eagerness learned to use them. Their excitement at the new and unfamiliar drew them to delve into their fundamental mechanics. It seemed natural to them: how could such a large part of their lives remain a mystery? As they once learned together how to tie nets, how to sail and fish, so they worked to comprehend the world of electrical circuits and wires. Reading books in a language they still struggled to comprehend, they slowly began to learn a new art. Over time, they knew the inner workings of every electrical contraption in their home, and the way to fix them.

They moved to the city, where they could work at their new profession. People were less inquisitive there. They loved secretly, hidden from prying eyes. To the outside world they were merely partners, but in the privacy of their home they became lovers. For five years, their passion for one another never waned. Though they missed their families, they found comfort in the thought that this way was better for everyone.

This bliss lasted until the day an earthquake wracked through the neighboring country. Alarmed, they turned to the news, which revealed that the reason for it was a volcanic eruption in a scarcely populated, distant island. This information was of no particular interest in their city, and it took the two of them a while to realize its significance. Only once before had they used a map to try and understand where they came from. The memory of the map unnerved them for several days, flickering threateningly in the back of their minds. At the end of one long evening, during which they both raised their concerns, they found the map and looked at it in utter horror, realizing that the name the outside world had given their island matched the one they had heard on the news.

The sorrow that flooded them when they realized the extent of their loss was second only to the guilt. Their entire families, their childhood friends, had all perished. The peaceful life they had envisioned for them came to an abrupt end. All that was left was the memory of their parents, telling of their joy in the knowledge that their sons will be there to herald the future.

Every day they spent together became tainted with shame and guilt. The fire of their passion went out, and only friendship and love remained to keep them side by side, supporting and comforting each other in their shared pain. But even comfort was accompanied by the bitter tang of shame.

The bolder of the two opted to further their shared life without looking back into the past. But the other, the more levelheaded one, understood that chapter of their lives had ended. On that last night he took his companion's hand in his own and smiled sadly, and they both understood. Passion returned to their hearts that night, and then was gone forever.

That morning, they parted. Divided their belongings between them and moved to opposite sides of town. The thought of seeing each other was more than they could bear, but so was the thought of not being able to. They made their separate residences and lived their lives with a loneliness that they knew would never be appeased.

They took wives. As their friends and families always knew they would. Or, perhaps it would be better to say that their wives took them, as they themselves found it difficult at first. They were good husbands, though at times their desire was lacking. You would be hard-pressed to find better men than they were, and over the years they became fine fathers, and fine grandfathers.

Occasionally, one of them would consider visiting the other, or try to find out some news about him. But they would be deterred by the thought of what to say. The pain and sorrow that arose at the idea of the life they could have shared stood strong between them, maintaining the distance.

Spring turned to summer, and summer to autumn. The years leaked away, like water through an invisible hole in the boat. The young men became middle aged men, who became old men. Their story was never told, but a legend was in the making, that which told of two old men, the last of their people, who would not speak to each other.

That is the end of the story, but it does not conclude there. Because they were not the last of their people. Not really. They begot sons, to carry on the legacy of their ancestors. Although the old men refused to meet, their sons were curious about their people, about the past that was lost. Overcome by that curiosity, one of them eventually called the other, and they decided to meet.

They brought their children with them, allowing them to play as they attempted to make conversation about a place that none of them really knew, apart from through stories. Following an initial awkwardness and a careful fumble for words, the two found themselves battling embarrassment. They stared into space, wondering if this really was a good idea after all.

"The children are getting along well," remarked one of them. "It's as if they've known each other their entire lives."

"Friendship is in the blood," said the other, and the first nodded in surprised agreement.

They both smiled when they realized who had taught them that saying. They continued seeking out other similarities, digging through their invisible past in the hope of unearthing the place their fathers left behind, even if only in their imaginations.

And the boys were laughing in the background. "Dad, there're the grandkids of Lori the sparrow, there're the grandkids of Kurkur the goose."

Doubt and I

Over the course of the long war between us, we each gather our troops to destroy the other. He attacks with the memories of every failure I've ever known, and I repay it in kind with praise I've received and fragments of still valuable words. From time to time, one of us seems to gain the upper hand (him, more often than me), and the other must flee, take cover and recuperate in hiding. I know that eventually we will be forced to engage in face-to-face combat. It will then wear the form of a colossal beast, and I will ward it off with ever-tiring arms. It is not a battle I can win. I have never won it before. In this manner, I have lost every person that I used to be.

Size

Sometimes when I meet someone I used to know, I wear for their sake the person I once was. I do this warily, as it seems to me that I must have grown since our paths last crossed, and that the old outfit would no longer suit me as it did. But, no. It goes almost completely unnoticed. Only through the eye slits, perhaps, could one tell that underneath it hides someone entirely different.

The Reader

I have books that know when something is wrong. From the shelf, they gaze at me as I come into the room, shrug off a long coat, toss a scarf onto the back of a chair with shaking hands, and sprawl over the bed in wrinkled clothes. They silently tut at each other, the rustling and crumpling of their pages falling on tired ears. Again, they whisper as I sigh, he is thinking of her again. How grueling it must be, to be human, they agree amongst themselves. The story is long since over, yet the person is still being written.

Garden

The whole incident arose from quite a small matter.

As it happened, the man looked out his window, past the windowsill, and the view of the garden suddenly induced a great calm within him. The man hadn't paid his rent for two months now, and the landlady had already begun threatening him with unceremonious dislodgement into the street.

Although he had, until that moment, been of the opinion that he really had no particular need for an apartment, as he would spend most of his time in the street, the view from the window incited the troublesome, disconcerting thought that on the day he evicts the premises, some stranger would live there in his place. The thought arose, lodged itself in his throat, of this hoodlum, this garish coxcomb, walking barefoot on his floor, trying on clothes in his room, even eating upon his table without the slightest modicum of shame.

Still, the thought might have been tolerable, if not for the view that unfurled before him. He would forbear and hold his tongue, as he considered himself an amicable and peaceful man, who could easily turn a blind eye at the coxcomb's affront. 'Although,' he mused, 'that utter stranger, once he had quenched his thirst from my waters, eroded the floor with his bare feet and slept in my room – wouldn't simply ignore this windowsill.' Of that he was sure.

Oh, how he was haunted by that image. In anxious delirium, he imagined his hidden treasure revealing itself to that coxcomb. Furthermore, it was clear that he would not be able to fully appreciate it. 'Out of the question!' he resolved, as he had forgone every one of the raider's affronts, but this final one was by far the most unthinkable. 'He will not have my room without a struggle,' declared the man, as he sprung from his seat, grabbed his coat and promptly stormed out the door. If the landlady would like her rent, then she would have it, even if that meant that he would be forced to attain for himself a measure of employment. The windowsill was far more precious to him than he thought possible.

As he came running, he happened upon the old landlady as she was sweeping the entryway to the building. Her eyes spotted him, missing nothing, and her face donned a special kind of ire. She immediately began scolding him for idle loitering and the long delay in his payments. He was quick to respond, silencing her with a quick hand motion and a guarantee that all was being taken care of.

"And just how, pray tell, is this care-taking coming about?" she asked, her brow furrowing in suspicion.

"I am, at this very moment, on my way to an interview at a renowned office," said he, unblinking. "And should I gain employment there, I will be at liberty to pay your fee by tomorrow. And if not tomorrow, then surely sometime during the following weeks."

The old woman clapped her hands and croaked. "Employment? Employment, he says! And this is fact?"

"Upon my word," he declared, impatient. Even though he was not, in fact, on his way to an interview, he was certain beyond doubt that any renowned office would consider itself lucky to employ a man such as he.

"Upon your word?" scoffed the crone, "Your word guaranteed me my payment two months ago. And you go like this?"

She instantly began busying herself around him, fixing his hair, straightening a crease here, removing a stray thread there. Finally she tutted, signaling that she did all that could be done.

"It is fortunate that you are at least handsome. Were you both unsightly and unkempt, you would be destined for unemployment for a long time yet."

He scruffily bowed his gratitude. And if there was some slight mockery in the bow, that was understandable. And really, it was good-humored mockery. The hag smiled at him obliviously, as his charms could be boundless when he so wished it. Not for nothing had he managed to maintain his residence for so long.

"Go on, then," she said to him, waving the broom with slightly reddened cheeks.

He smiled back at her and walked away lightheartedly, his eyes probing and his legs quick.

His search was fortunately brief, as he soon happened upon a sign reading "HELP WANTED!" in large, bold print. He stopped to meditate on this: the place was relatively close to his apartment, and therefore quite convenient. However, he was suddenly struck by a spot of dejection. Why must he accord with this folly? Certainly, he could eschew the rent for another month at least, based on charm alone. What business did he have with employment? Was he truly afraid that an imaginary coxcomb would attempt to take his place? Why, that was absolute hogwash.

He had just about turned to leave, when suddenly he spotted a young man examining the sign from the other side of the street. He was exceedingly foppish, impeccably dressed, his suit fashionably cut and his cheeks spotlessly shaven. Moreover, he was walking, right before his very eyes, toward the office.

'Ah, the villain!' thought he, 'It is my job that he is after. He will not be satiated by merely taking my very home, but now also covets all that which I hold dear, , and wishes to deprive me of it, with the avarice that afflicts those who have never wanted for a single thing. Just like those ravens, who crave every glistening object they lay their greedy little eyes on, and even more so if it is not theirs.'

He glared hostilely at the stranger, perhaps even pulling his upper lip back from his teeth as a wild beast would. The youth halted, and looked at him hesitantly.

'He now knows that he cannot fool me,' thought the man. 'And so he hesitates. But what to do now? Even if I were to call for a policeman, he will surely claim that, while the coxcomb's measures are indeed deplorable, he had not actually taken any illegal means to harm me. That is, after all, the core of his guile. Neither can I simply lunge at him, that most likely being the essence of his plot. We stand in front of my place of employment, and he is after my job. Ha, villain!'

He immediately smoothed his face into a smiling guise, bowed courteously and opened the office door for his rival, gesturing toward it. The coxcomb nodded in thanks, his apprehension melted in the face of kindness, and walked in as suggested.

'Ha,' he applauded himself. 'See how easily I outwit him.'

The two walked inside and were received by a narrow-eyed scribe.

"How may I help the gentlemen?" he asked, his eyes scrutinizing them.

"It appears that there is a position here in need of filling?" said the coxcomb, undeterred.

The man nodded silently, acknowledging the similarity of their goals. The necessity of acceding to his nemesis irked him endlessly.

The scribe nodded again and gestured for them to take a seat while they waited their turns. Again, his eyes inspected them, and he seemed to approve of the coxcomb's immaculate attire. His gaze then came to land on the slovenly appearance of the other candidate, only to immediately recoil sideways in repulsion. The man now reckoned that the scribe appeared to be in cahoots with the coxcomb, which all but added to his motivation to gain the upper hand.

It was some time before the scribe called his name. He arose benevolently from his seat, dipped his head at the two conspirators and boldly walked into the office.

He was greeted by a high-ranking clerk. He even turned a blind eye to the man's dishevelment and extended his hand for a firm handshake. The man responded in equal force, realizing instantly that here was a man of stature. His silver tongue hurriedly complimented the high-ranking clerk on his exquisite taste, and he grinned at him widely, not once, but twice.

"To my understanding, the gentleman is here for the position?"

He replied that yes, he was, and persisted to meet the clerk's gaze straight on, unflinchingly.

The interview went on for a while. He revealed his life story at great length and detail, and though he might have, on occasion, embellished here and there, that was but a trivial matter. Eventually the high ranking clerk stood up, shook his hand firmly a second time, and asked that he arrive there the following day dressed in his finest suit. And though he possessed no such thing, he thought it prudent to avoid mentioning it, as he was certain that people of that stature do not concern themselves with such minutiae.

Upon leaving the room, he threw a haughty glance at the scribe, and even daringly shot a sly smile toward the coxcomb who dared defy him.

When he returned home, he lingered shortly to share these excellent tidings with the old woman. While she squawked happily, he took the opportunity to borrow an old dusty suit, once the property of some absent son who had long since stopped visiting.

In his room, he tossed the suit on the bed as if he had lost all interest in it, and heavily sat himself down beside it. 'How much longer must I keep this up before the coxcomb ceases his machinations against me?' he wondered.

Fatigued, he lay to sleep dressed in his disheveled attire, and immediately fell into dream. He was looking through the same aperture, staring at the same vision which had prompted him to leave his room that very morning. This time, though, there was a variation in the scene. There he was, the coxcomb, sullying the garden with his steps, crows eagerly circling around him. Suddenly the coxcomb raised his head and smiled. It was a disconcerting smile, one that gave his face the veneer of an eternally-grinning skull. Those crows, black-winged Jackdaws, raised their black beady eyes as well and, noticing the hidden spectator, flocked hurriedly toward the open window. The man cried out, but dared not close the window, lest the coxcomb be allowed to persist in his transgression. He tried to knock away the vexing birds with his hand, but to no avail. One of them managed to reach him, and its sharp beak immediately plunged into his eye socket, pecking and burrowing as if in search. He cried out in horror and pain, his life's blood dripping, streaming down his face, and he awoke with a start, clutching his head, drenched in cold sweat.

He rose from his bed in alarm, tossing around his sheets. He then rushed to the mirror to carefully examine his face, and managed to don a smile of relief, pondering the foolishness of confusing dream with reality.

Morning found him washed and scrubbed, dressed in his dilapidated suit. He took pains to tidy his beard and wear perfume, even going so far as trying – and failing – to give his hair some semblance of uniformity. It was as if his heart was set: 'I cannot fail!'

He went, smartly dressed and pressed, as if riding into battle. Passing by the landlady he bowed so solemnly and elaborately that she was forced to flee the room, flushed and speechless.

Upon reaching the office, he greeted everyone with both words and gesticulations. He even expressed the utmost civility toward the clerk from the other day who had sought his downfall, lest future suspicions arise from that avenue.

The smile left his face the instant he stepped into the office. Right there, as threateningly insolent as ever, stood the coxcomb, grinning cryptically.

"What are you doing here?" he said, raising his voice.

"Why, this is my place of employment," the coxcomb seemed astonished by his tone.

"Impossible," replied he, "I have just been hired for this very position."

"And why wouldn't you be? Please note, there are two desks in this room. We have clearly both been hired with the same purpose in mind."

'This villain will not be readily swayed.' He pondered. 'Scandalous, that I must now work alongside him. And of course, he relies on my agitation, on my inclination to turn back. Ah, the wily minx. See how he sticks out his hand, as if in greeting. See how tidy and immaculate he is, as if to boast his success. But, no matter. I can outwit him – he covets my life, but shall receive no part of it!'

He bowed extravagantly, wore his finest expression and began by introducing himself. He then shook the lout's hand, patted his villainous back and partook in some flattery, but not too much, so as not to create the impression of adulation, such as those spineless, eager-to-please sycophants.

Once they had done away with introductions, the two sat down and got to work. That very day the high-ranking clerk praised their boundless diligence. As, each time the coxcomb would perform well, immediately his colleague would make every effort to surpass him, lest the coxcomb slander him as a malingerer and succeed in that way in taking what was his.

As the high clerk sung their praise, he peeked at the coxcomb and saw, in his eyes, something dark. But a moment had passed, a single blink, and the darkness was nowhere to be seen, substituted by pride.

A cold finger reached down his spine. He could not even hear what remained of the clerk's commendations. If a passerby would crack open his skull with a brick, he would likely not have noticed. Such was the extent of the dread that had gripped him that he was certain that his hair stood on end, like the bristled fur of a frightened cat.

The high clerk halted his rambling and looked at him with concern. Then he patted him amiably on the shoulder and warned him of the perils of overworking, before releasing them to their duties and concerning himself with his own.

The man composed himself instantly and guaranteed that he was well. He jokingly added that if it were possible, he would continue working in place of going home. This pleased the high clerk, who responded with a declaration that he would certainly go far in this company. Throwing a scrutinizing glance at his suit, he additionally promised – and indeed, followed through – an advanced payment out of his salary for the purchase of a new suit.

He thanked him, and shot a victorious look at the coxcomb, but his rival merely gave an enthusiastic nod and agreed wholeheartedly. For a moment his confidence was shaken, but he recalled the secret look in the coxcomb's eye, ground his teeth in a grin and swore in his heart, 'he shall receive nothing.'

When he returned home, he took care to visit the landlady and offer her the rent he owed her. She, however, declined the payment, saying that he needn't rush, that she was, in fact, more the capable of sustaining herself for quite a long while. Of far greater importance, she stressed, was the acquisition of a new suit. He shrugged and agreed to everything, even permitting her to choose the suit and the tailor to fix it.

In his room, he disrobed and immediately sunk into his bed in a dreamless slumber.

He had been working for a week. He did his best, in everything, to excel and outshine his bitter foe. He had toiled days and evenings, imposing a grim toll on his spare time. Yet somehow, through some wonder, or vicious intent, the coxcomb still defied him.

A day came, a week into his employment, when the coxcomb approached him come evening to inquire whether he would like to join himself, and several of their colleagues, for some form of recreation or another. Naturally, suspicion arose in him instantly. Why was he inviting him? It was possible that some sort of plot was afoot. Or perhaps, this was in fact the plot – that his own suspicions would hinder him from becoming a part of the group, creating a propitious window of opportunity for the coxcomb to recruit their colleagues to his conspiracy, as he did with the disreputable clerk.

He therefore accepted the offer with a wide grin and a bright expression, and went out with them, clandestinely assuring that no foul play was in the works. He entertained them with his humor and wit, endearing himself among clerks of all ranks and functions. He went as far as drinking excessively and, while drunkenly gripping the coxcomb in a tight embrace, singing a drinking song which – though lacking any music – was a song nonetheless. And all that time his actions were meticulously planned and calculated, and even the song was sung merely to elude suspicion.

When he eventually returned to his room, he fell into the deep sleep known only to children and fools.

The following day he was greeted warmly by all, and from that day on, wherever the coxcomb was invited, so too was he.

Months passed, during which he paid his rent on time, and sometimes in advance. He jested with superiors and subordinates alike, and his work was done with the utmost gravity and attentiveness. It surprised no one to learn that he was to be promoted before anyone else.

On the day of the promotion he was overjoyed. Finally, he had escaped the clutches of that impudent coxcomb. No longer will he wrack his brain at night, worrying whether he will somehow manage to snag everything he worked to achieve. No more worries about those invasive eyes, scanning and prodding into a view that was his alone to see.

But as he walked to his new office, he happened upon the afore-mentioned coxcomb, who was for no apparent reason even tidier and more immaculately dressed than ever.

"And what is all this?" he inquired.

"Have you not heard? I have also been promoted recently, and my new office is positioned directly across from yours. You can imagine my delight upon finding out."

He had no choice other than blurting out a congratulatory mumble and fleeing into the safety of his office. From the depths of his soul, he wished terrible agony and various tortures upon the villain, who dared mock him at every turn.

He was now compelled to persist with his work relentlessly. He would work during the day and at night carouse with his colleagues and acquaintances, and the coxcomb most of all. The two were, by this point, extremely well-liked by both their superiors and their coworkers.

Months turned to years. The man had long ago relieved his scruffy clothes with the aim of competing properly with his impeccably-clad rival. Promotion begat promotion, and suddenly the man found him-self in the position of that very same high ranking clerk, interviewing candidates for his old position. And behold, the same loathsome scribe was sitting at the counter and receiving the candidates. He was older now, gray of hair and a bit plumper than was considered proper.

An idea sparked in his mind: 'Here is a man who employs every idle moment of his time to plot against me. Something must be done to amend this.' He therefore decided to promote the scribe. 'Thus,' he concluded, 'He shall be too occupied by work to allow time for scheming.' He made a mental note to act on this as soon as possible.

When the next candidate entered the room, the man got up to shake his hand. It was a young, disheveled sort of man, his clothes tattered and threadbare, and he fully intended to send him back on his way without a second glance. But there the young man was, shaking his hand forcefully, and directing at him a fierce gaze to match his own. He began musing that this young man was reminiscent of himself, back in those days. When he observed the skillful etiquette he exhibited, he thought 'he must also face some young coxcomb, determined to rain ruination upon him and his,' and so he swore that this lad would go far and hired him for the post.

Once he left, another young man walked in, familiarly foppish and impeccably well-mannered. 'Ah, and here is that prospective coxcomb now,' he thought, 'And a serendipitous opportunity to save a kindred spirit from oncoming calamity.' He sent the junior coxcomb on his way several minutes later, and was awash with elation at his good deed. He therefore summoned the narrow-eyed scribe and promoted him instantly, placing him as a supervisor over the young man he had just hired. The scribe was so astounded that he could barely muster a few stuttered words of gratitude, and never noticed the sly smile on his employer's lips.

The years marched on tirelessly, his star ever-rising. He would address his superiors with words tailored, shaped and fashioned into pure silver. He would treat his subordinates with consummate courtesy. And yet each rung he ascended, the coxcomb was right there at his side, ceaselessly breathing down his neck. Eventually, the time came when the two had reached a truly exalted position, as the office they came to seeking work all those years ago had also expanded unrecognizably.

He never forwent his small rental apartment. He insisted on occupying the same room, that humble compartment, knowing that the coxcomb was always looming, just waiting for him to pack his belongings and leave. If anything, he was accumulating ever more causes for concern, as every promotion made him aware of even more things for the coxcomb to covet. It was clear to him that one day, there would only be room for one of them to progress. Therefore, he persisted in his friendly demeanor toward his archrival, spending every available moment in his company. Only by clinging onto him like a leech would the opportunity to bring about his downfall finally present itself.

One day, upon arriving at the office, he was greeted by the same narrow-eyed scribe he had promoted all those years ago. His hair had receded, his cheeks rounded out, but his face gleamed with contentment achieved by very few.

The scribe raised his hat with a slight bow and excitedly bid him welcome. The man smiled perfunctorily and turned to continue on his way. However, the scribe was not finished.

"Sir, I've been meaning to address you for a long while, and I am not overly blessed with courage. Indeed, I confess that only in seeing you now have I finally rid myself of doubt, and can finally utter those words which I had so hesitated to speak. Please, listen to the ramblings of a narrow-minded old man until they run dry, and if by the end of it you feel that some injustice has taken place, tell me, and I will leave your presence and never again burden you with mine."

The man nodded listlessly, sensing something weighty and unpleasant down this path.

Once granted permission, the scribe burst into speech: "Surely you are aware, sir, that all those years ago, upon meeting you for the first time, I harbored nothing but ill will toward you. To me, you appeared unkempt, a degenerate who malingers his way through life. I confess to hoping beyond hope that one day you would be tossed out of this establishment, never to return. Of that I am ashamed now, and for it I beg your forgiveness. Because such is not the full extent of my sins. Even when you had unquestionably disproved my assumption, I retained the suspicion that you are nothing but a conceited youth, flaunting his frivolity, whose wit masks his falsehood and who employs his pretense as wool to pull over the eyes of others. And while you climbed diligently to the top, I remained a simple pencil-pusher, as I was on the day we met. Jealousy consumed me, jealousy and a deep, foul hatred for my fellow man."

Here the scribe paused briefly and lowered his eyes in humility. The man's knuckles were whitening and rage was wreaking havoc inside of him. But the scribe had more to say, and he straightened his gaze once more: "One day, astoundingly, you summoned me to your office. Once more, I am forced to confess, I had believed you spotted my hidden animosity and wished to rid yourself of my presence once and for all. You cannot imagine my astonishment when in lieu of this you were kind enough to raise me up from my lowly post. The shame that flooded me then was so great that I dared not speak to you, lest you look at my face and instantly become aware of my transgressions. Moreover, following your endorsement, others began noticing me, as your word carries a heavy weight in the eyes of the superiors – and so I was awarded with even more praise, ever more acknowledgement. However, I did not feel worthy of those. I might have come to beg your forgiveness earlier, if I hadn't failed you further, but that simple task you appointed me to perform, that young man you asked me to supervise, he up and left without a word just a few days later. And I, being the loathsome creature that I am, did not come to you for fear of your response. And now, sir, I fall to my knees and beg of you, to absolve the ignorance, the narrow-mindedness, and the sorrow that afflicts the hearts of men."

And fall to his knees he did. The sight of it was quite ridiculous, but neither of them paid it any heed.

The man stood there for some time and said nothing. Eventually he muttered something, seemingly at no one in particular, and went to his office.

He informed his secretary that he was not to be disturbed with trifles that day and sat in his chair. For many hours, he sat there.

The following day he began examining his environment through fresh eyes. Indeed, he was in the right to suspect the scribe for wishing him ill. He confessed to it himself. Undoubtedly, therefore, he must also be right in suspecting the coxcomb, and not merely fabricating such things. Although the scribe abandoned his schemes, there was no reason to assume that the same was true for the coxcomb.

This profound suspicion led him to examine every word in his conversations with the coxcomb. And there were many such conversations, as he had not spent all that time with the coxcomb in vain. They revolved around a great many things, work and women, this acquaintance and that one. But he was wary in his speech, as he feared that he was not as alert as he once was.

One evening, the two went out together. He decided to test the coxcomb, relaying to him the scribe's tale, peeking through his pint to observe his reaction.

The coxcomb shrugged and smilingly said that he did not remember that scribe.

The man twisted his grinding teeth into a grin, and left the matter alone.

The two drank excessively that night, and left the pub leaning on one another. The coxcomb slurred, matter-of-factly, that his home was quite far, and was therefore considering spending the night at his friend's place, if it was not too much trouble.

The man shoved him away at once, leaping away on drink-slanted legs. Eyes wild, fists clenched, he cried at the coxcomb that he was a villain and a scoundrel.

As the coxcomb stared at him perplexedly, a crow that suddenly lost its prey, he turned his back to him and ran away like a man possessed.

Immediately upon arriving home he locked and bolted the door, as well as the window. Far into the morning, he was haunted by the words of the coxcomb, who conspired to enter his room through deception and subterfuge. At long last, after all those years, his true colors were revealed.

He left his room late that morning, his eyes swelled and his head reeling, locked the door behind him, twice for good measure, and went to work.

When he arrived the secretary approached him, and it seemed that her face was a mask of deep, penetrating mockery. She notified him, quite formally, that mister something-or-other was involved in an accident last night, and met his end on the way to the hospital. He blinked twice, opened his eyes and realized that, astonishingly, the cadaver was, in fact, the coxcomb.

The man thanked her and walked into his office. At first, he imagined that he would feel relieved with that burden lifted from his heart. No more will he be haunted by the coxcomb. At last, he was free to resume his work.

But as the minutes elapsed, he found that he had lost the will to do so. What had seemed at first to be relief was without warning revealed as emptiness, and that emptiness was pulsing inside of him, ever more fervently. He placed his head in his hands and contemplated the matter.

'Could it be,' he asked himself, 'that I am the very same as that youth that I hired all those years ago? Had I actually done him a kindness by ridding him of his adversary, the future coxcomb? Come to think of it, the coxcomb was the very cause of my high stature, the foundation of my aspirations.'

And while he was contemplating, he closed his eyes, as he had also spent the previous night worrying. He then stirred and found himself walking down the street in the wee hours of the night.

Even as he walked, he realized that he was dreaming. After all, he had just been in his office. He thought he heard a dog bark in the distance, and turned back, trying to assess its whereabouts. Suddenly he spotted a human figure, lying prostrate on the road before him. He hurried toward it, and to his astonishment found that it was none other than the coxcomb.

He was still cognizant, and his face maintained the same features that he knew. Or perhaps, not quite the same. He seemed more like he did on the day they first met, but his body was broken, mangled. A kind of crushed vessel composed of rent flesh and tendons, pulverized bone. There was a clean bone poking whitely out of his foot, like those carcasses rotting on the desert floor for innumerable years, picked clean by vultures.

Despite all this, the one truly horrifying sight, the one that appalled him above all else, was the state of the coxcomb's clothes – rumpled and ensanguined with blood. He, whose attire had always been a monument to perfection.

He kneeled beside him, making every effort not to look at his garments. Bile rose in his throat and it was becoming extremely hard to swallow. His eyes alternated between staring at the coxcomb and recoiling from him.

The coxcomb turned his smooth face toward him and said, somewhat roughly,

"Ah, my friend. It is truly fitting that you, my oldest companion, will see me through this most terminal of paths. And, truthfully, I must confess that there are some things I must pass on before I go, things which concern you."

He bit his lip, flooded with horror and aversion. He could almost smell the stench of the cadaver rising in his nostrils.

'This is nothing but a delusion, woven by an overactive mind,' he said as if to himself, 'and I know well that none of it is real. Why pay heed to the words of the dead, to ghostly whispers?'

The cadaver smiled through bloodstained teeth. "While I am indeed no longer among the living, and while this is indeed the product of thine own delirium, you are guilt-ridden, your hands stained with my life's blood. Therefore, preference notwithstanding, listen you shall."

He lowered his glance, and indeed, his hands were bloody. He listened, then, in spite of himself, as he knew this final kindness would cost him nothing.

"Hearken, my friend, and pay heed," spoke the dead man. "You must surely be aware that, during our long years of friendship, I envied you with the utmost invidiousness, for your charm and comeliness. Everything you touched turned to gold, and you were rewarded with well-deserved praise. And I, struggling never to straggle, never to lag behind. You remember that dark look in my eye all those years ago. How I hated you then. Just as that scribe who begged for forgiveness, so do I ask to repent for my wrongs, if you will permit it?"

Upon hearing those words, the man shed a tear, and felt a tang of bitter regret over his actions. Had he possibly misjudged the coxcomb? And those irksome, vexing thoughts, as if the coxcomb was pursuing him, coveting all that was his, indeed, his very life – how, in fact, had they come to reside in his mind in the first place?

"Oh, what woeful judgment, that only at death's door do you finally tell me these things," said the man. "Is there nothing to be done? Perhaps it is not yet late. I can summon a doctor forthwith, and at the hospital they shall remold you once more into human form."

The dying man shook his head. "The time for scalpel, knife and clamp is gone. But I have one, final request of you…"

He leaned over the coxcomb attentively, disregarding the absence of his breath.

The deathly whisper was serpentine, entreating compliance. "Take me to your room, reveal to me the mirage you witnessed. The same sight that I had been coveting all my life, that which I tried to rip from your clutches."

He stood, and the coxcomb's eyes followed him like the hollow sockets of a skull.

"From beyond the grave still you seek to disrupt me?" he cried. "Still, you pursue my treasures. You shall not have that which is precious to me, you hear? You shall not!"

The coxcomb began croaking with laughter, and the man turned tail and ran, leaving him behind.

His head rose from his hands with a start. He wiped the sand from his eyes, dazed.

He did not know how long he slept. But it was far past twilight, and the night was well into its course.

He left his office and locked the door behind him. As he made his way home, he searched his surroundings, seemingly looking for something he was missing.

'Can it be that it is the coxcomb I seek?' he thought. 'It was but a daydream, a reverie, was it not?'

Amongst himself he mused that, were the coxcomb among the living, they would most likely be on their way to some merriment or other. For a moment, he stopped in his tracks. 'Could it be that I am missing the wretched villain?' and indeed, he was. He suddenly felt as if that void could only be filled by the sight of his sworn enemy.

But on his way home, he met no one.

He walked into his room. He scanned it with a scrutinizing glance and realized that it had not changed in the slightest. It even seemed somewhat dilapidated, not worthy of him in the slightest.

He stood in front of the mirror and stared. Facing him was an old man. His hair whitening around his temples, his appearance distinguished, well-groomed, his moustache trimmed and neat. His attire would not have shamed even the coxcomb – in fact, they were practically identical in style and cut.

Melancholy descended upon him. 'Indeed, I look to be nearly a coxcomb myself'. A voice, sound and sensible in tone, whispered: 'and what is wrong with that? Your post demands it, your stature permits it. Why so glum?'

'Yet,' he disputed, 'if there is no shame in it, why had I despised the coxcomb for all those years?'

'While you indeed vilified him,' replied the voice, 'you were inseparable from him, as well. Your days were entwined with his. Employ your soul as a touchstone, and you shall find neither hatred nor contempt.'

In face of his own conscience, he fell silent.

'In that case,' he pondered, 'I had erred. I killed my friend, murdered him with these bare hands. But how can this be? And what of all the plots, his scheming against me? He confessed to them all.'

'Although,' he began to reconsider, 'In fact, he had not. It was but a dream, a delusion of my own making.'

He glanced at the mirror once more, and this time did not look away. He found himself desperately clutching for the coxcomb's name, but it refused to reveal itself. He closed his eyes and scrutinized his memory in search, but to no avail.

"Oh, is there such a thing more loathsome, more abominable and despicable than the unyielding passage of time? Such a thing more futile than words, once the opportune moment to speak them has passed? Of all I wish to tell you, all I long to speak of – nothing! Your life spilled out like sand between my fingers, and even as I grasped on to it, I never once considered that they it not last."

He gathered and heaped his now overflowing sorrow, throwing words into the space of the room. A sort of transient eulogy, a final funeral.

When the words had run out, he found himself in front of the window, gazing at the garden as he had done eons ago.

"That same mirage… that same lost garden that I now witness. I clung to it with a vengeance, with a flaming, whirling sword. And see now, my friend, I would happily give it to you, if only to hear your voice once more."

He leaned further and felt that his face was wet with bitter tears, but did not wipe them away. His eyes looked far into the distance, seeking that which was no more. A flash of colorful fabric at the bottom of the windowsill led him on, his head faint.

He was envisaging that the ground was growing ever nearer, spinning about, and the coxcomb was nowhere to be found. And the night was very dark, even the starlight extinguished. And, deprived of sleep and nourishment, he fell to his back and lost consciousness.

His eyes reluctantly fluttered open to the morning light, as if in opposition. But the habit of early rising was formed over many years, and joined forces with the urge to live to overcome lethargy. He found himself lying on his back, exhausted beyond words.

He lay there for a long while, and for the first time in many years did not go to work.

Eventually, he rose to his feet and, a slave to routine, began grooming and tidying himself. He did not recognize his reflection in the mirror.

His steps were heavy and his shoulders hunched as he left his home. Acquaintances who raised their hand in greeting felt that they bothered him, and there was no sign of his previously merry demeanor. Some had begun to mutter that old age was suddenly upon him.

This day, for a change, he did not head for his office. He felt in his gut that he could not bear even another moment of that insipid cell.

Instead, he wandered the halls in a daze. When those began closing in on him, he fled into the street. There he met the coxcomb.

His jaw dropped at the sight of the same streak of festive colors, and a joyful cry nearly escaped his throat. However, upon closer inspection, he realized that the man approaching him was the young coxcomb, the one who, many years ago, sought out the man's old position, and was rejected by him. In fact, he looked nothing like his friend. His face was freckled, nothing like the coxcomb's smooth olive skin. As for their cloths, only the cut was similar – and only his muddied mind could be blamed for confusing the two in the first place.

The cry caught in his throat and dissipated into nothing. For a moment, his heart overflowed.

This young man, although his clothes were spotless and fashionably cut, had undoubtedly seen better days. The years of his youth were gone, never to return. His face had weathered with age, and if he were a different, scruffier man, no doubt it would be covered in stubble.

"I know you," said the young coxcomb. "You are that same famed high-ranking clerk who wouldn't hire me all those years ago. In fact, at the time, I was furious at your refusal. In my rage, I swore never to return. But return I did, crawling on my knees, as the world is not the good and simple place I imagined it to be."

He blinked once, maybe twice, thinking: 'does this man truly believe that salvation may be achieved here, that he is standing in the presence of a savior? Indeed, the lad knows nothing of the world. '

He straightened his shoulders and directed his gaze at him. "Are you saying that you have no other hope left, outside of this very office from which I sent you away already?"

"Verily," he admitted. "When you and I first met, I would have spat upon such a pathetic display of humility. But I now see that all tenderness and grace in the world are but a mirage, and corruption has spread everywhere. Therefore, I beg of you – anywhere I turn has cast me out unceremoniously, as your name is renowned far and wide as a man of stature and class, and our history is known by all."

He raised his eyes in a kind of bewilderment, as he had never given a second thought to the consequences of that day's actions.

"I have no position to offer you," he said, and noticing that the young man did not turn away, he added, "However, I was about to retire to my home. As harsh and unkind the world may seem to you now, I aim to drape this young head with some hoary wisdom. And perhaps the sight that you would now spit on, will take on a different hue from beyond my windowsill."

The young coxcomb nodded slowly and, directing his glance at the heavens, he smiled lightly. It was an infectious sort of smile, and soon the old man found himself smiling as well, as he hadn't in many years.

The two walked away side by side. Their backs were not hunched as they walked, but upright and firm. Although their steps were not light, liveliness still surged through their strides.

The End

And then there are those people who are unhappy with the ending. So they rip out the final page and label the story 'unfinished'.

If you ask them how it ends, they will smile wistfully and say: It didn't. And one hand will nervously slide into a pocket, to fiddle with the remnants of a torn page.

CPSIA information can be obtained
at www.ICGtesting.com
Printed in the USA
FSOW02n1143291217
42883FS